Peter,

You may li—
because of the story but because
it's like a voice dialog I conducted
with my selves.

[signature]

CHOOSING THE STONE

Choosing the Stone

A 21st Century Fable

DW HOHLBEIN

For Visala

CONTENTS

PART I. PROLOGUE

On them that worship the Ruthless Will,
On them that dream, doth His judgment wait.
Dreams of the proud man, making great and greater ever
Things which are not of God.
In wide and devious coverts, hunter-wise,
He coucheth Time's unhasting stride,
Following, following, him whose eyes
Look not to Heaven. For all is vain,
The pulse of the heart, the plot of the brain,
That striveth beyond the laws that live.
And is thy Faith so much to give,
Is it so hard a thing to see,
That the Spirit of God, whate'er it be,
The Law that abides and changes not, ages long,
The Eternal and Nature-born—these things be strong?

EURIPIDES

Episode 0

Clotho stops spinning. Something is disturbing the tapestry. The warp is rippling. Lachesis puts down her measuring tape and Atropos lets go of her shears. They can see the undulations roiling the warp, like the rippling waves of a bay or a field of wind-ruffled grass. Some powerful force is moving. The sisters wonder if the disturbance has to do with Ge's distress, her suffering due to human lawlessness.

The sisters have noticed that they are weaving more and more souls into the tapestry who do not follow the Law either out of ignorance or willful pride or both, out of a mistaken belief that they are not subject to the Law and answer only to themselves. Entranced as they are by the Creation's ceaseless generation of changing forms, they die without knowing they are time's prisoners, completely unaware of the eternal. When Atropos cuts their thread, these confused souls, chained to matter and memory, are immediately dragged down to earth, into darkness, before they have even a momentary glimpse of reality. Their spirit sinks back into the material of Creation to join the churn of becoming, and they must again wander as shades waiting to be reborn. Lachesis is having difficulty determining where and when they might transmigrate in order to give them a chance to gain the knowledge and understanding of the Law that would allow them to die properly, with hope.

The rippling of the tapestry ceases, and their work recommences, as it must. They are time itself--spinning, measuring, cutting, spinning, measuring, cutting--and their work does not cease until another great exhalation, when all movement stops, when everything is at rest again for another long night.

Episode 1

They are exploring the kitchen dimly lit by solar-powered lamps, talking about what to make for dinner. As promised, there is plenty of food available. Plutarch notices an Instant Pot and ventures, "Chili?"

–Sure, sounds good.

–Who knows how to use this thing?

–It's just a pressure cooker, see? Just have to make sure the lid is fastened right.

Several hours ago Clea had met them where the road to Hyperborea meets the mountain highway, taking the five of them 20 miles or so in a faded Subaru to the lodge. As instructed, they had all made their way to the designated intersection landmarked by a long-abandoned Sinclair gas station. It was still possible to see the outlines of a dinosaur on the rusting sign now propped up by a tree. From there, Clea took them the rest of the way on a one-lane asphalt road that soon became a very narrow, root-ruptured dirt road twisting through a pine forest.

No one in the car had the energy to carry on a conversation. For all of them, it had been a long day. Her passengers had just enough energy to find out where everyone lived, where they had started from in the morning, and how they got to the meeting place. Then only tired smiles all around. They were all second-guessing themselves about accepting their invitations now that they were in a car with the not unfriendly but not talkative Clea on their way to Hyperborea, not having any idea what they had signed up for beyond what the people who had invited them had told them, which was nothing but vague generalities about what a great experience it would be and how they should go. The price was right, though—pay what you can or pay nothing—and for two weeks at what sounded like a beautiful place, complete with hot springs. None of them could afford an actual two-week vacation anywhere, so why not? Clea, as they would discover would be her way, offered little information during the drive except to tell them as they pulled out of the abandoned gas station parking lot that it would be another hour or so before they arrived.

They parked just as the sun was dropping out. The lodge, sided with cedar boards and roofed with green metal, had two stories and a wide covered porch that wrapped around in a U. Stepping out of the car, the first thing they smelled was sulfur. Once inside, as expected, Clea asked for their phones, and in exchange she gave each of them a note with the name he or she would use while staying there. The instructions they had received after arranging their visit urged them to accept their names in good faith and humor, and while there in Hyperborea, to adopt them. The instructions had also asked them not to bring laptops, books, cards or games—just clothes, a flashlight, a toothbrush, and a blank journal and pen in case they wanted to write something.

After collecting their phones, she took the five guests to their rooms on the second floor of the lodge and left them to settle. Each room was small and more or less the same, the only differences being the type of bedside table lamp and the fabric and designs of the throw rugs. Every room had the same wicker chair at the same small empty table, the same pinewood dresser, and the same twin bed with the same bedding and two pillows. All had one screened window with a view of trees and either the river or the gardens. One person might describe the rooms as spartan, another might say they were cozy.

"Pinto or black beans?" Plutarch feels responsible to get dinner going since chili was his idea. "There's both." The rest of the cohort rummage around for knives to chop veggies.

–What about Clea? Does she eat with us?

–Who knows?

–Will we ever see her or our phones again? What are they going to do? Steal our identities?

"What did the letter say about mealtimes?" Hypatia doesn't remember any directions in the letter about eating with the 'staff.' "Let's make enough in case she comes back hungry."

There is a notebook with simple recipes on the maple counter lining two walls of the roomy kitchen/pantry. After an energetic group effort motivated by sudden hunger and aided by the One Pot, they are seated at a round oak table in the middle of the room eating chili. No one is talking. There are only the sloppy sounds of food being devoured. Light flickers from several candles bunched in the middle of the table. Earlier nervous comradery during meal prep is now the shyness of eating with strangers. They have traveled far without a meal. They are famished, and they are anxious.

Plutarch breaks the silence. "So what's with the names, anyway?"

Hypatia looks around the table. "You Googled 'Hyperborea' before agreeing to come here, right?" Everyone had. "The Greek names make sense. Hyperborea is a mythical land of the ancient Greeks. No one named Brad or Susan ever went to Hyperborea. I think it's part of the experience of being here."

"I like my name," Corinna says, "it's exotic."

"Me, too. The four syllables roll off the tongue."

"Mine has four syllables too, at least I think so, but how is it pronounced? Anyone want to give it a try?" Everyone tries to say "Hyperides," resulting in four different ways of saying it.

"How about we just call you 'Hyp'," offers Corinna.

Fatigue has infiltrated their bodies and minds after the adrenaline rush of getting food on the table. Everyone suddenly realizes there's no more energy left for talking, or anything else, and head up to their rooms. Some had traveled farther than others, but all had traveled for at least a day to get there and while traveling everyone had burned up a lot of emotional energy worrying about what they were getting themselves into. That anxiety had only intensified since getting picked up by the not-glib Clea, who, after taking their phones, giving them their names, and showing them their rooms, had disappeared.

* * *

Hyperborea is not a tourist destination or a lodging advertised online. Browse for it and you won't find anything except references to a mythical land in the far north beyond the boundaries of the known world, the home of the immortal Hyperboreans. Apollo reportedly spent the winter there, vacating the cold slope of Mt. Parnassus where in clement seasons he presided as the resident god at Delphi.

When he left for the winter, Dionysus took over the Delphic operation. Apollo's oracles also took the winter off while he was away, giving Dionysus free rein to instigate his orgiastic revels in the forest fueled by wine, revels which culminated in besotted Maenads tearing live animals apart—or so it's said. These rites were unbecoming of an Olympian, but since he was more an honorary than a rightful member of the pantheon, why should he care? And he didn't. And neither did his frenzied followers. While the immortals of Mt. Olympus may have stuck their perfect noses up at his antics, the mortals of earth really, really loved him.

But nothing resembling debauchery went on in Hyperborea. There the sun always shines and as Pindar describes:

Never the Muse is absent from their ways:

lyres clash and flutes cry
and everywhere maiden choruses whirling.
Neither disease nor bitter old age is mixed
in their sacred blood; far from labor and battle they live.

There is a rumor that degenerate Atlanteans once made plans to invade Hyperborea, though they ultimately thought better of it. The Hyperboreans after all were 10 feet tall, in excellent physical condition, and under the protection of Apollo. Atlantean skullduggery seems unlikely, considering that according to Plato the Atlanteans...

...despised everything but virtue, not caring for their present state of life, and thinking lightly on the possession of gold and other property, which seemed only a burden to them; neither were they intoxicated by luxury; nor did wealth deprive them of their self-control; but they were sober, and saw clearly that all these goods are increased by virtuous friendship with one another, and that by excessive zeal for them, and honor of them, the good of them is lost, and friendship perishes with them. By such reflections, and by the continuance in them of a divine nature, all that which we have described waxed and increased in them...

Whatever waxes always wanes, including the moral perfection of an ancient race of humanity from the Golden Age, so maybe the rumor is true:

...but when this divine portion began to fade away in them and became diluted too often and with too much of the mortal admixture, and the human nature got the upper-hand, then they, being unable to bear their fortune, became unseemly. To him who had an eye to see, they began to appear base, and had lost the fairest of their precious gifts; but to those who had no eye to see the true happiness, they still appeared glo-

*rious and blessed at the very time when they were filled with unright-
eous avarice and power.*

Everyone knows what happened to the Atlanteans. Zeus lost patience with their godlike pretentions and impious hypocrisy, their inexcusable hubris, so he manufactured a day and night of torrential rain that sank the continent of Atlantis to the bottom of the sea.

No one knows, though, what happened to the fabled race of polar giants, the immortal Hyperboreans. There are fanciful theories, but no witnesses or respected conjectures from famous ancient philosophers. The only evidence people can point to is intriguing stone and ice formations in the Arctic that with the proper amount of imagination, enhanced by suggestion—Do you see it now? Look! There's a tower, and it's surrounded by a wall!—might resemble the ruins of an ancient civilization. The theory is that Hyperborea was flash frozen somehow and with the polar cap now melting, evidence of the Hyperboreans is literally popping up out of the ice.

There is also the tale of the "Electric Wars," waged by aliens, a war that included the Hyperboreans who were also aliens sent here to "seed the earth." They were the ancient race responsible for all of the mysterious monoliths found all over the planet. They were big enough and strong enough to move the massive stones, and they had the help of advanced alien technology. The so-called Electric Wars wiped the Hyperboreans out, but not before some of them were saved by being reincarnated as the titans and gods of Greek mythology.

* * *

The five guests just arrived at present-day Hyperborea would enjoy these fantastic stories if they heard them. They are people still curious about the world and its mysteries; they are still interested in the unknown. They are interested in knowing in general, which is not a widespread interest in their time. People of their time are not so much interested in knowing as they are in being distracted, and the electronic technology designed to distract them dominates their attention to such an extent that they usually have no awareness of their surroundings, their senses being fully engaged in whatever is filling the screen held in front of their face and whatever sound is being transmitted through tiny amplifiers implanted in their ears.

Perception is captured and funneled into a small rectangular space filled with pixels. They may be sitting on a park bench next to a sweet-smelling jasmine under an old oak tree, there may be early spring robins hopping around them foraging for worms, there might be a sudden break in the clouds that lets a shaft of sunlight through for just a moment, but they would have no experience of any of these delightful events, and no memories of them. What they will remember is what they saw and heard from the data stream, and this is what they will talk about with people, and when they go to bed this is what they'll be thinking about, and this will be the last thing they see before closing their eyes.

The guests are also often distracted by these devices, it's unavoidable, but their consciousness has not been completely captured. They are still interested in learning about the world and themselves. Getting invited to a place named after a mythical paradise seemed to them an alluring break from the routine and the stress of everyday life. In ancient times they might well have been the first to sign up for the expedition beyond the Riphean Mountains to the home of Boreas, the North Wind. Their trip taken in mid-21st century is hardly an adventure in comparison.

They are also people who would never turn down an opportunity for a cheap vacation, no matter how sketchy it sounds, so they had contacted Clea about making reservations and received her charming handwritten letters of confirmation and instructions written on fine linen paper in an elegant cursive. They were to stay for two weeks, and on this first night, after their first meal together, they lay in their twin beds under hand-sewn quilts on a not-yet-chilly early September night looking at the stars and a waxing crescent moon through the screens covering their bedroom windows wondering the same thing: *now what?*

Episode 2

–What do you think of this group?

–I don't know, Trip, haven't had much of a chance to talk with them yet. They're nervous of course.

Clea and Triptolemos are soaking in the main pool near the lodge, greeting Eos as they do every morning. Sunlight is just starting to slant through the forest canopy. The main pool is the largest of three cement pools, all of them inlaid with a random assortment of tiles like those you can buy as souvenirs in curio shops. The pools are filled by sulfurous, steaming water falling from an elevated corroded pipe, the water spilling over downslope of the main pool to the lower two pools, each one smaller—and cooler--than the one above it. The hot mineral water eventually overflows the lowest pool making its way in spidery rivulets to the river.

–Their names are interesting, for sure, especially 'Plutarch.' He was my boss, you know, back in the day, an Apollonian priest at Delphi when I presided there as the Pythia, so he was officially my superior—or my pimp—depending on whether or not you were a recent convert to Christianity. If you were a Greek or Roman Christian, then Plutarch was doing the devil's work, using me and my spectacle to rip off pagan suckers who still believed in oracles, not to mention luring them to eternal damnation. Supposedly he actually respected my intellect, and we were friends despite my being a woman. Thought I was smart and capable. I do wonder about his getting that name. He's the first 'Plutarch' we've had for a visit.

–I get a vibe from this group.

–Me, too, though I'm not sure it's anything but having someone here named after my former boss. But no coincidences, right?

–First impression is these guys aren't going to be down with secrets.

* * *

In the hand-written letter the guests had received from Clea confirming reservation dates and providing instructions for their visit, they'd been asked to gather the first morning in the gazebo in the center of the main herb and flower garden. Clea and Triptolemos, having left the pool and now fully dressed, are making their way down the path to the garden, where the five guests, in various degrees of sleep-deprived daze, are waiting on a stone bench that circles around the perimeter of the gazebo. No one is talking. They assume Clea will fill them in on why they were invited, what to expect, what they're supposed to do while they're here, and after that, take questions. There's nothing to talk about until that happens.

"Morning, everyone," Clea says brightly, smiling. "Hope you got some sleep. It's hard the first night."

Murmured "mornings." They're unsure of their footing, afraid of violating an unknown protocol. There was nothing in the instructions they'd been given about what this meeting was for and what was expected of them, and they are still in the following instructions mode.

"Anyone having phone anxiety yet?" Everyone chuckles except Hyperides, who's not in the mood for obligatory pleasantries before the orientation spiel.

"I've got to get phones out of sight and out of mind for your time here to be meaningful, which is what you want, right? A meaningful time? No one wants their time wasted. Of course 'meaningful' is so vague as to be meaningless, and whatever meaning each of you gathers from your time here will no doubt be completely different, or maybe not, who knows? But I assume you want your time here to be meaningful since you all made considerable effort to get here, and you came despite the unusual conditions outlined in the letter I sent, conditions that put off a lot of people, and understandably so. Most of the people who are invited decline, you know, but not you. So Triptolemos...

–Trip....

...and I are going to do everything we can to help you get the most from your two weeks, which means no phones, which, in time, hopefully, you will understand."

"OK," Trip says, smoothly taking the floor from Clea. "I'm the gardener and maintenance guy here and Clea is like the MC. Guests are welcome to help me fix things, so don't hesitate to offer your assistance! And I always need help in the gardens; don't be shy about pitching in."

Smiling, he continues his pitch. "Working in the gardens is a meaningful...ha!...way to spend your time here, despite what you might imagine paradise to be like, which is what Hyperborea is supposed to be, right? And who works in paradise? Who works in the land of golden apple trees and swans where people live forever? Doesn't everybody just lounge around eating grapes? This place is not that kind of paradise. For one thing––no grapes. There is always work that needs doing, believe me. We don't have grapes but we do have a lot of old apple trees, and there's pear and almond and plum and peach trees. No swans, though."

He stops talking, not having anything left to say, but then keeps going. "Anyway, where, exactly, does it say work is not something done in paradise? Sitting around for eternity drinking sweet nectar and playing the flute doesn't seem that wonderful to me..."

Rescuing him, Clea interrupts Trip's redundant ramble: "Like Trip said, you all must have looked up Hyperborea before agreeing to come here and discovered it's the name of a mythical paradise that existed in some prehistoric era. You may even be thinking that being here must have something to do with getting away from it all, since to reach this place in the distant past you had to head north and not stop until you travelled beyond the edge of the world. You had to keep going through the misty sea until you found paradise. That was getting away from it all for sure. Well, believe it or not, you made it!"

Silence. The guests are glancing at each other with worried expressions. This was not going the way they had mapped out in their minds. Clea was talking a lot but not communicating anything. She was talking in circles not telling them what they were hoping to hear, such as this is the reason you were invited; this is what you'll be doing while you're here and why; this is what we hope you will gain from your experience; this is what to do in case of emergencies; these are the rules and regulations while you're here, etc., etc. They had questions. None were being answered.

–You did your Googling before agreeing to come, right?

Mumbled "Yesses" and some "uh huhs."

–Getting away from it all is the general idea, with an emphasis on the word all, and so phones have to go away, and laptops are not allowed, because face it, there's no getting away from all of it as long as your phones or laptops--all your screens--are available, up there in your room or down in the public areas or wherever--though there's no connection here anyway--no matter how far north or south, east or west you go, and since the earth is not flat despite what some xtians, even now, continue to insist...

"Fucking idiots," Hyperides mutters, sotto voce.

...there's really nowhere to go on this earth except around and around, and there's no way to stop whatever you're thinking, doing, or saying and actually relax completely, getting away from it all, if you have a phone or a laptop available. There's no way to resist those insidious devices designed to keep you on edge 24/7, because you're all addicted. Everyone in One America is addicted, which is great for business, but not so great for anything meaningful.

Clea looks around. "Anyone here believe the earth is flat or that it was created 6,000 years ago and we humans lived in harmony with dinosaurs?"

They all laugh nervously, wondering if they're supposed to laugh.

–Good. Didn't think so. We don't want to draw attention to ourselves and our place here which, with all the hush-hush, I imagine you have figured out already. We don't know how the OAP Dominionists might react to our hidden paradise, and we definitely don't want to find out. Anyway, about the phones, you know you would not be able to resist...

Hypatia interrupts: "So, Clea, is that what we're doing here? Dealing with our addiction to the data stream?"

...not a bad thing to deal with, but please, friends, I understand. Of course you are anxious to know why you were invited and what you're doing here, but the thing is I can't say why each of you is here. That's for you to discover––or not. And it really doesn't matter if you do, and it doesn't matter if you don't.

–So what does matter?

Clea stops to think for a moment. "Well, Plutarch, I guess I would say that everything matters. Everyone matters. Every thought and every word matters. Every movement matters. Every breath. What doesn't matter is why it matters, because who really knows why?"

Clea stops talking. Her spiel floats in the middle of the gazebo like a cartoon bubble. The guests are alert now, hoping they won't miss Clea letting drop something--anything--useful, something specific. Some clarifying bit of information. They above all else want direction, but Clea is not providing any, and Trip is not helping. He seems content to sit there with them, his face friendly but implacable. The sun breaks out above the trees, and the air gets warmer. The frogs stop croaking and flying insects start waking up.

After a minute or so, Clea continues. "OK, I know you all have expectations and fantasies about what's going to happen now that you're here, but can I ask you to let those go? Expectations and fantasies are like the chicken and the egg: fantasies lead to expectations; expectations lead to fantasies; one leads to the other in an endless loop of delusion. There's never a clear path from expectations and fantasies to reality. They muck up your chances to have direct experience.

Their minds are now furiously mulling and coming up with nothing. What is she talking about and why?

"I'm being too vague, I know...*factually* speaking, why are you here right now in this gazebo, in this garden, listening to my mumbo jumbo?" She doesn't expect anyone to say anything, and no one does, because she knows the question makes no sense to them.

–You're thinking too hard. It's simple. Someone invited you. You decided you wanted to come. That's why you're here. You were called and you answered. You came even though you knew you would be asked to go by some weird name and stay somewhere extremely remote for two weeks without your phone or your laptop, bringing nothing but some clothes. So you want to know why you came? How would I know? Only you can tell me that. So I'll wait for you to tell me when you have figured it out.

Triptolemos is gone, though no one noticed when he left. They will learn that he has a way of disappearing and reappearing mysteriously. He is up at the lodge making them buckwheat pancakes with huckleberries. Clea is clearly done talking but stays with the group, waiting for them to decide to move.

Finally, after an awkward period of silence during which no one moves , Corinna asks what she believes is a fairly harmless question that won't get Clea going again, because she is ready for the orientation to end, not for Clea to start another nonsensical rant.

"Is clothing optional in the pools?"

"Of course, but really, it's much better to soak without clothes. You're in direct contact with the water and the air, so you get the full effect."

Clea smiles. To everyone's relief, she doesn't elaborate. No one else says anything. They're afraid to ask questions now, and they have enough to think about anyway. Or rather, they are tired of thinking, wondering, and worrying. It's a beautiful day in paradise. There's no sense in wasting it.

Episode 3

After their surprise breakfast and while still enjoying the taste of wild huckleberries, Plutarch suggests that as a way of staying connected they meet at sunset every day to make dinner and talk about their day. "But no one should feel obliged. Like Clea said, everyone is here for his or her own reasons and maybe that doesn't include hanging out with other people and sharing."

Hypatia adds her support, "I think it's a good idea."

Corinna and Pausanias shake their heads in agreement, and Hyp gives a thumbs up.

"Clea did give us things to think about," Plutarch points out. "It seems like it would be interesting to hear from everyone why they came. Why did each of us respond to the call as she put it?"

"What we're doing here, despite Clea dismissing it, has not been answered. What's the point? The goal? Travel to a place where we can escape our fucked-up world? Sounds great. But to accomplish what? Clear our minds? Relax? That's it?" Hyperides, the public defender, is agitated, and at 40, the oldest of the cohort. Too many unanswered questions and not knowing the Hyperborean agenda disturbs him. He is sure there is an agenda. There's always an agenda.

--And yes, I do have phone anxiety. There are people who need my help trying to reach me right now. It's not easy to get that out of my mind.

Pausanias has had enough of the hashing out. The sun is up. He wants to explore, build rock pools, see what's swimming, crawling, and flying around. Maybe there are still butterflies here pollinating Hyperborea.

"Look, I get that everyone's anxious. Everyone's wanting direction now that we've run out of instructions from the letter.

But it's pretty obvious that Clea is more interested in confusing us than answering questions we might have and that's how it's going to be at least for now, and even if that's how it's going to be the whole time, maybe we'll understand why and what for in two weeks. Anyway, we're here. Shouldn't we try to get into the spirit of this thing, whatever it is?" Corinna is nodding her head.

Hyperides, feeling like he just got reprimanded, is thinking that he's the odd man out, literally, there being five of them, three men, two women, leaving the odd person out, and that person seems to be him. He is the oldest. The youngsters of the group, Corinna and Pausanias, seem to share feelings of wanderlust. Plutarch and Hypatia seem to be taking on the role of group parents. But he's not bothered. He knows he has no reason to feel resentful, and he doesn't--he prefers being the odd man out anyway.

Hyperides, Plutarch wrote about the number 5:

...since two makes the first of the even numbers and three the first of the odd, and five is produced by the union of these numbers, very naturally five has come to be honored as being the first number created out of the first numbers; and it has received the name of 'marriage' because of the resemblance of the even number to the female and of the odd number to the male. For in the division of numbers into two equal factors, the even number separates completely and leaves a certain receptive opening, and, as it were, a space within itself; but in the odd, when it undergoes this process, there is always left over from the division a generative middle part. For in no combination of these two numbers is there produced from the two an even number, but in all combinations an odd.

In a group of five, someone has to be the odd one out. It's not personal, it's math.

* * *

For some, paradise is decadence—luxurious furnishings and bedding, designer lighting and landscaping, imported tiles lining an infinity pool, silver settings, precious china, linen napkins to wipe your mouth, cushy seats from which to take in mountain or ocean views through huge windows cleaned twice a day, stone fireplaces to lounge in front of while waiting for your gourmet meal to be prepared by a famous chef, oily massages in the spa, cocktails at the antique bar or drinks wherever you happen to be sitting, soothing soundtracks in the background, staff available in every corner to attend to your whims—and for those people Hyperborea would be no paradise, but the gang of five, on their first full morning, spreading out onto the property under a blue sky and a gauzy late-summer sun, taking in for the first time since they arrived at dusk the night before the forested hillside above the lodge, the steaming river bank mottled with yellow, brown, and orange hot-water algae, the fast-moving freestone river, the herb garden peppered with bees, feel blessed to find themselves in this rare natural wonderland. A place that seems to exist completely outside their fallen, poisoned, loud and smoky world covered with shoddy rectangular pastel apartment boxes made of recycled materials.

They are exhilarated by the natural beauty, by the air, by the sounds and the smells, but their visceral exhilaration is also the exhilaration of relief. They had all entertained fantasies about the place and had brought with them many expectations, and Hyperborea so far, despite Clea's obtuseness, more than meets their expectations and exceeds their fantasies. They feel safe for now. They can relax and enjoy themselves. Isn't that why they're there? That must be why. This is why! And it's not too difficult to relax when you're soaking in 106-degree mineral water in a tiled pool looking up through half-closed eyes at sugar pines and maple trees, listening to the birds.

Episode 4

Corinna and Pausanias make their way up the hill to explore the forest above the lodge compound, taking the first trail they see. They're walking, not hiking, as the trail is dry packed dirt and quite broad, and the elevation gain is minimal. The path has the ease of a guided nature walk, a trail designed for casual tourists wearing tennis shoes or sandals. The trees surrounding them as they walk are old and tall with spacious pine-needled avenues between them. Manzanita shrubs, nettles, and some poison oak form the underbrush. It's the land of the squirrels.

Pausanias is the first to talk: "Is it OK to get personal while we're here? I don't remember any instructions in the letter about that, and Clea didn't lay down any rules this morning, so...

–No worries, Pau—can I call you 'Pau'?

–Sure...so how do you spend your time when you're not in paradise?

–Lots of ways, but if you're asking what I do, mainly I do art. Video art, though I'm not into it much these days.

–No?

–Everything I think of seems trite, considering, you know, the state of the planet and the political nightmare that never ends. Making art seems pointless. I can't get pumped for a project. And finding an audience for my art or anyone's for that matter is tough. You would think with everyone so addicted to their screens like Clea said, spending every waking moment in the data stream, that video art would be a popular thing, but actually it isn't at all. For sure, there are a lot--a lot--of videos, but art? Everything competing with art for attention requires so much less effort and provides so much more immediate gratification. What I'm trying to say is no one gives a shit about art.

–I give a shit about art.

–Really, Pau? How? Do you go to shows? Keep up on what's happening in the arts? Do you actually buy someone's art? I mean, besides downloading movies and music, which are entertainment, what art do you pay attention to? Art is low priority for most people, and I get it, everyone's just struggling to get by however they can. It's not like the Boomer days when people had disposable income and hosted dinner parties and wanted to have something to talk about, something on their walls someone could ask about to start a conversation while they were waiting for the tiramisu. 'Where did you get that? Is that a painting or a photograph?' Those days are gone. We're living in the human jungle now just trying to survive and pay our bills. And forget about gallery shows. What galleries? They're all out of business. Those cosmopolitan urban neighborhoods that used to feature art galleries are boarded up, homes for squatters and rats...

–OK, you're right, but if I had money and threw dinner parties I'd have paintings on the wall and cool videos by Corinna to show my dinner guests.

–Ha!...right. What about you, Pau?

–I used to write a blog called 'The Travel Miser' that got some views and attracted some advertisers. I wrote about my travels and provided itineraries for people without much money...people like me. I'd make suggestions about what to see, where to stay, where to eat, things to avoid, everything that was a must see or do or a must not see or do if you had very little to spend. My itineraries were pretty popular among a certain crowd—you know, people who would come to a place like this.

–Not anymore?

–Airfare got too expensive years ago. I can still drive places, but the price of gas is getting too high for that, even though I drive an old Honda hybrid that gets like 75 miles to the gallon—360,000 miles and still going. Flying is too scary with deregulation anyway. There's a plane crashing somewhere every day now instead of like every six months or so. Flying is turning into Russian roulette.

–I've never flown anywhere. Never had the money.

–These days I'm just getting by with my old Honda, taking people places, delivering stuff. Don't know what I'll do for money if it ever dies. It's all I've got. I might have to do what some of my friends do––volunteer to be subjects in medical experiments.

–That sounds pretty desperate, man.

–They've all been OK so far. Side effects haven't been too bad. Sometimes you just need some cash, which you can't get by foraging for food behind restaurants or checking the data stream for free stuff.

–I guess if you've run out of things to sell and are really hard up...

Their conversation is interrupted by a sign on the trail:

AUTHORIZED GUESTS ONLY BEYOND THIS POINT

–Huh, that's disturbing. Are we authorized?

–I don't think so. Seems like Clea would have let us know.

–Does this mean there are other "authorized" guests here somewhere?

–Maybe we're authorized but don't know it. That seems more likely. This sign could be for people who shouldn't be here. Trespassers.

–Do we dare ignore it?

–You mean keep going?

–Yeah, maybe just a little further just to see what the deal is. Maybe we'll find some authorized guests.

–I wouldn't. I don't know why, but Clea scares me, Corinna. I really don't want to break any of the rules here, even though I don't know what the rules are. It freaks me out how she so easily assumes authority over us and we accept it––and she's what? Our host?

–Well, I bet the other three all question her authority, but yeah, it is interesting how we all fall in line. The thing is, though, we already more or less conceded authority to her when we agreed to come here and follow the instructions she sent.

–Can you see anything past the sign?

–Just the trail; it bends to the right, and you can't see where it goes. Don't see anything but more trees. And I don't see any authorized guests roaming around, either.

* * *

Just as Corinna and Pausanias without a word between them ventured up into the woods, without a word Plutarch and Hypatia went down to the river. Hyperides was inclined to follow until he spotted Trip on a ladder picking apples. Maybe he needed some help. Maybe he could get some information from him.

–What can I do to help?

–Thanks...Hyperides?...how about collecting the apples on the ground and adding them to those bins over there? He points. Use that bucket to haul them.

–Sure.

Hyp starts gathering apples lying below the orchard ladder Trip is perched on while thinking of a way to start a conversation. "I never lived anywhere like this where I could have a garden, even if I had wanted to. If I'm honest, though, I never had any interest in gardening."

–Always be honest, Hyperides.

"They all call me Hyp by the way. No one could figure out how to say it, so thanks for teaching me how to pronounce my new name." He stops talking, tries to think of something to say that will lead to some inside information. "So...honestly...I don't really like digging around in the dirt.

–Did you ever try it?

–Not really. Never had the opportunity.

–By 'not really' I take it you never have actually got down on your knees with a trowel in your hand and dug into the earth. It's OK, Hyp, gardening's not for everyone, but for me, it's everything. It's life. I can't imagine not spending my time tending to plants, replenishing the soil, watching things grow, die, and then coming back again, experiencing the joy of spring—everybody poking up out of the ground ready to give their all again, making their offering, then resting until coming back to life again next spring. One thing you can count on is plants. It's hard on the knees, though, and you're always dirty.

–My knees are good, and I don't care about getting dirty, but I guess I've never been drawn to the earth or really even noticed plants or trees. Living in the city makes it easy not to notice.

–Understood. It's not just being surrounded by roads, buildings, and cars instead of plants and trees, it's the constant noise. There are still a lot of birds living in the city, but you can't hear them, so you never look up and see them.

After working in silence for a while, Hyperides asks, "So Trip, how long have you been working here in Hyperborea, anyway? Did you create these gardens?"

Triptolemos laughs. "These gardens and orchards are way older than me." He knows Hyperides is fishing for information. Clea keeps them in the dark and people have a hard time with that at first. "Been living here since I was a teenager, actually."

Hyperides gets back to picking up apples. It's comforting to have something useful to do, something normal, on his first day here in what is an abnormal and anxiety-inducing situation, at least for him. He had been hoping that the meeting with Clea this morning would ease the anxiety of not knowing what this place is all about, of not knowing what to expect, but the effect of the meeting was to generate more uncertainty and more anxiety. He helps Trip move the orchard ladder to the next tree. There are half a dozen gnarly old apple trees that need their fruit harvested, enough apples to fill several large bins.

–What are you going to do with all these?

–Dehydrate them, make cider, applesauce, pies, butter—keep them stored in the cellar to eat through the winter. See that cider press over there?

Hyperides sees what he's pointing to. It looks like a wooden barrel with a giant screw mounted on top.

–You can make some fresh apple juice with that if you want. I'll show you how. It's easy.

Hyperides is trying hard to come up with what he hopes seems to be another innocent question. "So you've been here since you were a kid? You grew up around here? We didn't see any town coming in yesterday."

–Nearest town with anything resembling services is about 25 miles away. It's a ways for sure. Clea and I have been hanging around this place since we were little kids. This land has been in the family a long time. It's our inheritance.

"Oh, nice." Hyperides is thrown off now. What Trip described is not what he expected. He remembers Clea's lecture on expectations and smiles inwardly. "So, this is like your family business, then."

–Not really how we think of it. It's our life, and we are so blessed to have the opportunity to live here. We try to show our gratitude as much as we can to this land and the life it sustains. Count those blessings, Hyperides, every day, and especially today. Look around—you're in paradise, right?

* * *

Hypatia points out the colorful formations of salt crystals in the algae covering the rock-strewn slope above the river. "It's like a living abstract painting!" She and Plutarch kneel down to examine the miniature salt sculptures and to get a closer look at the algae that seems to be thriving in the hot mineral water bathing the rocks. "These crystals look like baby stalactites. Like you see in caves. Do you think there are caves around here? I did see bats flying around the lodge last night when we arrived."

"Have you ever been in a cave?" Plutarch asks.

–The Carlsbad Caverns in New Mexico. When I was a kid. Doubt if it's open anymore, but I remember the amazing crystal icicles hanging from the top of the caves and there were other ones like spikes growing up from the floor. Stalagmites? Everything was lit up with spotlights. We walked on the boardwalks whispering our excitement. I can still see it clearly in my mind. At one point in the tour they turn off the lights so you can experience total darkness. It was definitely total! It was like being underwater in an ocean of pure black. Very disorienting.

"That park may still be open," Plutarch says, "but it would be enter-at-your-own-risk. Sign this document waiving all your rights before entering. There wouldn't be anyone there paid to maintain the place and make sure it was safe. I remember going to some national parks with my parents when the Park Service was still operating—barely--keeping up some of the facilities, like the restrooms—except in the winter; then you were on your own, and it was dangerous with all the hunters around. There was even a ranger station at the Old Faithful geyser in Yellowstone with a park ranger staffing it when I was there. They had maps and brochures. The National Park Service is long gone. Nobody's managing the parks anymore. The wildlife should take over, but the animals are getting slaughtered by outdoor 'sportsmen' with automatic rifles. It's like going back in time about 200 years in Yellowstone: giant herds of buffalo are being decimated again. The Lamar Valley is littered with Buffalo carcasses getting picked at by vultures.

–You remember Yellowstone pretty well.

–I do. It made an impression. There were so many animals! When we were there we literally drove—very slowly—through buffalo herds crossing the road. I remember the black bears and mountain goats wandering around. Really magical.

–Nature is not exactly high priority in One America. And caves? Caves are where demons live.

Plutarch and Hypatia discover they are both teachers. Hypatia actually has a mechanical engineering degree and had once been hired for an entry-level position by Boeing, but her career in aerospace had not lasted long. "I was the only woman in my group and One America is a man's world. I was the token female, not a respected professional colleague. The men wanted a date not my input on the projects we were working on. I wasn't clueless. I went into the job knowing what to expect, but the reality was intolerable."

–It's easy to imagine what you had to deal with.

–After leaving Boeing I managed to get a job teaching math...in a public school if you can believe that. I could not and would not teach in a Dominionist school. There's no way I could handle the lunchroom.

–Only in California would you be able to find a public school.

–I'm pretty sure there are still public schools scattered along both coasts. Boston still has some.

–I was a member of the adjunct faculty in the humanities department at a community college, a part-time teacher paid on an hourly basis. We were just stop gaps in the dying days of the American liberal arts education. I mainly taught composition. English 101 was the last course to go. It had been such a mainstay for so long, a requirement no matter what your major, but the Boomers died, and their kids all graduated, and English 101 went with them. It's hard to imagine getting a college degree without taking English 101, but that's One America—no legacy must be left alive. No one needs writing skills however primitive anyway. Do kids still learn cursive writing in school in case you wanted to write a letter?

–Like the one we got from Clea? And in the mail no less! I almost threw it out with the junk mail, but the envelope was so nice. Such high-quality stationery couldn't be junk.

–What a shock to get an actual letter; it was like time traveling back to the 20th century. Maybe now there's no need to be able to print, either, when you can just talk to your phone and your message pops up on the screen, complete with emojis. And won't the implants be available soon so all we will have to do is think what we want to say? They'll want us all to have the chip. The OAP will probably offer the procedure for free, and then they'll make it mandatory in order to capture people like us who resist getting the operation. They will not only know everything about our likes and dislikes, they'll know what we're saying and to whom and in what tone and where we are at all times.

–Paranoid, aren't you? No, they don't teach cursive anymore, but I think kids still learn the alphabet and how to print letters. At least they do in my school. Spelling, though, forget it.

While they were talking, they had stripped and entered one of the rock pools along the river collecting scalding mineral water trickling down the bank. Water from the river lapped over the rocks into the pool, cooling it down to hot bath temperature. They found some flat rocks to sit on and listened to the rushing of the river and the clattering of the rocks underwater.

"What do you think?" Hypatia is ready to cool off. "Is it safe to go in the river? The current looks pretty strong."

–I'd slip out over there and then hang on to that big rock.

–OK, here goes.

The river is cold, but not too cold. Actually, it is the perfect coldness after the hot soak, and the current is not as strong as it looks and sounds. Hypatia lies on her back and stretches out in the river, anchoring herself by clinging with one hand to a cleft in the big rock, and lets the cool water flow over her, taking away the heat from the pool and washing away her thoughts. She lies there with her eyes closed for a long time, long enough that every pore of her body is murmuring its joy.

–Nice?

"You have no idea," Hypatia says, "it's heavenly."

* * *

There's a story about how Hypatia dealt with a suitor.

Hypatia was born, raised, and educated in Alexandria. In nature more noble than her father, she was not satisfied with her education in mathematics by her father but also gained knowledge of philosophy, the other not ignoble study. Donning the robe of a scholar, the lady made appearances around the center of the city, expounding in public to those willing to listen on Plato or Aristotle or any other philosopher.

In teaching also she achieved the peak of excellence, and though naturally modest and fair-minded, she remained unwed, and she was so exceedingly beautiful and fair of form that one of her colleagues fell in love with her. And because he could not control his passion he made his affections obvious to her.

There are some uninformed stories that Hypatia cured him of his sickness with music, but the truth long ago reported is that the tales of music were nonsense, and that she brought out one of her feminine napkins and threw it at him. Having displayed the evidence of her unclean nature she said: "It is this you love, young man, not beauty"; and he, put off by shame and horror at this unseemly display, disposed his heart more temperately.

If she did that now, she'd probably be sued, if not arrested.

Episode 5

Hyperides figured out how to operate the cider press (put apples in barrel, turn big steel screw attached to flat wooden circle at the top of the barrel and squish the juice out), and so they have fresh apple juice to drink. Everyone is feeling a glow from the beautiful September day, especially Hyperides, who not only provided the juice that everyone is raving about but who had brought the interesting news of Clea and Trip's sibling relationship. Corinna and Pau take their turn, reporting on the "authorized guests" signs they had encountered on the trail, which leads to a lot of speculation, triggering Plutarch who asks if anyone has ever watched the old TV show "Lost."

–Really, no one has seen it? Haven't any of you gotten hooked on watching those shows that used to be broadcast in 'prime time'? It was prime time: the whole family fed and happy, cocktails, soda, and snacks in hand, kids in pajamas, and no responsibilities until the alarm goes off in the morning.

No one has seen the show. Plutarch, undeterred, is inspired now to lecture. "Watching favorite shows was a family ritual back in the day, the thing to look forward to. The shows were like mini holidays breaking up the monotonous work week. Gather in the living room and snuggle together on the couch with popcorn or ice cream just before the show is scheduled to start. Sweet anticipation as the opening images appear and the theme song kicks in. What's going to happen this week? Then the next day at work or at school talk about what happened and what you think is going to happen. Such a cohesive social force that was never replaced."

"There's a dissertation topic for someone," Hyperides offers drily. "if anyone still pursues a graduate degree in sociology."

"I'm sure it's been analyzed every which way by now," Hypatia says dismissively. Plutarch is like a human broadcasting system that needs to be unplugged before he embarrasses himself, and Hypatia and Hyperides are trying to send him a message, but he doesn't take the hints from his new friends. Hints are often lost on him.

Plutarch rambles on. "'Lost' was about survivors from a plane that crashes on a remote tropical island. They have no idea where they are, but they discover crazy and inexplicable things on the beach and in the jungle that get weirder and more impossible to explain until the end of the final season. By then all of the plot lines and bizarre happenings have become so byzantine and logically incompatible as to be impossible to explain, so the show ended without a clear resolution. People were not happy. They had invested six years of their lives and many hours of precious prime time following the show trying to figure out what was going on, developing theories and abandoning them for new theories, only to find out in the last episode that 'it was only a dream' or 'they were in purgatory,' theories that had been long abandoned and scoffed at as way too simple, way too easy by Lost fans. The showrunners could not possibly betray fans with such nonsense. But they did."

"Have you managed to forgive them, Plutarch?" snarks Hyperides.

Hypatia piles on, "What did Clea say about expectations, huh?"

"Are you going anywhere with this?" asks Pausanias, exasperated.

–No, I haven't forgiven them, Hyp. Their copout was unforgiveable, and yes, I'm going somewhere with this. The show has something to do with us. A big plot line had to do with the 'Others,' people the survivors kept hearing at night or catching glimpses of in the jungle or finding random signs of on the beach. There seemed to be people sharing the island with them, but they weren't entirely sure. Maybe it was just their imagination, or maybe they weren't people at all. Maybe they were ghosts or demons. Maybe we are sharing this place with authorized guests or maybe not.

Corinna chimes in: "Same thing happened with 'Game of Thrones'—people were really angry about how it ended, but I thought the ending was about as good as you could expect, just as long as your expectations were set very low. Maybe that's the fate of any popular show that has a long run. After so many years, everyone has his or her own idea of how it should end."

Hyperides intervenes: "Umm, no doubt there are other old TV shows that share plots with our present story. Shouldn't we find out from Clea if we're actually authorized guests or not, and if not, why not? Are there 'Others' we should be aware of?" After hearing about the sign, his giddiness from providing the news about Clea and Trip and making apple juice has faded. The prospect of other guests they are unaware of with unknown privileges is upsetting. Why keep it a secret?

On cue, Clea walks into the kitchen. "Smells good. Enough for me?" Corinna makes room for her to pull up a chair, and Pausanias brings her some potato stew.

–Nice day, huh? What did you all do?

Hypatia remarks on the beautiful colors of the algae covering the riverbank and gushes about hanging out on the river. "The water is so clean and comforting. I felt held by it. Like it was welcoming me. Soaking in the pools along the river and then cooling off over and over again was so relaxing."

–Stops the mind doesn't it?

–Yeah, it really does, and so effortlessly. I don't remember thinking of anything. I just remember how my body felt.

–And Corinna and Pausanias you took one of the trails? You're probably wondering what the sign about "authorized guests" is all about?"

So we're being watched? What the fuck?! Hyperides mutters to himself.

"We're all wondering," said Plutarch.

–Of course.

Hyperides asks, "So are there other guests somewhere?"

–Not right now, no. The area past the sign are for people who have been here before. That's how you become 'authorized.' If you do choose to come back, you'll be staying in some other facilities.

Clea senses her sister's amusement concerning the group's fixation on the word "authorized," not to mention her using the word "facilities."

Their hysterical attachment to words, as if they are the word. And their unconscious entitlement. I deserve to be authorized. Why am I not authorized? What do I have to do to be authorized?

–Everyone OK with that?

–Sure.

–Yeah.

But no one was really OK with that. They would be "authorized" to do what? What facilities? Mostly the idea that they could—or would?—possibly return was unsettling. Really? Why would they? How would they?

Clea goes back to her meal and the talk stops until they start clearing the table and washing dishes. "Hyperides, Trip said that he told you about our being brother and sister."

–Yup."

–Were you surprised?

–I guess I was surprised.

–Why?

"Because like you said this morning, we make up stories in our heads, we fantasize," Corinna offers before Hyp has a chance to answer. "I thought you and Trip must be married or at least be committed partners, living the off-the-grid dream, away from all the bullshit, making enough money with your word-of-mouth AirBnB to pay for those giant batteries that are powering everything around here."

–Yeah, we're going to have to replace those someday when we can't recharge the cells any longer.

Hyperides adds, "I was surprised because you're both marrying age. I'm not much older than you and have already been married and divorced. So neither of you plans on ever getting married, having kids?"

Hyp is the only one in the group who has been married. In the ride from the highway to the lodge, marital status and kids had been the second topic to cover after where are you from, where do you live. No one is married and no one has kids, but it would have been more unusual if they all had spouses and families. The new norm is not to get married, not to have children. Having kids seems irresponsible considering the uncertainty and outright terror about the future of the planet.

They're imagining they've been kidnapped by a cult that lures single 30-something adults here to groom them as sex slaves.

Clea doesn't need her sister to tell her what they're thinking. The paranoid fantasies that inevitably surface in the first couple of days are predictable. Fear, violence, and sex: the three pillars of the human mind.

-This might be a good time to tell you about my family and the history of this place, at least the short version, since it's getting late...

Episode 6

Clea proceeds to tell them the backstory.

Our great, great grandparents bought this land back in the 1920s, more than a century ago, planning to develop a resort. Hot springs were popular. Mineral water was widely believed to have magical medicinal effects, able to cure just about anything, but most people went just to soothe their aches and pains from working so hard every day. A lot of the spas in those days had what they called 'corn holes.' You would sit on a bench on a deck over hot mineral water enjoying a cigarette you had just rolled and stick your poor corned up feet into a hole in the platform and soak those corns away. This was before everyone sat on their ass every day in an office in front of a computer monitor. Have no idea if you can get corns on your ass.

The only problem was getting here. The closest train station was 80 miles away, and the closest road was not much more than a wagon trail where the highway is now. But by then cars were getting mass produced and were more affordable, roads were getting improved, and more and more people were driving. The allure of hot springs was strong. People would go to a lot of trouble to get the cure, and so after they built a small lodge, they made a go of it. People would camp out or stay in the lodge for a fee. Guests could pay for meals if they wanted. They had a little canteen where they sold stuff guests might need. But their resort met the same end as just about every other hot spring spa in the day: the lodge burned down. By then they were too old to consider rebuilding and starting over.

Our great grandparents inherited the land, rebuilt the lodge, and tried to get the place going again. They had some success, and their rustic resort became fairly well known, but once again, fire struck, and the lodge burned down—it's not like there was a fire station nearby—and they didn't have the money or the desire for another resurrection.

Our grandparents had no intention of rebuilding the resort. They wanted the place to themselves. Their dream was to live off the land and off the grid. Permaculture gardening, solar power, geothermal energy, back to nature peace and quiet. For many years they had to deal with people curious about the hot springs they had heard about—could they possibly camp anywhere nearby and have a soak? Grandma and grandpa were polite but firm. "No." "Go away." "You're not welcome." Eventually word got around; plus they put up No Trespassing signs everywhere, and people stopped coming. They did as little as possible to maintain the road in off the highway to discourage the curious. They worked hard and built and planted a lot of what you see.

Our mom was their only child. Living in such a remote place, she was lonely, so they decided to send her to a private boarding school, which after adjusting to life in the outside world, she really loved. After going away to college, where she met dad, she never came back here to live. They live on the foggy north coast where mom works as a librarian and dad is a marine biologist.

As you can imagine, we very much looked forward to our visits to grandma and grandpa's awesome place. We loved it here so much. Grandma and grandpa would teach us about the plants, the herbs, the trees, the fungi, the river, the animals, the fish. They told us how everything in nature has lessons for us if we pay attention, and they taught us how to pay attention. They showed us how the solar system that powers the place works and how to manage the gardens. They were committed stewards of the land when so many people were foolishly denying that climate change was happening and that human beings had any responsibility to nature at all, when supposedly intelligent people were actually speculating that humanity was moving into a 'post-nature' phase of evolution, rationalizing that the death of earth was inevitable, that the human race is destined to travel into space and colonize other planets. Nihilist bullshit peddled by greedy capitalists who didn't want to stop making money at the expense of the environment, who didn't care what they destroyed or what they killed as long as they kept making money. The same people who built the habitats orbiting the earth right now waiting to rescue them when they've taken everything they can from the planet and left it uninhabitable.

"Tell us how you really feel, Clea!" Hyperides appreciates his host's politics. So do the others. They are glad to be on what feels like a vacation in a remote wonderland away from the everyday stress of living in America resisting the Dominionist OAP. Constant effort and imagination is required by the majority of Americans to pay for basic necessities like shelter and food––food that is suspect nutritionally, if not toxic, as there are no longer government agencies making sure that food being sold is safe. Very few people now take a chance on store-bought meat. And water? You better have some kind of technology that tests for lead and kills parasites before you drink any water.

Now they're fantasizing about being recruits to a secret rebel enclave in the wilderness.

Yeah, but they're not entirely wrong.

I guess it's becoming clear that the Dominionists and OAP are not welcome here, but it goes both ways: we would definitely not be welcome in their homes unless we kept our mouths shut. Enough—it's depressing.

Our grandparents taught us that we are a part of nature, not separate from it, not superior to it, that we are bound by its laws.

How can we not be? We're not machines, and we'll never be machines, no matter what future some may dream of for humanity. No AI will ever be human because no AI will ever have a soul.

Our parents loved grandma and grandpa and loved this place, but they are city people. Visiting is nice, but they never considered moving back despite the devastation to the environment caused by OAP policies––or lack of them––and their criminal disregard for basic human rights.

Trip and I, though, desperately wanted out, and after high school, rather than go to college, we asked our grandparents if we could stay with them. We saw no point in our parents investing huge amounts of money on degrees that would probably not get us a job, much less an education. We were vehemently opposed to the One America Party, and it was the graduates of Dominionist schools who got hired out of school, not suspected supporters of the resistance. And our older sister, Themis, was already living here. She went to live with them before finishing high school. She couldn't cope. She's a special person. Very sensitive. Intuitive. And very opinionated, extremely strong-minded.

As if I have a choice.

Our parents understood, and our grandma and grandpa were ecstatic to have us live here to work on the land and keep the place going. They were getting old and needed help. After they died, we just stayed on. Our parents are happy we did. They didn't want the responsibility of maintaining the place, and they are glad we are someplace where we can live close to nature and not have to deal with repressive power politics. Somehow the world leaves us alone here, and we hope it stays that way. It was our sister's idea to start this word-of-mouth, offline 'business,' though we don't think of it as a business. I mean it's not like we're making a profit. For us it's a project, an endeavor, a good work. It's sharing our good fortune. A place like this is so precious now, and it's not OK to keep it all to ourselves.

Hypatia interrupts: "Why not OK?"

Triptolemos had come in while she was talking, though no one had noticed. He stands in the doorway, his head almost touching the top of the frame. He, like his sister, has a deep tan from spending so much time outdoors, and his muscles show through a heavy shirt. His friendly, ironic expression doesn't seem to change.

–Why not OK, Trip?

–What is not OK?

–Why is it not OK for us to keep this place to ourselves?

–Because it would be selfish.

–Elaborate please, brother.

–Because it would be...unbalanced. There's a lot of land, water, buildings, gardens, food, trees, air—there's just a lot here, way more than just the three of us are entitled to. *Nothing in excess*, you know. Look at the world you're escaping from right now. Everything in excess and completely unbalanced, like a top that's lost all of its momentum and is just careening around. Like a teeter totter that has a hundred people on one end and one person high up in the air on the other and the hundred people all jump off every now and then and the one person on top comes crashing down. Like a sailboat with really high wind pushing it one way, and huge swells pushing it another way, and the people on board keep moving from one side to the other trying to keep the boat from capsizing.

–Right, but I want to add something. Yes, it would be unbalanced for us to hide out here just by ourselves, but also we want to share the place with like-minded people hoping that together we can create some kind of counterbalance to the destructive imbalances existing in the world. We believe that restoring balance to any degree, however small, is important, especially now. If all we can do is get people to appreciate nature in a deep way, and those people leave here and spread some of their love of nature to others, then we have accomplished something to counteract the apathy of most people regarding the destruction of their planet, their home. Think of it as adding people to the high end of the teeter totter, one by one.

"Um, Themis? Another sister?" Corinna asks for everyone.

Tell them the story of my name. Finding out there's another sister is freaking them out.

Good idea...

–So, yeah, our sister...By way of introduction, I'll tell you the story mom told us about how she got her name.

Mom and dad couldn't decide on a name, which happens a lot with the first child. Mom's hippy parents––our grandparents––and their friends suggested names like Juniper or Phoebe but their co-workers and friends tossed out names like Helen––'So sophisticated but down-to-earth'––or Samantha––'Sam, for short, so cute!' They were torn. Nothing they heard or read or thought of themselves sounded right. Then mom, who was due any day, had one of those vivid dreams in which everything is high def, and when you wake up, you remember every detail. She told us about her dream one night when I asked her how she came up the weird name, Themis, and why Trip and I didn't have names like that...

"Wait," said Hypatia, "what were your names then?"

–Well, I was Zoe and Triptolemos was Charles...

–Chuck

"Chucky." They both laugh. "He's the baby."

...Anyway, in her dream she was in a procession of people walking up a hill at night. The moon was lighting everything up. People in the procession were quite serious, not talking, 'focused' is how she described them. She felt focused, too, though she didn't know what was going on. There were a lot of people, maybe a hundred or so. When they got to the top of the hill, the procession continued on, descending into a ravine. There was a creek running through the ravine and what looked like an opening in the hillside on the other side of the creek. Those in the procession ahead of her were walking down toward the creek and some were already wading through it. They were heading to the opening. It looked like it might be a cave. She could feel everyone getting excited—'ramped up' she said.

Then suddenly the dark opening across the creek lit up with a brilliant white light. The light was intense, blinding. In the dream she knew it was not light of this world, and it frightened her. She could see faint humanlike images in the light, like silhouettes, not actual bodies, more like thin, two-dimensional stick figures draped in gossamer. They were suspended in the light and slowly floating upward. It reminded her of those lamps in kids' rooms that have designs cut out of the shade and when turned on project images on the wall. She couldn't look at them for long. It was too bright. People in the procession seemed drawn to the light, and she thought they were going into the cave, but she couldn't see the opening anymore. She was scared and didn't want to follow them. She heard people around her saying "Themis," even though she couldn't tell if they were actually talking. It was more like she was hearing it in her head. It sounded to her like a prayer or a hymn.

That's when she woke herself up. The dream was getting too intense for her. She felt like if she got too close to the light it would swallow her up. She would be lost in it, become one of the silhouettes. But she could still clearly hear the name *Themis* in her head when she woke up, as if the name had been rung by a bell, and she knew without a doubt that it was supposed to be her daughter's name.

Trip had disappeared as he always does without anyone noticing. For a big man, he makes surprisingly little noise. No one is talking. Finally, Corinna says, "So how is it that you're now Clea and Triptolemos?"

–That was our sister's call. This whole thing is her idea: inviting people to come here, the names, the two-week stay. We follow her lead. She's the conductor, and we're the orchestra, I guess....So can we leave it at that? Because it's late, I'm tired of talking, and I'm ready for bed.

Clea is already heading toward the door and casts them a rueful smile.

* * *

–Great, the more we find out, the more we don't know.

–Yeah, but you know what they say, Hyp, the more you know the more you know how much you don't know. Or something like that.

"Close enough, Pausanias." Plutarch can't remember exactly how it went either. "Seems like we should meet our conductor while we're here; otherwise, how do we know what to play?"

"Are you sure we're part of the orchestra? Aren't we just sitting in the audience?" asks Hypatia.

–Maybe, but Clea talked about getting like-minded people together to restore balance to an unbalanced world. That's supposed to be us, which sounds like we're not expected just to be passively sitting in the audience.

–What I'm wondering right now is where do Clea and Trip and big sister Themis sleep, anyway?

"I was wondering the same thing," muses Pausanias, "must be in those other facilities Clea told us about."

* * *

Plutarch is lying in bed, his thoughts swirling around by free association. *We're not here just to watch and listen. If her sister is the conductor, then Clea is revealing the score, what the conductor wants us to play. Why should we play? Except why wouldn't we? We're here aren't we? We chose to be here. We choose to stay...well, we can't really leave now...We could walk out to the highway if we had to...then what? ...Why not learn the piece and play? No one likes to be manipulated, at least without knowing why...I think everyone's feeling manipulated, especially Hyperides. His pride is on alert. He doesn't like to be anyone's fool...It was nice hanging out with Hypatia today...Don't think we're supposed to be hooking up here...there's the moon...Is that an owl?*

* * *

Hypatia is looking out her bedroom window. She can see the moon reflected in the river. Waiting for sleep to come, she is thinking, *I feel like I'm meant to be here, that it's important, and fooling around with Plutarch is not why I'm here. I hope he doesn't hit on me.*

* * *

While brushing his teeth, Hyperides is thinking, *Until we meet the big sister, we're not going to know what's going on...sensitive, intuitive, how? Is she psychic or what? Why am I fantasizing about her?*

* * *

Corinna is sitting in the wicker chair by the window, looking at the moon shadows of the trees, working out a video project in her head. She wants to capture Hyperborea in an AV piece. Audio of rocks tumbling and clattering along the bottom of the river. An osprey perched at the top of a cedar tree. Video of deer munching on fallen apples under the trees. She is energized like she hasn't been in a long time, and not just because she is feeling creative. Triptolemos has something to do with it. She is fascinated by how he moves like a big cat. Silently.

* * *

Pausanias is sitting in an Adirondack chair on the lodge porch enjoying the comfortable fall evening. He's not sleepy. He's thinking in spurts. *I really want to see what is beyond that sign on the trail. I want to see everything around here...don't know if Corinna or anyone else cares...don't think I will be able to resist disobeying that sign...want to walk along the river as far as possible...*

The world is still very much with them.

Of course it is. Let me sleep.

Episode 7

Up at dawn, Plutarch makes a pot of coffee and waits in the kitchen for everyone else to come down. After last night's revelations he's eager to hear everyone's thoughts, and he wants them to hear his. The perfect weather of September is staying perfect: cloudless sky, slight breeze, still warm. The Hyperborean climate is pleasant indeed. First to arrive is Hyperides who goes straight to the coffee without a word, followed by Corinna, who puts water on for tea. Hypatia and Pausanias arrive together and pour themselves the rest of the coffee.

–More?

"Yes, please, thanks, Plutarch." After just a couple of days hanging out with him, Hypatia can read Plutarch easily, as can everyone else. When he is about to say something, his body stiffens a little and his eyes roll up slightly. He's thinking about what he's going to say, rehearsing in his head. "You look like you have something to say."

–I was hoping we could all talk after breakfast before going off to do whatever it is we're going to do today. I'd like to hear what everyone is thinking about what we heard from Clea and Trip last night.

Pausanias says, "You mean about sister Themis, the conductor?

–Yes, about her and about everything else Clea said to us yesterday. Just what everybody's been thinking about. This is a pretty crazy scene we're in.

–You want to hear what everyone thinks about what the hell is going on?

–Exactly, Hyp, what's going on.

–It's hard to know where to start. I have a lot of thoughts and a lot of feelings.

"So do we all, Hyperides." Corinna isn't that keen on spending a lot of time trying to figure things out. In her experience things always have a way of figuring things out themselves. Analysis and theorizing are not required and to her mind a waste of time. Maybe not a complete waste of time so much as almost always a relatively poor use of time relative to all the other ways time could be used.

"Would everyone be willing to take a soak in the main pool this morning and share thoughts? Would that be OK?" Plutarch needs to talk not so much to consider what everyone has to say but to release his thoughts to make room for other thoughts waiting in the wings.

After breakfast, everyone walks to the main pool and strips down. They arrange themselves around the edge of the pool, elbows or heads resting on the coping and legs sticking out into the center, toes almost touching. The main pool is the hottest, between 106 and 108 degrees, and once immersed, no one wants to talk as they get used to the heat. Their bodies are completely relaxing as limbs, backs, and skin reach a pleasurable homeostasis with the water. Their minds follow, becoming watery, and even Plutarch is unable to say anything for a while.

"Maybe we should move down to the next pool," Pausanias suggests, after they had been luxuriating with their eyes closed and their minds stopped for some time. "This pool is not so good for talking."

It takes a while, but eventually they all slip into the next pool down, which feels like a hot bath instead of a steam room. Though this pool is smaller, they all fit, from Pausanias the tallest to Corinna the shortest. So close together, they can't not check each other out--skinny Pau, tall Hypatia, Corinna's spiky red hair--and they start to feel self-conscious, which gets the conversation started. Plutarch throws out some questions:

"What's everyone thinking? What's everyone feeling after last night?

Oh for fuck's sake, thinks Hyperides, as does everyone else. *I didn't come here to be in an encounter group.*

The theory that they are being groomed as sex slaves is raised and rejected as absurd, but the notion that they are being recruited into a secret guerilla army to revolt against the OAP seems at least plausible considering Clea's unabashed hostility toward One America and the state church. While the theory is remotely conceivable, they can only laugh at the thought of Clea and Trip leading them into a fire fight against a militia of angry OAP gun nuts in camo. So what then? No one thinks they're there just to chill out, but what else is there to do?

–That's the question, isn't it? What else are we supposed to do here besides soak in hot mineral water until we shrivel up?

"We were given a journal and a pen, presumably to write something, Hyperides," offers Plutarch. He had begun on the first night. He didn't want to forget anything important, and not knowing what might be important or not, he is noting down pretty much everything.

"Already started," says Pausanias, who is keeping a blog he hoped would get some attention in the data stream after they went back to the world.

"Me, too," adds Hypatia.

If things go wrong here, I might have to record stuff for evidence, Hyperides muses. *I better start writing stuff down. Contemporaneous notes.*

"Trip did ask us to help him in the gardens." Corinna is thinking of doing just that once she feels it is OK to excuse herself. "And there are bees to take care of. I love bees."

"I don't think Clea just randomly tells stories, and I imagine the details she includes are significant. I thought about what she told us last night, and I think it's pretty obvious that they hope we study nature and try to learn something, like they did when they moved here to live with their grandparents. They want us to develop our relationship with nature and go back into the world urging others to do the same. You know: take time to smell the flowers instead of texting. When else in our lives have we or will we have an opportunity to actually do that?" Hypatia had done a lot of thinking lying in bed the night before.

–I mean we're in this amazing place, like a dream world—hot mineral water burbling up everywhere, the river, the trees, the beautiful gardens, the birds—and we have been relieved of everything that normally dominates our attention. There's no place for us to go and nothing we're obligated to do, and now we're wondering what we're supposed to do here? Clea said it was her sister's idea to share the place, that it would be self-ish—unbalanced—to keep it just for themselves. Can't we just take it on face value that that's all this is? They want us to enjoy the blessings of this place for two weeks. Does it have to be anything more than that?

"No," Plutarch says, "it doesn't, but somehow it feels like there's more to this than a random act of kindness."

Pausanias is getting impatient. "So? Is it that important to figure this shit out? It's only our second—well third, I guess, but the travel day doesn't count—day here, and it seems like Clea shows up to give us hints or clues or whatever, but maybe we're just making this way more complicated than it actually is like Hypatia says, so anyway, my feeling is that we figure out what we, I mean what each of us wants to do and do it and take it day by day and see what Clea or Trip have to say or maybe we'll even hear from the older sister, the conductor, and then come to our conclusions or have more questions or whatever. Actually, I'm not that concerned with the why and what for. I'm most interested in finding out what's around the bend in the river. Can I go now? Please?"

Corinna's smiling, "Agree. Don't we have enough annoying conspiracy theories to deal with in the outside world? Why do we have to keep on with that in beautiful, serene Hyperborea?"

Plutarch gets it, but that doesn't mean he's going to stop trying to figure out why and what for. It's what he does, what he's always done, it's all he's really interested in, but already after just two days away from the data stream and from all that is habitual, he's sensing something happening, a crack opening up in his consciousness that is completely unconcerned with why and what for, something inside him that is comfortable with what? Not thinking? A stopped mind? He's just sensing it, like déjà vu, like a floater flashing in his peripheral vision, but he can't deny it's there. It occurs to him that he should pay attention to that.

Hyperides is irritated. He is not convinced there is anything to figure out or at least anything to figure out that matters.

Hypatia intervenes on the group's behalf, "Honestly, Plutarch, do we have to get into all of this right now? It's all going to come out in the wash. And we've already done a lot of laundry in the last hour or so. Remember Clea saying that we will each discover on our own why we were called and why we responded, or maybe we won't. She also said it doesn't really matter. It's only our second full day. Is it OK to just take advantage of our being here and just be here instead of always talking about it?"

Pausanias and Corinna are already getting out of the pool while Hypatia is still talking. And Plutarch is already following different thought threads that had been waiting their turn. "Of course, that's fine, Hypatia. Good plan."

Hyperides is thinking, *I want to meet Themis. Why the hell am I obsessing about her?*

Episode 8

There are a number of gardens scattered around the property and Corinna finds Triptolemos collecting acorn and butternut squash from one of the vegetable gardens seemingly dedicated to gourds, tubers, and roots. Glancing around she can see the green feathery tops of carrots and many varieties of striped and colorful squash. There are some very tall plants that tower over one corner, and she has no idea what they are. *This gives me an opening*, she thinks, as she walks up behind Trip.

–Is this dinner tonight?"

–Sure. Easy to make a soup out of these. Are you all enjoying the vegetarian diet or not so much?

–For me, it's not a change except for the fact that everything is so amazingly fresh and good! I think there's only one carnivore in the group.

–Let me guess...

–Yeah, Hyperides, but he's dealing with it. He says he may finally lose the 20 pounds he's been trying to lose since college.

Trip turns back to his work.

–So what is that super tall plant over there, anyway?

–Those are Jerusalem artichokes, sunchokes. They require zero care. They just grow. They shoot up tall like the sunflower they are, but you dig them up like potatoes. They're really hard, knobby guys, but if you know how to cook them, they're tasty enough with a lot of oil, salt and pepper. Emphasis on 'a lot.'

–I imagine we're going to find them on the kitchen counter one of these nights.

"If you want to try them. There's a recipe in the book." Trip turns around and looks at Corinna. "I'm going to head over to check on the bees. Want to come?"

–Yes, definitely! I was hoping you would ask at some point while we were here.

–OK then. I'll take these up to the lodge and be back.

Corinna falls in behind Triptolemos as he heads for a narrow path beyond the gardens. The sun is high above the oaks and pines that form a semicircle around the lodge and grounds. She is enjoying being with the mysterious nature-lover who seems always to be around then suddenly not around, who walks without making a noise despite his being a big man wearing heavy leather boots. She checks to see if he leaves boot prints in the dirt path. He does, but he doesn't raise dust. He moves as if he were on an invisible people mover.

There are numerous plants still flowering on both sides of the path—asters, daisies, blackberries, and many others she can't identify—and there are the bees busy among them. The path opens up onto a clearing with a simple three-sided roofed shelter housing four hives. The hives are surrounded by a solar powered electric fence, which Trip powers down so they can get to the hives.

–What does the fence keep out?

–Bears. You must know how they feel about honey. Didn't your mom read you Winnie the Pooh?

–No, I grew up on Harry Potter, and there were no bears in that world. Do they come around much?

–Not anymore. They've learned. It stings, but it doesn't hurt them too much.

Bees are clustered around the entrances to their hives, waiting to get in after landing with their pollen load or waiting to zoom out to get more. The bees taking off shoot out in all directions from the shelter following their flight paths. She wishes she could just stand there all day watching. She loves bees, but she has never had a chance to be around them in the city, to walk in a garden filled with them, to even spot them here or there. Parks in the city were left to go wild when government funding for their upkeep ceased, and most parks are now habitats for coyotes, rats, squirrels, feral pets and wildflowers, but very few bees. Pesticides have decimated them. If feeling lucky or just desperate, the homeless sleep in the parks, hoping to get a night's rest without getting picked up for vagrancy and thrown in jail.

If you're wealthy enough, with the help of those sentenced to community service you can create your own private flower garden that attracts a few bees and hummingbirds and maybe even butterflies, but Corinna is hardly wealthy. She has a small room in an old house she shares with a fluctuating number of people, usually between four and eight, but sometimes more than eight. She is lucky to have her own room—even though it is actually a closet, but a custom closet soundproofed with egg cartons—and to be able to keep it considering her shaky financial situation, but her housemates aren't any better off, so she is able to hold on to it.

There is no place around her house to plant a garden anyway. Setback regulations are a thing of the past, and buildings are crammed together forming monotone block-long towering monoliths. It is not a given that anything would grow anyway, and if a plant did manage to sprout and reach for the hazy sun, it would probably be thin and sickly. Soil is contaminated, the air smoky, the weather unpredictable. Regular rainfall can't be counted on. Drought is the norm, punctuated by spurts of heavy torrential downpours that wash away the soil and the plants it barely supports.

How is this place of abundance even possible? she wonders. *The air, the water, the plants, the trees: it is like we have time-traveled back hundreds of years.*

-Oh my God, Trip, if you only knew how much I love bees! Thank you for bringing me here. This makes it all worth it!

-Who doesn't love bees, huh? I mean, unless you're allergic, but even then you can love them from a distance.

Maybe you were a bee maiden, Corinna.

There are certain holy ones, sisters born—three virgins gifted with wings: their heads are besprinkled with white meal, and they dwell under a ridge of Parnassus. These are teachers of divination apart from Apollo, the art which he practiced while yet a boy following herds. From their home they fly now here, now there, feeding on honeycomb and bringing all things to pass. And when they are inspired through eating yellow honey, they are willing to speak the truth; but if they be deprived of the gods' sweet food, then they speak falsely, as they swarm in and out together.

They were oracles, Corinna.

Triptolemos walks directly into the shelter swarming with bees.

-Whoa, aren't you going to get stung!

-No worries, Corinna, they know me, and the only reason they'd sting me is if they felt I was a threat. I wouldn't be here doing this if I were in an angry mood, which I'm not. I'm happy. I'm happy you are here loving the bees, and so are they. No fear! You can get closer if you want. You're not angry are you?

-No.

-Afraid?

-A little.

-Try coming closer. Slowly.

By now Triptolemos is walking among the bees who form a hazy bee cloud around him, landing randomly all over his body and then flying away.

–C'mon, Corinna, you'll be OK, I promise. Come and say hello to the bees; they will be glad to meet you, and they'll remember you next time you visit.

–Really? You're sure?

Corinna ventures into the shelter very slowly, thinking no fear, no fear, Triptolemos will protect me. She feels so much trust in him. She feels the trust and relaxes. She can almost hear his voice inside her head saying in his soothing tone, It's OK, Corinna, no worries. The voice is so real, so convincing, she not only believes it, she thinks it must actually be his voice. The bees start flying around her, sometimes landing. Are they tickling her? Is she imagining it? They land, meet her, and fly away. Land, meet her, and fly away. She feels so much love for them. She can't remember feeling this kind of love before. So pure. Nothing in it or behind it. Nothing expected. And no fear. Only love.

She walks very slowly among the hives as Trip checks their frames. She feels like she might faint—no swoon, like a love-struck young woman of the 19th century. She floats out of the shelter leaving the bees behind, a few still interested and following her. Trip is smiling at her with that way he has of smiling as if he knows something delightful that no one else knows, and she thinks, "is it the bees I love or Trip or both or all of it?" And then she thinks, "it doesn't matter."

–See? The bees like you. What's not to like?

Corinna is still in a daze and doesn't answer. She misses the fact that Trip just blatantly flirted with her. He keeps looking at her and smiling for a while, then turns back toward the shelter.

"I want to get some beeswax and honey; do you want to hang around and see how it works?"

–Uh, yeah. Of course. That sounds great. I would love that.

–OK, then. I'll get some trays and you can see what to do.

–I did notice the beeswax candles on the kitchen table.

–That's right. The only place candles are allowed. Can't have them in the rooms. Too dangerous. You heard Clea's story.

–Hey, Trip. I have to ask you, how is this place even possible?

–What do you mean?

–I mean, like, the whole place, Hyperborea, the trees, the thriving plants, the beautiful flowers, the bees, the river with clean water, the fresh air—Where's the smoke? Where's the haze?--all the birds, and it's just you and Clea and Themis. Where is everybody? How is this possible these days when everywhere you go things are turning to shit?

"Just lucky, I guess." Triptolemos smiles his Cheshire cat smile.

–C'mon, Trip, you know what I mean.

–Well, it is quite remote, a long way from any cities and sources of pollution. We're surrounded by forested mountains in a hidden valley, and there's only one highway that gets you anywhere close, and that's a highway that goes nowhere that anyone goes anymore. Tourists used to drive on the road for the scenic beauty. It was one of those special byways that only the curious would take. Now curious types can't afford to explore faraway places, so hardly anyone takes this road. You remember coming here. It took a while. You only came because you knew we were waiting.

–Right, but still, it seems miraculous.

–OK, I confess, it's a miracle. Enjoy!

Episode 9

Hypatia's Journal

My second full day here started with oatmeal with blackberries and honey. The honey is sooo good. Corinna told us at dinner about Triptolemos taking her to meet the bees and what an amazing experience it was to have them land on her and not be afraid. I'm pretty sure the experience was made all the more memorable by her being there with Trip. Who wouldn't be interested in him? The way he moves—or doesn't move—it's like he's doing quantum jumps from one place to the next. But I am not going to be distracted while I'm here. I'm supposed to be paying attention, or is it I'm supposed to be stopping my mind? Maybe it's not possible to really pay attention without stopping the mind. What is it Clea?

Talk about an interesting person. Clea is just so in command. I'm not sure what it is she does or is supposed to do, but she's perfect at it.

Corinna told us about how they extracted honey from trays they pulled out of the hive. Trip into inserted the trays into this barrel contraption and then turned a crank spinning them. The centrifugal motion flung the honey to the sides of the barrel, then they opened a tap at the bottom and collected the honey that poured out. And that's what we have to enjoy every day in our tea, in our oatmeal, and on our toast (if someone makes bread). Apparently, the beeswax they carved away from the trays is what our candles are made out of.

Pausanias told us about actually meeting an "Other" somewhere down the river. So now we know there are locals. The fellow was carrying a gun and wondered what Pausanias was "doing around here." Of most interest to us is that this fellow expressed surprise that Pausanias was a guest of the "people livng up the river in the old hot springs place." He said, "those folks keep to themselves and make it clear they aren't to be bothered." He talked about getting "bad feelings" whenever he got close to the property and about one time when a "big man popped up out of nowhere" when he accidentally trespassed while hunting. Triptolemos would be scary just showing up like he does and suddenly confronting you, though it's hard to imagine Trip looking fierce. The guy is probably just paranoid, living out here with how many other Others in the middle of nowhere.

I will not be distracted. I haven't talked to the others about my reaction to what Clea said yesterday morning in the gazebo about being "called." I felt a jolt, because she put into words what I've been feeling since I was first invited to come here by someone I knew from school.

She had texted me suggesting we get together for coffee, which was strange since we hadn't been in touch since finishing our engineering degrees, and even while in school together we had not really been friends. After a few minutes of small talk around what we had been doing, mainly trading stories of discrimination and humiliation as female engineers (at least I had been offered a job), she handed me a pretty card decorated with images of wildflowers and said, "This is an invitation to a very special place, and I think you should go. I think it will be good for you. Don't open the card just now. Wait until you get home."

Really? What? But as soon as she handed me the card, I knew it was something I had been waiting for, something I had been expecting. I felt a thrill. Head to toe. It was like getting a phone call I had been anticipating for a long time. I guess all my life. I already knew I would go before I opened the card. I knew I was supposed to go, and since I arrived two days ago, that feeling has grown into I belong here. I'm home. It's unsettling and a little scary, but still I have never felt such contentment as I felt yesterday lying in the river cooling off. I was a leaf floating on the rushing water, looking up at the sky, but the water was not sending me headlong downstream, it was holding me, cradling me, and I trusted the water to keep me safe as if it were my mother and I was its baby. I knew it wouldn't let me go. The water was teaching me that there's nothing to be afraid of.

I managed to cut short the group pow wow called by Plutarch. It was obvious that only Plutarch and maybe Hyperides were interested in discussing why we're here, what does it all mean, blah, blah, blah. I know I want to be here, and I don't care why. I went down to the river again and started building another hot pool to soak in. It took a lot of trial and error to get the rocks arranged just right for the optimum balance of hot water coming down from the hillside with cold water seeping in through cracks in the rocks on the river side, but there was no hurry, and I was not hurrying.

Plutarch and Hyp saw what I was doing and came down. They wanted to help. I didn't really want them to. I am an engineer after all and capable of designing and constructing a rock enclosure, but it wasn't my pride being challenged that made me feel like I didn't want their help; I just wanted to be alone with the rocks and the water. I should have told them how I feel. They would have understood. Why didn't I? Just habit I suppose. Go along to get along.

The two men and I made an almost perfect pool, big enough for all three of us, with just the right balance of hot and cold, and I found some flat rocks for seats. They were impressed by my design and my eye for just the right rocks placed in just the right spots. Nice of them to be nice I suppose, but I wasn't building the pool to gain their approval or to impress them, I was trying to learn a lesson from the rocks. Since you want to know, Plutarch, that's what we're here for. You might understand if you can get out of your head. The rocks speak if you are able to listen.

Later in the afternoon before dinner, I picked a lot of black-berries and baked a pie, the first pie I ever made. Everybody said it was really good. It was definitely tasty, thanks to the honey.

* * *

Pausanias's Blog

I couldn't wait to get out of the pool and start walking up the river. Thank you Hypatia for speaking up and ending that non-sense. I'd rather walk than talk any day, especially here. We've been given an awesome gift out of the blue and it's not right to spend our precious time here theorizing about why we're here and what it all means. You're not supposed to look a gift horse in the mouth, right? Plutarch is an anxious type, in his head too much. I feel sorry for him. I thought Corinna might come with me like she did yesterday (or did I go with her?), but she went off with Triptolemos for a bee encounter, which experience she re-lated in breathless detail during dinner (hmm, snarky, am I jeal-ous?). Corinna, though, obviously has a thing for bees, not just for Trip. She mentioned that on the first day here when we took our walk in the woods.

We all wonder what's up with the three grown siblings in their 30s all living here together. Who knows? Maybe Hyper-boreans have to take a vow of celibacy to qualify for immortal-ity. Do immortals have children who are immortal? And where do they live, anyway? They're not sleeping in the lodge, unless there's a secret basement underneath the oak floor. Not out of the question, considering.

The three Greeks must be fronting some sort of back-to-na-ture religious cult, and we're in the meet and greet phase of the sell. There's the aura of mystery, the suggestion of some secret to be revealed, the allusions Clea makes to spiritual principles, just the whole chill out, live-in-the-moment message. What else could it be? We're the donkeys and Clea is dangling the carrots. Now the third sister, the 'special' one with intuition, is brought into the story. Can't wait for her dramatic appearance. Probably timed for a full moon (must check the moon tonight).

What's going on here is obvious to me, but maybe not to everyone else. I don't know and don't care. Hanging out here with the cult is way better than having to sit through a time-share pitch in order to get a free weekend in a three-bedroom condo in Florida––what's left of Florida. It's such a relief to get away from the stress of living in a world on the verge of environmental collapse and in a disintegrating country desecrated by the OAP.

Maybe I can stay here if I agree to convert? How bad can it be? The person who invited me here was adamant about how I would love this place. And I do love it! I'm happy to wait for the veil to be lifted and then we'll see just what we've got ourselves into. In the meantime, I'm going to explore and enjoy myself in beautiful Hyperborea. When I die and my life flashes before me, these two weeks might turn out to be the highlight.

Observant as always Pausanias. You once wrote about a place like this and even mention me:

On what is called the Gaeum (sanctuary of Earth) is an altar of Earth; it too is of ashes. In more ancient days they say that there was an oracle also of Earth in this place. On what is called the Stomium (Mouth) the altar to Themis has been built. All round the altar of Zeus Descender runs a fence; this altar is near the great altar made of the ashes. The reader must remember that the altars have not been enumerated in the order in which they stand, but the order followed by my narrative is

that followed by the Eleans in their sacrifices. By the sacred enclosure of
Pelops is an altar of Dionysus and the Graces in common; between them
is an altar of the Muses, and next to these an altar of the Nymphs.

You wrote about a lot of places, though more dispassionately
then. Now you're a modern cynic.

Today I started my exploration of the river. I followed a faint
trail along the near bank (the lodge side) that led northwesterly
upriver. It didn't last long, and soon I had to make my way
by climbing the bank and bushwhacking through moderately
heavy brush or hiking alongside the river whenever a strand of
rocks wide enough to form a trail was exposed.

The sun was shining in a cloudless blue sky as it has since
we arrived, just like in mythological Hyperborea. As it passes
by the lodge the river is flowing through a fairly narrow, deep
cut, creating a strong current, but once I'd made it about a mile
upstream from the lodge, the river turned in a sharp bow and
widened out. It was much shallower and slow moving, like a
small lake, with pebbles on the bottom instead of rocks. There
were rocky beaches and even some sand beaches on both sides,
and it was easy to wade across—only about six to eight inches
deep in the middle. Poplars, alders, cottonwoods, but mostly wil-
lows lined the banks. So peaceful. I took my boots off and waded
to the other side where there was a sandy spot and lay down in
the sun. I closed my eyes and listened to the birds. Then I heard
something moving in the woods behind me and scrambled up.
Someone said, "Hey, man. What's up?"

The man was in his 50's, maybe older, wearing blue jeans, a
flannel shirt, and a faded baseball cap. I couldn't make out the
logo on it. He had a full black beard that ended at his shirt col-
lar and was carrying a small-caliber rifle, which he kept pointed

down, thankfully. He was not menacing, but I was startled. Being in Hyperborea for a few days had lulled me into feeling that no one else existed in the world, but here he was, one of Plutarch's Others. And he had a gun.

I said, "Just talking a walk. It's so nice here."

–Yeah, but like walking from where to where? You're not from around here. I don't usually run into people when I'm out hunting squirrels, but here you are.

"Plenty of squirrels around here, that's for sure." The squirrel hunter was waiting for me to answer his question, while I tried to decide how I should answer.

–So, squirrels, huh?

–Dinner.

"Oh, yeah." After living on nothing but grains, nuts, and vegetables for the last three days, the thought of eating a squirrel turned my stomach.

–Would like to know what you're doing out here if you don't mind.

"I'm, uh, staying with"...I was thinking, is it OK to use their Greek names? What should I say? Finally I said, "you know, the people up the river about a mile from here."

–At the old hot springs place?

–Yeah. I'm visiting them for a couple of weeks. They invited me.

His face was more concerned now. "Those people aren't the friendliest sort. Surprised they have friends. Never met anyone out here that stayed with them. Usually, it's someone hungry hoping there's fish in the river here."

–I like to explore. I used to write a travel blog. Guess I can't help looking around wherever I am.

"What's it like there with them?" he asked. "Whenever I get near their property, I get a bad feeling, like butterflies in my stomach. Once this big guy just appeared out of nowhere across the river from me. He was staring me down letting me know I'd better not cross."

–That must have been Trip. He's a nice guy, and so is his sister. They're good people. They just like their privacy. People still come around looking for the hot springs.

–Folks living around here know to leave them alone.

–So you live close by?

–Close enough.

–You and your family? Are there a lot of people living in these woods?

He didn't answer.

–Must be tough to live out here.

–Better than dumpster diving in the city and trying to stay out of prison—no one wants to do their so-called 'community service.' They scoop up people like me and that's that. You're someone's slave for life.

–Yeah, everything these days is pretty fucked up. I gotta say being here is like finding an oasis in the desert.

–Got that right. There's water still clean enough, wood to burn, and food. Some trout left in the river and animals to hunt.

It seemed as if his curiosity was satisfied and the conversation was over, so I said, "Is it OK for me to keep walking up-river?"

–It's a free country. At least here it is. I can't stop you.

–But do you mind? I don't want to trespass.

–We don't own anything around here, so you can't be trespassing.

I told him, "OK, I'm just going to keep walking a bit further today. I'll keep to the river."

The man disappeared into the trees. I wondered how many Others were living out here, surviving...or living, depending on your perspective. All of the displaced and dispossessed people in the cities—the climate refugees, the destitute, the homeless, the working poor, the people like me who are barely hanging on to the little they've got—are they, and are we, living or surviving?

As long as my car keeps running I have a way to make money, but if the battery goes out, I won't be able to fix it. I might be able to barter with someone who can fix it. Go to the junk yard and pull a hybrid battery from an old Civic and hope it's still good, find someone who can switch them out, promise to let them use the car or something. I'm only a few days and a hundred miles or so away from that world, and I'm feeling lighter, happier. Definitely not thinking about having to leave, and if I think about that, which I'm doing right now, I'm definitely feeling like I don't want to leave.

* * *

"She's very tall," Hyperides says, watching Hypatia walking down to the river.

–Yes, she is, and really smart. She has an engineering degree. Used to work for Boeing in their aerospace division.

–Used to?

Plutarch is getting uncomfortable with the way the conversation is headed. "Maybe it's not appropriate to be talking about personal details that people here share with you."

–You worry too much, man.

Plutarch smiles in acknowledgement. "It shouldn't take too much imagination to guess what happened. Woman engineer working with a bunch of sexist men who don't respect her and are threatened by her intelligence and competence."

–Not to mention her looks.

–Her professional input was not solicited nor appreciated, ever, and she basically said screw it, I'm done.

–It sucks to lose a professional job that actually pays well.

–She's a math teacher now, in a public school no less.

–I work for the people, too, as a public defender. I try to keep innocent people accused of the crime of being poor out of jail. Like public schools there are still pockets of legal resistance on the coasts. Did you know that the vagrancy patrols now wear jackets with "VP Police" in big block letters on the back? They're no longer private gangs of thugs terrorizing helpless people. Now they get paid by the police to roam the streets looking for people who fit the very wide profile of doesn't have a home, doesn't have money, doesn't have ID, doesn't have credit, addict, mentally ill, looks funny. If the government ever decides to look toward Hyperborea you can be sure they'll arrest whoever is here and shut it down. Socialist pagan nature worshippers! Then someone will bribe someone to have the opportunity to buy the land, and the buyer will try to make a profit by developing it. Paradise lost...

Did you ever read Milton, Hyperides? He wrote this famous line:

Farewell happy fields, where joy forever dwells. Hail, horrors, hail.

These men with VP on their backs know nothing about happy fields or joy. For them it's better to reign in hell than serve in heaven, and so they make a hell to reign in.

...They hustle our clients to the police, who detain them and try to make some charge stick. What these sadists do is sanctioned by the OAP and the church, so there are no issues with legality or guilt. No issues at all. They are fucking patriots. I'm the traitor. My job is to represent the people they detain and make a case for why they shouldn't be sentenced to community service and forced to work as a so-called *productive citizen of One America*.

–Which means doing jobs that the OAP and church members won't do and don't want to pay someone to do. Jobs that machines and robots still can't do or do profitably.

–That's pretty much it, though it's not always just labor they are forced to do. Once they've been assigned to community service they are essentially slaves who must obey their masters or be sent back to prison. Some of the masters don't have actual work for them. They are only interested in private entertainment. Life gets pretty boring when you have it all.

–Depressing and horrifying.

–Honestly, Plutarch, it's brutal. I don't win too many cases, and it's not because I'm a lousy lawyer. Most of my clients get sentenced to community service, and all I can do is wish them luck. Makes me feel like shit knowing that they will probably be doing their so-called service for the rest of their lives.

Hyperides has a pained expression on his face. "You have noticed my cynical edge, haven't you? I'm not unaware of the impression I make. I'm obviously suspicious about this place and what we're doing here, but I'm not sure how much of that is due to the work I'm doing, which keeps me in a paranoid mind set. I don't think we're going to really understand why we've been invited until we hear from the big sister. This is all her idea, right? So what the hell is the idea?"

–It must be incredibly frustrating, trying to fight back knowing that you are virtually powerless...I have some thoughts about what Hyperborea is about, but I don't have confidence they are on the mark. I feel like their heart is in the right place. Clea and Trip both seem genuinely sincere. I trust them, but I get why you might not. I can't imagine doing what you do. I couldn't handle it.

–It is extremely frustrating, but what's the alternative? Give up? I have to say, though, despite my suspicion, this vacation in nature's wonderland is a welcome rest. I can't remember feeling this relaxed maybe ever.

–It is pretty nice here...

–Should we go down and help Hypatia build a pool?

–I guess, but I don't think she's looking for our help.

–I don't suppose she is, considering she's an engineer, but I haven't had a soak by the river yet.

Episode 10

–Wow, Trip left us some eggs! Anyone not eat eggs?

Corinna declines, but otherwise all share Hyp's excitement and eagerly anticipate the protein.

"Has anyone seen chickens around here?" Plutarch asks. "How could we not know there are chickens?"

–Scrambled OK?

–Hey, I'm going out exploring again today. Anyone interested? Maybe we will find where the chickens are hiding.

–I'll go with you.

–Hope you have shoes that can get wet, Hyp.

Hypatia isn't listening. She wants her eggs and then wants to be alone. Corinna plans to spend the day working in the gardens with Trip. There is mulching to do, and he is going to show her how to turn the compost, which is steaming away in several large piles contained by wire frames. "They're alive!" he said, pointing them out to her when walking back from the bee encounter. Plutarch promises to make bread.

* * *

Plutarch's Journal

What Pausanias and Hyp discovered today confirms what I already thought after Clea's welcome-to-Hyperborea talk on the first morning. I can't say it's a cult yet, but it's something cultish, like a secret society, and at some point they will reveal the secret, probably in a dramatic flourish, though I hope not. For now I trust Clea not to be running a con. I really like her, not just what she says, but her. If the reveal comes with bells and whistles and then a condescending pitch as if we're gullible idiots willing to trade our integrity (and hand over our money) for wish-fulfilling fantasies I will be greatly disappointed.

I'm thinking of a book titled "The Secret" published a few years before I was born (I think) that is still selling strong and that generated an impressive product line of videos and merchandise that is still available today. I think the great 'secret' was the power of positive thinking, which no one with any common sense could possibly question as extremely useful in life. Always thinking you're going to fail or the worst is going to happen is obviously a self-defeating approach except to those it's not obvious, but to promote common sense as "The Secret" with a capital "S" is disingenuous. For whom is this a secret? Only those people stupid enough to go online and buy all the 'Secret' stuff. I feel sorry for them. People so desperate for quick fixes and false hope that engaging in positive thinking to the degree necessary to actually change their lives and raise them out of their misery is probably impossible. But that's the point, isn't it? Keep them buying the newest products that will supposedly help them become successful and happy. If using the Secret actually worked it would put the peddlers of the Secret out of business. That's not a viable business plan.

We are all more or less convinced that what was already obvious is almost certainly true to some extent. The only question is the extent. Strangely, though, after hearing about the wellspring in the forest—or should it be called a fountainhead? Or 'the tank'? I was as unconcerned as Corinna always is, which I suppose is because I already suspected there would be some sacred site hidden on the property where we would be taken in the middle of the night under a full moon. Of course it would be a hot spring, and it seems that our friends have discovered it prematurely. Or maybe not. Maybe it was meant to be.

Clea does seem to anticipate us. I know that Hyperides thinks we're being monitored. He's been scouting for cameras but hasn't found any yet, but as he points out, it's pretty easy to hide them in the trees. My lack of concern, which is not my usual response, is in keeping with a general mood of unconcern that continues to grow in my consciousness every day I'm here. Hyperborea has that effect. Days without accessing the data stream. Days without agendas. Hours passing without notice. Minutes going by without thoughts. The outside is the inside. Rocks are furniture. Breezes tossing tree branches around is entertainment. Listening to the different birds and trying to mimic their calls is a pastime. At the end of two weeks, I may reach a point of ultimate nonconcern about anything except whatever is immediate in that moment. My consciousness may be occupied entirely by each moment instead of hovering beside the moment, inspecting it. If I understood Clea on the first day, that may be the goal here.

Is that good or bad?

Not the right question. Is that something I desire or not?

I should say that I wasn't unconcerned about the bread I made today with rye flour and sunflower seeds. I was proud of it and glad everyone loved it.

* * *

Corinna joins Trip at the compost bins. "Thanks for the eggs, man! Even though I don't eat them, everyone else was ecstatic, especially Hyp. The gang devoured them! So where are the chickens anyway? We haven't seen or heard them. How much property do you have here that you can hide chickens?"

–A lot. 200 acres? 300? I don't really know. We've never done an official survey. I'm not sure if there ever was an official survey.

–And all yours...nice.

–Plenty of room to hide chickens. I'll take you to them, but there's work to do first. Grab that pitchfork.

–Trip, this will be the first time in my life I've ever held a pitchfork. I didn't even think pitchforks were something anyone used anymore, just something you see in a movie.

This is the first time Corinna has held any tool outside of a hammer or screwdriver and the first time she's ever done anything that could be called yardwork. She is thinking rapid-fire, Corinna style, *I should be wearing overalls and a red bandana. No...dungarees and a flannel shirt. Where did that word 'dungarees' come from? What are dungarees? I shouldn't be wearing my flip flops that's for sure. This compost is going to get all over my feet and between my toes. Jeez, those pitching forks look deadly.*

–If you hang out with me, it won't be the last time you'll have that pitchfork in your hands: the compost needs turning every few days.

–So I'm drafted, and you haven't even seen me pitch yet!

–See how it's steaming? All the microscopic creatures in there are heating it up. How hot is it?

Corinna checks the gauge stuck in the middle of the pile. "It says 90 degrees! Holy shit!"

–Yeah, that's too hot for the worms, so we should turn it. It heats up at the bottom. The bottom material that's cooking away needs to be moved up to the top to cool down, and the stuff at the top needs to be moved down to get it cooking. Then do it again and again until it's done. Pretty much a never-ending process since we always need more compost.

–So is it done when you stick the pitchfork into the middle, pull it out, and the forks are clean?

Trip laughs, "More like the opposite of baking a cake. It's done when you pull the pitchfork out and there's nice dark stuff sticking to it...but you don't need to test it that way. It's just done when you think it's cooked enough to be decent growing material. Sometimes it's just not that good, just good enough."

–It's hard to believe these piles of twigs and grass and leaves and whatever else is in there turns into soil just by sitting there.

–Like I said, it's full of tiny things that are alive. The pile seems to just be sitting there, but it's actually a bundle of molecular movement, creating heat—it's like a little earthy sun.

Corinna shoves the pitchfork down into the pile and pulls out a smoking mass. It is heavy and smells...it smells like she imagines it would smell if her head were buried underground. It is suffocating and intoxicating. "Oh my God, look at all of the worms!" The earthy mass is writhing. Images of snake pits from horror movies are popping up in her mind, except these are worms, and it isn't a pit, it's a pitchfork full of worms, and she is holding it. She isn't afraid or grossed out. She's entranced. *What an image! I wish I had my camera. Why don't I have my camera?! A closeup showing the patterns of writhing worms cutting to other images of similar patterns in nature--clouds, schools of fish, whatever writhes like these worms.*

–Yo, Corinna, the idea is to dump that on top and then get another load and another and so on.

–But these worms, they're amazing. I've never seen anything like this. It's so cool.

"You're going to see a lot of worms today," Trip smiles. "They're basically making these piles of stuff into soil. They eat all of these branches and leaves and poop it out as soil. It's more complicated than that, but I can't remember the chemistry. The main thing is that worms can actually eat the material in these piles and turn it into something we can grow food in. That's nature for you. Everything has a purpose."

"When you said *it's alive*, I didn't imagine it being this alive." Corinna laughs.

Triptolemos faces Corinna and says emphatically, almost solemnly, "everything is alive." He wants her to understand that he means what he is saying. "Not just the things you think of as alive, like all of these plants and trees...us. Everything. The rocks, the mineral water, the air we breathe."

Corinna doesn't know what to say, and if she did, she wouldn't be able to speak just yet. She feels as if Trip has somehow entered into her and is holding her from the inside out. Holding her in outstretched arms and speaking to her as if she were a child. *I understand, Trip. I understand what you're telling me. I just realized I already knew that. Thank you for reminding me.*

* * *

Hypatia wants to be alone. As soon as she finishes the veggie scramble Hyperides made for breakfast she heads for the river under another blue sky and warm sun. *Is it going to be this nice every day we're here?* She is planning to follow Pau's route along the river to the place where it broadens out and forms a lake. *I wonder if I'll meet the squirrel hunter. I hope not.*

She is losing interest in hanging out with her companions, not that their company is tiresome or unwanted, but her inner voice is telling her to be alone with nature. When will she ever have such a chance again? *So take it*, is what she's hearing. In her tiny apartment which, thankfully, she can afford and has to herself, she is often alone, but she's not really alone: there's the furniture, books, pictures, and bric-a-brac that every human accumulates, objects that figure in the history of her life, that have associations, trigger memories, evoke feelings, so she's not alone, she's there with her past selves, remembering who gave her that chair, how excited she was to find that lamp, thinking she should read that book again, wondering if it's time to think about getting a new mattress, where this mug came from, what happened to her favorite pen? Why isn't it where it's supposed to be? Guess I'll check my email. OK, whoever's texting just stop, the alerts are annoying. "Being alone with nature" is a cliche, but maybe it's the only time a human being can actually be alone. There's just you, a homo sapien, a part of nature, alone with all the other parts that with you comprise the whole. There's nothing separating you from you, nothing from your past, nothing that will be a part of your future. Nothing dividing you into pieces. Nothing urging you to do this or that. Nothing that re-animates any of your past selves. There's just you, your "I," being who you are when you're not distracted, when you're present, just you the observer, the witness playing your part.

This is why you are.

Whoa, got to be careful. Caught up in her thoughts, Hypatia slips and barely regains her balance on the wet rocks along the river. She has to step from one large rock to the next to make her way and hope that she chooses well. The river is widening and slowing as she leaves the lodge behind. She can see tiny fish darting around in the shallow water. Sparrows and swallows are wheeling across from trees on one bank to trees on the other. And eventually there is the lake Pausanias described, the river maybe 75 yards or more across and now very shallow and barely moving, just rippling, and there's the beach on the other side. Nice. Warm sand.

She takes her shoes off to dry and lies on her back scooching around to make herself comfortable. At first all she's aware of is the warmth of the sand, how the sand feels sifting through her fingers and moving between her toes; then she notices the different sounds of the birds—there are so many, and they are so distinct. Tweets and warbles, sharp cries, soft twitters. If she focuses on their bird talk it gets louder and louder and after a while instead of being random bursts of chatter their talking becomes a wall of sound. If she shifts her awareness to the sounds of the river, the same progression happens from noticing the different sounds of the water flowing over rocks and lapping up onto the beach to picking out all of the variations of sound and hearing each of them distinctly, to all of the sounds intensifying and blending together and getting so loud that she feels overwhelmed, as if the river is going to wash over her like an ocean wave. It actually does sound like an ocean wave, and she breaks out of her reverie, a little frightened.

When she opens her eyes, she's not hearing anything anymore, and she watches the branches and leaves of the trees above her on the bank being swirled by breezes coming and going. At some point she sees what she thinks must be an eagle circling overhead. She's not thinking about anything; she's nothing but awareness, observing, watching, seeing, feeling, understanding the Good.

I'm alone, but I'm part of the all.
Beauty surrounds me.
I don't need anything.
I don't want anything.

Episode 11

–Which way, Pausanias?

–Just follow the river. Be careful. The rocks are slippery and not always stable stepping stones.

Pausanias wants to go farther downriver, past where he'd encountered the squirrel hunter. "I should have introduced myself and got his name," he tells Hyp as they make their way along the bank, "but I wasn't in the social mode after being here for a few days."

They scramble along the river where they can and whack their way through the forest when they have to, each carrying a stout driftwood branch to smack aside the brush. Hyperides is happy to have something to do and somewhere to go even though their destination is just "farther than yesterday." Pausanias just wants to see what's around the next bend, and then the next and the next. When they get to the severe bow where the river widens out, they see Hypatia lying on a small sandy beach across from them.

–Should we say hi?

–I'd rather keep moving, Hyp, if you don't mind. Anyway, she obviously came out here to be alone.

–Right. Ever since the first day when she was soaking in the pools by the river she's been doing her own thing even when we're all together.

–She's a thoughtful person.

–Did you know she's an aerospace engineer? Or was...she didn't get along with her sexist male colleagues.

–I bet she didn't.

They clear the elbow of the river, climbing over old driftwood logs that have been piling up there for what? Centuries? Some of the old logs serve as garden beds for cedar trees and ferns but mainly it's just a massive conglomerate of oversized forest debris that floated this far and got stuck in the ever-growing pile. They can see quite a way downriver now as it straightens out and narrows down, the trees on both sides leaning over and shading the water. There is no sign of human habitation. No Others. No smoke. Just thick forest.

"I wish I knew how to fish. This looks like a place that has fish, and I'd like to catch some, clean them, and eat them." Hyperides is really hungry for protein.

–Your father didn't teach you to fish?

–Nope. Do fathers even do that anymore?

–I'm sure they do some places. Places that still have fish. I wouldn't feel safe wandering around in a national forest anymore, too many preppers living off the land shooting at anything that moves.

–What are we doing out here then, Pau?

–Good question. For some reason it feels safe. Trip will protect us! Still, I don't think we should go too deep into the woods.

They're about a mile and a half from the lodge and walking along the river here is easier. The current is not as strong as it is at the lodge, the water deeper and blacker from the shade of the overhanging trees, no rapids, and there is pebbly beach along both sides. Pausanias suddenly yelps. Butterflies. Monarchs. They're pollinating milkweed and verbena growing on the edge of the forest bordering the river where there's some sun. He moves up closer to watch them and Hyperides joins him.

Pausanias stays very still and whispers, "I've never seen a Monarch butterfly, except in the butterfly house of a zoo."

–Neither have I. Aren't they endangered?

–Since before I was born. I thought they were extinct.

Pausanias is grateful for somehow being at a place in the world where Monarch butterflies still exist. "I'm so glad I came here, Hyp, just to see this."

–Just to see butterflies?

–Not just just. To me it's a friggin' miracle. I've traveled a lot, all over the world and been through all the states, and butterflies are a rare sight. I can't imagine what it was like when everyone who had a garden had butterflies. Kids actually used to have butterfly collections. It was a popular hobby, just like collecting stamps used to be. They'd go out in the back yard with their net and find another specimen to pin up for their collection.

Hyperides is listening but distracted. He sees something that looks like it might be a trail and moves toward it, breaking the spell. Pau reluctantly follows him. "Guess we should see where it goes. Are we still in Hyperborean territory here?"

–Don't know, but it's definitely a trail that is used. Not sure it's a good idea to go too far, considering.

–OK, let's try it for a little while, see if it follows the river or goes deeper into the woods.

The trail is narrow, allowing only one person at a time, and it does follow along the river, which they never lose sight of through the trees. After walking just five minutes, steadily gaining elevation, they emerge from the trees and are looking down at the river about 100 feet below. They are overlooking a shallow ravine, the river having narrowed, and the banks are now small bluffs on either side. The water is dark and deep, flowing slowly. It's a magical setting, but the rock structure on the edge of the bluff adds an extra jolt of mystery. It looks like it might be a well: circular, mortared brick, about three feet high. Flat river rocks embedded in the ground surround it forming a two-foot wide skirt all the way around.

"Uh, this is something someone made for a reason," Hyp is nervous now. Who does this belong to and are they around?

"It's not a well, but it's filled with water...mineral water. It's hot. See the steam? Smell the sulfur?" Pausanias sticks his hand in the water. "Nice. Not too hot, but hot enough. What an awesome place to soak. It must be placed right over a spring."

"There's a trail down to the river from here," Hyperides is scanning the area, "and there's wax from candles along the edge of this...a...tank?"

They decide not to linger not knowing who might be responsible for the tank and whether or not they might be close by. People definitely use it and not too long ago. The ground around the tank is packed dirt, clear of brush, grass, moss, and the trail down to the river is obviously used. On their way back they decide there's a good chance the tank is on Hyperborean property and something used by guests or maybe just by the siblings.

–It's so far from the lodge. Who would come all this way just to soak? It's not like it's that easy to get here.

–There might be a decent trail through the forest back to the lodge, or back to the 'authorized' guest facilities.

–There's just enough room for one person. Maybe it's for people like Hypatia who want solitude, who just want to be alone with their thoughts.

"Or who want to stop thinking entirely." Pausanias thinks this is the more likely goal of a session in the tank. On the walk back, he and Hyp share their theories on what's going on in Hyperborea, and they are in general agreement that the siblings are anything from an eccentric iconoclastic mini-cult of some kind and looking for some company—if not actually trolling for possible mates—to being the pleasant non-threatening front of a larger, scarier cult with perhaps more serious aims. Both are in agreement as to what is coming: the reveal, the lifting of the veil, followed by the pitch.

–I'll tell you, Hyp, if the conditions for staying on here are not too weird and not too expensive, I'm all in, and so what if they're looking to hook up with the right like-minded people? I'm available and would love to live here. What am I losing out on if I stay? Going broke and then getting charged with community service and having to work for some rich OAP asshole?

–I get it, Pau, but I'm not there. I'd feel like a coward if I just said fuck it I'm out of here.

Your always feel your duty to the Law, Hyperides. Once you said in court:

If men are to be happy, the voice of law, and not a ruler's threats, must reign supreme; if they are free, no groundless charge, but only proof of guilt, must cause them apprehension; nor must the safety of our citizens depend on those who slander them and truckle to their masters but on the force of law alone.

Episode 12

Hypatia is the first of the gang of five to come into the kitchen. She is hoping to find eggs left for them again, but instead of eggs, Clea is sitting at the table drinking tea.

–Oh, hey.

–Hey, how're you doing?

–Doing great, fantastic really. I spent yesterday lying on a little beach by the river basically listening to all of the sounds of that spot—the water, the birds, the trees, the wind. It was so relaxing. I don't remember thinking of anything. My memories are of sounds, and the memories are so vivid.

–So glad you're taking such good advantage of your time here.

–That's funny, Clea. Most people would consider my time wasted.

–Most people throw away all of their time as if time is worthless. I bet you feel like lying on that beach yesterday was one of the best uses of your time ever.

–Pretty much. Maybe the best day of my life.

–That makes me happy, Hypatia.

One by one the others come in and join the breakfast club.

–No eggs today, Clea?

–Not yet, Hyperides, but later. Trip is going to make a spinach quiche for you all. We're inviting you to dinner at our place—or I should say our places.

–Really? That's exciting, and not because of the quiche. We've all been wondering where you sleep and hang out.

"A quiche sounds good, too," added Plutarch. "Thanks for inviting us."

–I'll be here about an hour before sunset to show you the way, and Trip will bring you back. It will be dark by then.

*** *** ***

–I told them you were making a quiche, Trip.
–I bet they were surprised.
–I'd say thrilled.

The men are convinced we're a cult, which I suppose we are, but they don't feel like we're sinister—yet.

Our hobbit homes ought to put them at ease.

Clea, though, is not at ease. This is the first group ever to be invited to their forest enclave—for dinner, even! Where is everyone going to sit? Poor Trip, he's going to have to be cooking all day. And poor Corinna, what's she going to do without him?

Something's going on that her sister hasn't felt ready to let her in on, which is not good. It means either Themis isn't clear on what's going on or she feels the need to keep it from her for some reason. One or the other or both is unsettling. Themis is usually confident about what she knows...what she "remembers"...and Clea actually can't remember when she kept something from her.

Don't worry, sis, you know there's never need for worry.

Go away. You're breaking our agreement.

When Themis first entered her mind, adding another voice to compete with her own inner voice, Clea felt at once the necessity of creating boundaries. Having a sister who not only could basically read her mind but who had access to sources of information too fantastic to comprehend, a sister who could somehow project her voice inside her mind, was to put it as mildly as possible, disconcerting.

She and Themis talked it through, and talked some more, as it was not easy to determine the boundaries they needed to agree on and how they would be enforced. Clea above all else wanted to protect her right to inner privacy. She didn't want to feel as if her sister were eavesdropping on her or monitoring her, which it turns out is problematic as Themis tried to describe how she is somehow able to see or read or access...

"I don't know how to explain, Clea, but it's as if I'm able to access the data stream of the universe...there's no time or space, just the data, all of it—or maybe not all, how would I know?—including your thoughts and Trip's..." which to Clea sounded terrifying and ridiculous and absurd, but Themis could talk to her as if she were talking to herself, so however impossible it was for Themis to claim she had these...powers...she seemed at least to have that power.

They came to an agreement with a lot of leeway. Themis was not to intrude except when necessary. No checking in to see how she is doing or just to chat. How she is doing is her private domain, and she'll let her sister know if she wants to talk about it or not. Any chatting should be done with their outside voices. Necessary should be unambiguously necessary. Of course, Themis took liberties. They are sisters.

Clea is feeling as if something necessary is coming, and it makes her nervous. From the start there was something about this particular group––and not just one of the guests being named Plutarch––that felt different, and Triptolemos felt it too.

Episode 13

Themis had already been living with her grandparents for several years before Zoe and Charles came to live with them after graduating from high school. Like Themis, they were completely disillusioned with life in One America. Their economic prospects were severely compromised by their being in the resistance, but they were not particularly ambitious. Their wanting to live remotely and off-the-grid wasn't just because they were not going to be able to establish credit, buy a house, and live a life relatively free of financial stress––they wanted to escape because they were choking on the country's air that was no longer just oxygen and nitrogen but also equal parts anxiety, anger, and frustration. Inhale resentment and rage, exhale exhaustion and self-pity. Inhale violent fantasies, exhale domestic abuse. Inhale sexual repression, exhale misogynistic slurs. Moments of joy and peace, of fulfillment and contentment, were like fleeting miracles.

They missed how they always felt at grandma and grandpa's place, where the air was clean and the water comforting. Where the trees whispered and the birds sang. Mom and dad understood when they explained how they felt, but they had no desire to go with them and start another life. They were firmly rooted and not willing to trade the acute pain of transplanting with the chronic pain of living in a country gone wrong. Their coping strategies were well developed by now.

Themis moved in with her grandparents when she was 13. School was impossible for her academically and socially. Coping with life in mid-21st century America was impossible for her. Everyone in the family understood. Themis was not just "special," she was completely different. Her grandparents welcomed her, her parents were afraid for her, and her siblings adored her, but none of them really knew what she was experiencing, which she tried to explain, but as she always told them, giving up in frustration, how do you explain the unexplainable? She quit trying and just let everyone in her family try to understand in his or her own way as time went by.

The first time she entered Clea's mind was when grandpa had his accident.

Zoe, I'm sorry, but you have to tell mom and dad that grandpa fell in the river and hit his head. He died. Please come when you can.

Clea didn't realize that she hadn't imagined what she heard until they reached grandma on the satellite phone checking to make sure grandpa was OK. Then she thought she was psychic until Themis confided in her. Then she didn't know what to think.

Grandma died a few years after Zoe and Charles came to live at Hyperborea. Themis told them after she had died peacefully in her sleep that she knew grandma was going to die and had prepared her for death. She was so lonely without grandpa and had just been waiting for them to come and settle in. Clea and Trip had not asked Themis what she meant about "preparing grandma for death." By then they were used to cryptic statements that from anyone other than her would have been considered crazy if not frightening. Soon after they had come to live there, they were forewarned by their grandma about the uncanny things Themis might tell them. She sat down with them in the fairy tale cob cottage she and grandpa had created and told them they needed to trust whatever Themis said, no matter how difficult to comprehend or believe.

"She knows things from places far away and times long ago. She knows the future. What she knows is not limited by time or space. Grandpa said she is someone who might have been called a shaman or a seer, a soothsayer or a witch. 'Maybe even a goddess,' he said, 'who knows?' She doesn't care about being called anything. She says she's supposed to help, and she says you two are going to help her do what she's supposed to do."

They asked grandma what Themis is supposed to do and how they're supposed to help, but she said she didn't know, and she wasn't sure that Themis knew either, but Themis did tell her and grandpa a story once. She said it was a myth from Indonesia.

At the time of creation, the sky was close to the earth, and the Creator, who lived in the sky, used to let down gifts attached to the end of a rope to the human beings living on earth. Once he let down a stone and the first man and first woman wouldn't take it. They asked the Creator "What are we supposed to do with this stone? It's worthless. Give us something else." The Creator took the rope with the stone back and then lowered it down again with a banana. The first parents ran to the banana and eagerly took it. Then the Creator's voice from the sky rang out and said "Because you have chosen the banana, your life shall be like its life. When the banana tree has offspring, the parent stem dies; so you shall die like the banana tree, and your children shall take your place. If you had taken the stone instead, your life would have been like the life of a stone: changeless and immortal." The first parents realized their mistake, but it was too late.

Themis laughed after telling the story and said that she was here on earth to try to get people to choose the stone instead of the banana. That human beings always choosing the banana is the reason everything is so wrong.

Clea remembers this now. Something is up because this dinner invitation is not the usual course of events with guests, not that they've had that many guests for comparison. Themis has always been extremely picky about who gets invited, though she doesn't explain how she decides who to invite, and they don't bother to ask, anticipating more questions and confusion as Themis attempts to explain.

Clea had improvised when asked about the "authorized guests" sign. They had put up the sign because they didn't want anyone wandering into their private glade, which is where the trail beyond the sign leads.

PART II. AGON

Would that I were not among the men of the fifth age, but either had died before or been born after. For now truly is a race of iron, and men never rest from labor and sorrow.

Strength is right and reverence ceases to be; the wicked hurt the worthy, speaking false words against them, and swear an oath upon them. Zelos, foul-mouthed envy, delighting in evil, with scowling face, goes along with wretched men one and all.

And Nemesis, just retribution, and Aidos, respect, shrouding their bright forms in pale mantles, leave the wide-wayed earth and go back to Olympos, forsaking the whole race of mortal men, and all that is left by them to mankind is wretched pain. And there is no defense against evil.

HESIOD

Tell the king that the carven hall is fallen in decay.
Apollo has no chapel left, no prophesying bay, no talking spring.
The stream is dry that had so much to say.

THE LAST ORACLE AT DELPHI

Episode 14

Clea is nervous as she comes up the stairs to the porch where everyone is waiting. Themis had told her she was going to make an appearance and meet the guests, and Clea can't predict what "meeting the guests" might mean. Her sister is reliable but not predictable. Themis does not normally meet the guests, much less agree to have them over for dinner at their fairy-tale enclave in the woods. The situation is unprecedented.

"Where are we eating, Trip?" Clea asks after venting her anxiety about Themis throwing a dinner party. Triptolemos as always is imperturbable. "We'll eat outside; it's the only table that's big enough, and it's right by the oven. What are you worried about, sis? It's not like she's going to trance out while we're eating."

–You can't be sure of anything with her.

–It's a good thing. They all want to meet her, and from what I can tell they are open to whatever she has to say.

–What she has to say, sure, but what about what she does?

–This group has come a long way in what?––four days?—I haven't kept track, but they haven't even been here a week and they've progressed quite a bit already. Has anyone yet even asked for their phone? Usually there's one or two who beg to have the phone back, if only to hold it.

–Right, but still, Themis might say or do anything. She's not always in complete control. You know how she changes, and we don't know when it will happen.

–Yeah, that would disturb them. Maybe just the men, though. Hypatia and Corinna seem like they're ready for anything, however odd.

–And what are you going to do about Corinna?

–What do you mean?

–You know what I mean.

–We're simpatico, that's all.

The bee maiden.

C'mon, we're talking here. If you want to join in, then come over and join in.

It's going to be fine. Meet and greet is all.

On their fourth full day in Hyperborea, the guests are preoccupied with the dinner date with the family. Anticipation dominates their consciousness, taking them out of the reverie that has been deepening since they arrived. That first night had felt like crossing a threshold, though if asked, no one would be able to describe the threshold or say when it had been crossed. Was it when they had piled into the Subaru after standing under the Sinclair dinosaur waiting for Clea? There hadn't been more than a few words exchanged between them before she pulled up. No one could think of anything to say beyond a nervous "is she even coming?"

But once in the car, the relief felt from realizing the invitation wasn't a prank and they were at least on their way to somewhere might have been when the dream started. Was it when Clea had taken their phones and given them their names? When they opened the folded piece of paper and tried to pronounce it silently to themselves? Or when they were eating the first meal they had prepared, five strangers seated around a candlelit table far away from anything familiar. Outside, it was darker than anywhere they had ever been. When they stopped talking, all they heard was the crazy croaking of frogs. Normally they would have all been a little nervous, but there was something about the atmosphere that put them at ease, though if any of them had been asked about the 'atmosphere' that first night he or she would have said, "Do you mean the candlelight?"

On their fourth day, they're familiar with the atmosphere and its ease. They've been breathing it, moving around in it, sleeping in it, so today it's unsettling not to be at ease, to have this future event pulling them out of the present and distancing them from the natural world surrounding them. The atmosphere is changed. It doesn't occur to any of them why it is all too easy to break the spell and hurtle them back into their habitual mindset so often controlled by an imagined future.

Clea had brought up the effects of expectations and fantasies on their first morning in the garden, but no one is remembering that today, except Hypatia, who does not take what Clea says lightly. She has hiked to the wellspring––the 'tank' that Pausanias and Hyperides found––and is soaking in it. Leaning forward, her arms draped over the front of the mortared bricks, she's looking out over the river to the woods on the other side watching the birds darting around eating insects. She feels her awareness being yanked away from the birds and the sensations of her body immersed in hot mineral water by thoughts about the evening, images of what their homes will look like, the furnishings, will there be music, will there be wine, and she doesn't like it.

She fights back against the infiltration of thoughts. She wants to experience what she's experiencing now, not get snared in the net of imagining experiences that may never happen no matter how pleasant the fantasies might be. She's remembering Clea's admonitions. This is exactly what she was talking about.

This is why I'm here. To learn. The guys think it's a cult, but they're wrong. It's a school.

Socrates Scholasticus notes your renown as a teacher, Hypatia...

There was a woman at Alexandria named Hypatia, daughter of the philosopher Theon, who made such attainments in literature and science as to far surpass all the philosophers of her own time. Having succeeded to the school of Plato and Plotinus, she explained the principles of philosophy to her auditors, many of whom came from a distance to receive her instructions. On account of her self-possession and ease of manner, which she had acquired in consequence of the cultivation of her mind, she not infrequently appeared in public in the presence of the magistrates. Neither did she feel abashed in coming to an assembly of men. For all men on account of her extraordinary dignity and virtue admired her the more.

A great teacher and now a brilliant student!

Unlike Hypatia, the rest of the guests are not in a wrestling match with their minds trying to maintain their meditation on nature. They are monitoring the sun, waiting for it to go down. They are not remembering what Clea had to say three days ago. Corinna is the least distracted, working alongside Triptolemos digging up potatoes and harvesting corn. The three men are exploring upriver but aren't making much progress as one of them will bring something up about the upcoming dinner party which gets them talking, slowing them up. Plus, the hiking is more difficult than going downriver, so when they reach the spot where the road they took from the highway ends, where it was washed out and covered by the river some time ago, they decide it's a sign. The place to stop and turn around.

"I wonder how far the road used to go. You can see it continues up that rise on the other side." Pausanias wants to ford the river and follow it. "There might be a town. Why else build the road?"

"I know you want to follow it, but we need to get back. See the sun?" Plutarch has no intention of getting back late no matter what his friends want to do. Clea said meet at sunset.

Hyperides adds, "Only way through now is build a bridge, unless you want to risk your life swimming across. It's pretty deep here, and the current is strong. I agree with Plutarch. Time to head back. Our hosts are expecting us."

Episode 15

Pausanias's Blog

Plutarch, Hyp and I explored up the river from the lodge. Hiking was difficult. No trail to speak of and no rocky beach to traverse, just finding or forcing a way through the underbrush. I showed them what poison oak looks like and warned them to be careful. Neither of them had ever had it, so they might not be as careful as they should.

We were all looking ahead to dinner with the sibs and sharing our thoughts about what we expected, so we weren't getting very far. Does getting invited to dinner mean we're part of the family now? We've only been here four days but it feels like we're a family. Plutarch agreed. He said it was surprising how fast and easily we've settled into life in Hyperborea. Maybe it's because Clea and Trip treat us like brothers and sisters. Hyperides said he's going to ask if we can meet Themis if she's not there for dinner. He's obsessed with her. He said, "What if she's not the innocent orchestra conductor but instead the manipulative puppet master?" He's suspicious because he sees no reason why she should be "hiding from us" as he puts it.

We decided it was time to turn around when we got to where the river had washed out the road we took in from the highway. We could see that the road continued on the other side of the river. I wanted to try to find a way across and follow the road, but Plutarch was anxious to get back. He's not someone who likes to be late. He's the guy who has to get to the airport early enough to sit for at least an hour at the gate waiting to board. I have no doubt that Plutarch has never missed a flight.

We joined the girls who were waiting on the porch and told them about the washed-out road and how it continued up the hill on the other side. Corinna said she'd go with me to try to cross the river and see where it went. "Maybe it leads to the hunter's place!"

Everyone was excited about seeing where our hosts live. We know so little about them, but I've enjoyed not knowing and am apprehensive about finding out. After tonight we will have so much more information about them that I'm afraid the mysterious will become the mundane. Our romantic fantasies will be brushed aside and replaced with commonplace details, and the great mystery of why we were invited here will turn out to be nothing more than three lonely eccentrics seeking company. I would rather they are a cult, dangerous or otherwise.

Clea came to escort us just as the sun was going down. Following her up the trail, I suddenly felt shy, but I realized it wasn't shyness I was feeling, it was shame. We were all so excited—for what? To get to know them? No, we were excited to see how they live—to gawk—we were voyeurs anticipating titillating revelations. We regarded them as stars of a show, not as possible friends, not as our fellow brothers and sisters. It was shame I was feeling.

We were so animated while waiting for Clea on the porch, but now we were quiet, walking apart, and I believe everyone might have been feeling a little shame themselves at our childish excitement, as if we were going to the zoo.

We were following the trail that Corinna and I had taken on the first day, and when we passed the sign about "authorized guests," we realized that all it took to be an authorized guest was an invitation to dinner. Five minutes of walking later the trees, which had been thick, opened up, and we were on the edge of a spacious glade surrounded by enormous oaks, big-leaf maples, and towering pines.

There were three small homes, or rather habitats, or maybe huts is the right word? They looked as if they had been molded out of giant balls of clay. There were no straight lines, even around windows and doors, just curves and shadows created by the curves. Clea told us they were made of cob, clay soil mixed with sand, straw, and water. Strong, durable, and moldable. Her grandma was the cob artist, and they had built their "hobbit homes" under her direction. The cob homes were arranged in a circle around an outdoor oven also made of cob that was molded so that a giant hood came up and over it providing shelter. Triptolemos was there checking on his quiches and behind him was a large maple-wood table with benches which was set for dinner with plates and forks. I was surprised to see what looked like a bottle of wine.

Hyperides said to Clea, "Wine?" and she explained that grandpa had made the wine, and since this was a special occasion, they thought they could at least offer it. Everyone sat down at the table. Looking around the compound I saw a couple of solar panel arrays, rain barrels, and what looked like a well house, also made of cob. One of the taller pines on the perimeter had a ladder hanging down from its lowest large branch. I blurted out, "What's that ladder for?" pointing toward the tree. Trip said it was how they got up to what he calls the "Eagle's Nest."

–Good reception for the satellite phone and our Ham radio. You didn't think we were totally out of touch with the world did you? Never know when we might need a helicopter in an emergency, and we like to check in on what's happening out there every now and then.

"Internet, too?" Plutarch asked.

–Supplied by One America Web (OAW), so the news is just propaganda, but there are some fairly reputable sources we can access. We've had to order some things online before, and we arrange for pick up at the highway. It's expensive, so a last resort.

I could tell everyone's fantasies were getting punctured, just as I thought might happen: Wine? Internet? Ordering stuff online? What's the next illusion to be popped? What was happening was what I feared. Our pleasant romantic fantasies getting replaced by dull reality.

Then Themis appeared. Had anyone seen her coming? She was suddenly there at the table, smiling, dark hair framing her face. She said, "It's not easy to get up there, Pausanias. That ladder just takes you to the first branch strong enough to support you; then you have to climb. It's not just hard, it's scary, especially when you get to the top and the wind's blowing." She swayed with her arms in the air imitating the treetop. "I don't go up there. That's Trip's domain. I'm not sure I'm even strong enough to pull myself up that ladder."

The conductor had arrived. The orchestra sat up straight on the benches and waited for direction.

"So does anyone want a little wine? Not much. Don't worry."

When she said, "Don't worry," I felt my mind and body relax, not necessarily in that order, and I saw that everyone felt the same. I saw my new friends loosen up and their faces soften. It was like a cloud had just passed over and the sun was back out. To describe Themis is to describe her voice, which is like an army of voices commanding you. Listening and then obeying is not a choice. Themis poured us each what amounted to maybe two thimblefuls of wine and made a toast: "to health!" It was as if we were having communion. No, it was communion.

Hyperides looked completely dumbfounded. Plutarch, for once, was speechless. Hypatia's eyes were closed, and she looked as if she were far away, somewhere, in her mind. Corinna was smiling--beaming, rather. Clea looked worried, and Trip, as usual, looked amused. I was trying to stay aware of what was happening so I could write about it, and it was not easy. A lot was happening on a lot of levels--physical, emotional, mental--both consciously and unconsciously. What is happening? That was the question.

Triptolemos brought two quiches over, and we ate, sharing bread and wine. At the time I thought, *this is a cult, and I hope it's an innocent, sweet nature cult or something like that because if Themis wants you in it, you're in it.*

And I was right.

* * *

Hypatia's Journal

It's late in the morning of the fifth day, at least that is my best guess. I wouldn't be surprised at all if it were actually the sixth or seventh or some other day. I'm not tracking time right now, and I don't know if I will again. Sound ridiculous? I agree. Everything I write this morning is going to sound pretty ridiculous. Last night we had dinner with the family at their home in the woods, but it was really dinner with Themis: Clea and Trip seemed to disappear after she arrived. Actually, when Themis arrived, everything seemed to disappear except her voice, which was mesmerizing. Whatever happened yesterday before dinner is unimportant. I'm not sure I would be able to remember it clearly anyway. I know I took a soak in the 'well' or the 'tank' or whatever we're calling it and watched the birds.

Everyone had been so excited about the dinner invitation. We were looking forward to getting some idea of who the three siblings are beyond their roles as Hyperborean hosts. I was mainly hoping to meet Themis, thinking she could help me understand why I feel like I belong here. I really don't want to leave and need to know if staying is a possibility.

Knowing that in a week I will be going back to my old life depresses me. I realize now how lonely I am. I don't have anyone.

No husband, no partner, no kids, no siblings. Do any of us here have siblings? No one ever mentions them, which is not so odd. Bringing children into the world is overloaded with political and moral considerations. Having just one kid is the norm—for those who want children at all—and a lot of couples don't. A lot of couples don't even bother with marriage.

I'm lucky to have my own place, but I'm lonely, and I don't have nature in my life. Until I came here, I had no idea I missed nature or that nature was something to miss. Now here I am immersed in nature, and I have siblings! I have a family. Or so it feels like anyway.

The men came back from their excursion and joined Corinna and me on the porch to wait for Clea to fetch us. They, especially, were flush with anticipation, or maybe just flushed from their hike, probably both, but once we were following Clea through the woods, the mood changed, and the animated talk stopped. I can't say why. Maybe we sensed that everything was going to change and felt some unconscious fear of that. Everything did change, but there was nothing to fear.

There were three 'hobbit homes,' as Clea called them, and rightly so, except they weren't built into a hill. Each was a stand-alone structure, and they were arranged in a circle around a large outdoor oven with a tall hood coming up from the back overhanging it about four feet or so. The hood was like a canopy that partially covered a beautiful wood table. Everything was made with cob, which we learned from Clea is clay mixed with sand, straw, and water. Clay cement. Their grandmother was the architect.

The oven is an amazing creation; it brought up an old image from childhood of the hookah-smoking caterpillar from Alice in Wonderland. How far down the rabbit hole are we anyway? I didn't think that far until Themis appeared, until she spoke.

Now I'm not sure of anything. I was the only person who saw her coming out of one of the huts and walking over to us. Even though everyone seated at the table should have seen her, I was the only person who could see her, as if she somehow singled me out.

What I'm trying to describe may not make a lot of sense. Mea culpa: you had to be there. She wasn't looking directly at me, but even though our eyes were not meeting, I felt her looking into me, and I swear I heard her say "Hi, Hypatia," except her mouth didn't move, and if she actually had said that loud enough for me to hear, everyone would have heard. But no one looked up, and no one heard. While she was looking into me, she was looking at everyone else as she made her way to the table where we were sitting. Her appearance startled everyone but me.

Why me, Themis? Is it because I realized today that this is a school?

Pausanias had spotted a rope ladder hanging down from one of the tallest trees surrounding the clearing, and Trip had just told us it led to their communications center, their link to the outside world. Themis said it's hard to get up there since you have to climb the tree after you manage to get up the rope ladder. Then she raised her arms and started swaying as if she were a tree in the wind and said it was scary going up to the "Eagle's Nest" as Trip called it.

Earlier we had been surprised by what looked like a bottle of wine on the table and as soon as Themis sat down between me and Corinna, she said, "Does anyone want a little wine? Not much. Don't worry." The effect of her voice was dramatic. We all (except for Clea) seemed to freeze for a moment and then reboot. Pent-up anticipation and nervous energy hissed away as if from a balloon, and we relaxed. She told us not to worry, and we followed orders. Clea had told us that Themis is the conductor, and she definitely is. Her voice is irresistible. She poured no more than a swallow of wine for everyone and raised her cup, toasting "To health!" And so we drank to health of all things, which, if you think about it, is a great thing to drink to. Then we shared the food that Trip had made.

While we ate, she told us how grandma was the cob artist while the grandchildren were the builders. Zoe and Charles came to live there, and building their homes was the first priority. Themis had already moved into hers. Guests would need the lodge, and they all would need a place to live. She apologized for the sign on the trail, but it was more effective at keeping guests from intruding than telling them to kindly respect their privacy. "You know how it is. It's just like with your devices, you can't stop yourself from peeking."

By the time we were finished eating it was dark but clear, and light from a waxing moon was flooding the clearing. We were all trying hard to be polite, holding back questions, pretending we weren't anxious to know everything about them and their lives. Clea brought out a teapot, poured, and asked "Well, is our place like you imagined?"

Plutarch said he had imagined a clearing in the forest, like in a fairy tale, but not the cob huts. How could he have imagined them? He had no idea anything like them existed. Corinna said it was pretty close to what she imagined since Clea had mentioned their "hobbit homes," but their actual homes were larger and more elaborate than she had pictured. No one had imagined the oven with the sculpted canopy hanging over it. Themis said, "Next time you visit, we can show you inside our homes. You're all welcome."

"Which one is yours, Themis?" Hyperides had not said a word since she had first spoken. Rather than talking he had been rather obviously looking at Themis, doing his best not to stare but not succeeding.

–Which do you think, Hyperides?

–That one (pointing). The one that looks like a bird cage.

–How'd you know?

–Because you're like a bird. You are a bird.

This is when everything changed.

Clea looked desperate. The rest of us were wondering what had just happened. Hyperides would never say anything like that, at least the Hyperides we had come to know, and it wasn't just the words he used, it was the way he said them with such solemn sincerity, with no trace of irony, no cynicism. He spoke with reverence, and we were all momentarily stunned.

Themis broke through the eerie silence that followed Hyp's bizarre announcement: "Wow, Hyperides, I never realized I built my house to look like a cage, but I'm seeing it now. Maybe that's why I always want to be outside where I can see the sky, where I can fly." Hyp kept his eyes on her but didn't reply. Themis was smiling at him, or I should say she was smiling for him. We were enveloped in the energetic glow generated by whatever was happening between them, until Themis abruptly asked if we wanted to see the geodesic dome grandpa had constructed before we went back to the lodge. "He and grandma did their yoga and meditated there. They'd play Indian bhajans and sing along."

Corinna asked, "What's a bhajan?"

–It's like a Hindu hymn made into a song with verses and a chorus. Very catchy Indian rhythms. Grandma loved to dance to them.

–What do you do there? The same thing?

–Come. I'll show you something we do there for our health, for the health of all, and since we toasted to that, it's perfect.

Themis was energized and energizing, and there was no way anyone in her orchestra was not going to follow her direction. Clea was having a really hard time keeping her composure. It was obvious to everyone that she didn't like this idea. "Themis, it's late. Maybe another time would be better."

"Clea, you know that there is no time better than any other time. Look, we're already on the way!" And so we were. Without even realizing it, we were following Themis on a well-worn path in the moonlight. Clea ran back for a lantern and caught up to us. It wasn't long before we entered another clearing, not as large as where we'd just had dinner, but large enough for a geodesic dome about 30 feet in diameter made of what seemed to be clear plastic triangles fit together. The entire structure rested on a platform about two feet above the ground. Once inside, everywhere we looked we could see stars, the moon, trees. The apex of the dome was about 15 feet above us.

It was not a living space. It was a temple. In the middle was a large rock shaped like an egg about four feet high. It was standing on its own flat base and was covered with carvings of flowers, vines, leaves, and geometric shapes. Clea brought the lantern close so we could see it better. Triptolemos was busy lighting candles around the perimeter of the dome. Plutarch asked, "Who did the artwork?"

"We all did, but grandpa started it. He got the tools and showed us how to use them," Clea replied.

I said, "What is it? It's not just decoration."

"It's the omphalos. It represents the center."

While talking, Themis was rolling out large gongs mounted on stands about six feet high. Each stand had a mallet with a fat felt head hanging from it. They had been stored behind screens along the wall. There were three of them. The largest was almost four feet across and the other two were slightly smaller. She was placing them next to the omphalos forming a triangular circle around it.

Themis said, "The omphalos is supposed to be the center of the world, not geographically, obviously, but spiritually, energetically."

"What center is it for you?" Pausanias asked.

–Do you mean just me or me and my sibs?

–For you, Themis. In what way is it a center for you?

–Hmm. Good question. Right now for me, Pausanias, it is the center of our evening, but that could change. One moment the center is here, the next moment the center is somewhere else. Aren't each of you the center of your own world? Every time you move, the center of the world moves with you. Regardless, the omphalos we're looking at marks the center of this dome perfectly. Grandpa made sure of that!

It's beyond me to describe in words the rest of the night in the dome. I'm an engineer, not a writer, but the most accomplished writer in the world, lying on her back with her eyes closed in a geodesic dome in the middle of a forest, would find it impossible to describe her experience once Themis started striking the gongs about four feet from her head. Once the vibrations of the gongs made the dome throb and the world disappear.

Episode 16

The guests are standing in a huddle, giving each other nervous looks, shrugging shoulders, not knowing what to say, wondering if this is that moment in a horror movie when the audience is yelling at the clueless characters on the screen "Get out of there you idiots!" But no one is afraid. Themis had said, "Don't worry," so they aren't worried.

They're nervous because they have no idea what is going on or what's expected of them. After Themis answers Pau's question about what the omphalos means to her, Plutarch thinks It's hard to believe, but Themis is actually more obtuse than Clea. He glances at Hyperides and sees that he is still in the state of shock that he's been in since Themis spoke to them at the dinner table. It was only a few hours ago that they had been hiking together talking about what they expected that evening and just minutes ago that the sometimes bitter, always ironic, world-weary defender of the poor and dispossessed had said to Themis, "You're a bird."

Since then, he hasn't spoken, and there's no chance to find out from him what is going on now that they are riding a sneaker wave of surprises. Where are they headed? Themis had appeared at the dinner table and using her voice as a baton had started conducting them, and now here they are in the family temple waiting for her to mark the next beat, literally, with the big felt mallets hanging from an array of huge gongs mounted on six-foot stands. She positions the gongs equidistant to each other around the omphalos while her guests watch and wait.

–OK. Are you all ready for tuning? As promised, it's good for your health!

Pausanias musters, "I guess." Then Hyperides suddenly speaks and emphatically says, "Yes!"

"Good. Over there by the laurel there are pads and blankets," Themis points toward one of four plants potted in large, brilliantly glazed ceramic urns that ring the perimeter of the dome. "You're going to be lying on the floor, and you'll be much more comfortable lying on the yoga mats covered by a blanket. There should be enough for everyone."

The orchestra members head over to the laurel bush. "Circular spaces are interesting aren't they? No corners. The plants mark the directions. The laurel is north, the lily is south, the juniper is west, and the olive is east. The lines from north to south and east to west cross at the omphalos forming a symbol of the sun. If you all can space yourselves evenly around the omphalos, lying with your heads toward the gongs about four feet away...

...Perfect. I'd suggest covering up with the blankets. It's a little cold on the floor." The five guests lying on the floor now form a pentagram around the omphalos, their heads ringed around it near the gongs and their feet pointing toward the perimeter of the dome.

So, everyone comfortable?" Murmurs of consent. "Close your eyes...Relax your body starting at the top of your head......your face......moving slowly down to your shoulders...now your arms......your hands and fingers......your chest......down each leg to your calves......your feet.....

The guests feel like jello. Themis's voice seems to relax their bodies from the inside out. "Fair warning: it will get pretty loud."

Themis strikes the Earth gong, its tone filling the dome. She strikes it again, harder, and the tone joins the first which is still reverberating throughout the dome. Then the Sun gong; then the Moon. Then she's playing them all, striking one, then another, sometimes hard, sometimes just a tap, sometimes with a

force in between, the tones reverberating one at a time or together, two, sometimes three together blending as one or somehow perfectly distinct, echoing throughout the dome and
funneling directly into their ears, their heads, their bodies, their
cells. Her playing speeds up. She forcefully strikes all of the
gongs one after the other with no beats in between, and the reverberating sound gets louder and louder still, so loud, so total,
that there is nothing but the sound of the gongs without and
within them. Then her playing slows down, softer, quieter, until
she's barely tapping just one gong, its tone now a whisper, now
almost inaudible, and now silence......until a gong is struck again,
and again, and again, the crescendos crashing against them in
waves and the diminuendos coming just in time to bring them
back from wherever the tsunami of sound carried them.

No one moves away from the gongs while Themis plays. No
one moves at all. No one is thinking. No one is caring where they
are or where they will be. No one is worried, and no one is wondering. Everyone is no one--Not one, not any, not me, not you.
Everyone is vibrating at the frequency Themis has created, each
point of the human pentangle arrayed around the omphalos a
resonance chamber within the larger resonance chamber that is
the dome, within the larger chamber, the earth, and larger still,
the solar system.

Was Themis singing? This is the first thought of the first
guest who becomes someone again. As each point of the pentagram sits up changing his or her frequency and resuming iden-
tity as a person not a point in a geometrical figure, he or she
remembers and feels, and each person's memories and feelings
are different. The separation and differentiation of egos begins,
and eventually they are all up, loosening limbs, lost in their
thoughts, remembering, and they are no longer one resonance
within the one resonance. There is a memory of that unity they

all shared that is more like an intuition, a deja vu, like the bliss from a dream that is lost the moment you wake up.

Themis is gone. The orchestra members are back to being guests. Hypatia, her blanket wrapped around her like a prayer shawl, is the first to speak and asks Clea if she can stay and sleep overnight in the dome.

–Are you OK, Hypatia?

–Yes, more OK than I think I've ever been. I don't want to leave here while I'm feeling this good. I want it to last. I'm afraid once I leave I won't remember any of it.

–I understand, Hypatia, I really do, but I'm worried about your being here by yourself all night.

–I'll be fine. Really. I won't leave the dome until it's light and I can find my way back.

"Hyperides, are you leaving?" Clea notices Hyp putting his rolled up pad and folded blanket back by the laurel bush. "Do you need Trip to guide you back?"

–I can find my way back.

–Are you sure? Trip expected to escort you all back to the lodge.

–It's no problem, Hyp. Even with the moonlight, it's pretty dark.

–There's only one trail and it's easy to follow. I'd like to be alone right now. But I have a question. Themis said we are welcome to visit. Is that true?

–If she says something, she means it. So yes.

–Is it OK just to knock on her door?

–I'm sure that's fine. She'll know you're coming and be there. No appointment necessary.

Hyperides does not question Clea regarding how Themis will know he's coming. He steps out of the dome letting in cool evening air. Everyone had followed his conversation with Clea with interest as they had planned on asking the same question. Corinna follows up: "So, it's OK for any of us who want to visit to come by and knock on anyone's door?"

–Sure, but if it's not Themis, we won't know you're coming, so you should probably arrange a time.

–Got it. Thanks.

Hypatia is still waiting to get permission. "So, Clea, can I stay here tonight? There are plenty of pads and blankets. I'll be perfectly comfortable, and I love looking up at the stars."

"How about if I come by to check on her?" Trip offers.

–Would that be OK, Hypatia? I would feel better about your staying then.

– If Trip doesn't mind, then sure.

"Sounds like fun," Corinna says, "a sleepover! Would it be alright if I stayed, too, Hypatia?"

Hypatia is now almost regretting asking, but she doesn't want to leave. "Of course, but I won't be much company. I don't want to stay up all night talking."

–I understand. It's not what I expect.

Episode 17

Early in the morning after her sister's performance, Clea is at her door, asking to be let in.

–We need to talk.

–Come in, then. But you can't stay too long, Hyperides will be here soon.

–Right, which is one of the reasons we need to talk.

The stress Clea was feeling the night before as Themis began the initiation of their guests––without their permission––without warning her or Trip, much less divulging reasons or discussing possible consequences, has morphed into anger. Why not consult with her? Why go rogue in such a dramatic, possibly––probably––irreversible way? She is used to her sister engaging in mischief for her own amusement, but what she did last night was not harmless play. She brought out the Oracle voice, then using the gongs, softly humming along the entire time, she entrained them, or as she so cavalierly put it, "tuned" them to resonate at the same frequency, synchronizing them and her. Well they're tuned, now what?

–Are you going to let me know what's going on? I know you're sure you know what you're doing...

–Faith, sister.

–All right. faith, which on my part you have no reason to doubt, considering. Still, last night was radical, even for you. You didn't give them a chance to think, much less make a choice. How is that in accord with the Law? I don't get it. You assaulted them. You used force without warning or consent which is not lawful and something you adamantly oppose. It's not Themis, sister!

–Of course, I understand and appreciate your concern, but it was necessary, and I am capable of using force as you put t in a lawful way. 'Assault' is too strong a word, Clea, and not fair. What I did was not violence. Listen, I needed to accelerate them. What you don't know and what I didn't know until last night is that what we've been preparing for since you moved here, the reason for our under-the-radar-word-of-mouth Hyperborean retreats, is going to happen soon. Do you understand what I'm saying? *They need to stay here with us as planned.* We can't risk their leaving now, because they may not make it back. I can't remember what precisely is going to happen, or the exact outcome, but I do know that we're not supposed to be left alone. And we couldn't have been stuck with a better group. This is how it is meant to be. How can I say it so it makes sense? I can't. This is how it happens. This is what I remember.

Is she saying what I think she's saying? These are the five who are going to—hopefully—ride out the apocalypse with us? Plutarch? Really? I knew it, and so did Trip. We both felt it.

Yes, I'm saying what you think I'm saying.

Tell me.

–You know this is what I remember and what we've been preparing for. The human race is going to face the consequences of its lawlessness, as it must. There are no other possible outcomes. We are going to face the music, which is ironically a very accurate way of putting it, just as all the other human races that have evolved and fallen have had to face the consequences of their abandoning the Law, but our case is unique in its severity, in its finality. Our transgressions are magnified to the nth degree by our sheer numbers. Our flaunting the Law is killing our Mother. We torture and maim Her and Her children with the same insolence and disregard with which we torture, maim, and kill our fellow human beings, our own brothers and sisters. So many of us now are dead inside having no respect or regard for anyone or anything but our own selfish gratification. The walking dead encounter life in any form and their instinct is to destroy it, even though in doing so they are killing themselves...

Themis has to pause to let go of her anguish and center herself.

...But you know all this...What's going to happen is an intervention, and there is no right word to use to identify the forces whose duty it is to intervene, as these forces always have when necessary. When the Law has to be upheld. You could use the word "celestial" or "cosmic" or "divine" or "transcendent," but none of these words come close to describing who or what these forces are, because they are incomprehensible to us. These are the same forces responsible for expressing the Law in all of our religious texts, and they are responsible for enforcing that Law. In the Christian Bible the Law is written: "Pride goeth before destruction, and a haughty spirit before a fall." This is the Law, plain and simple. There's nothing difficult to understand, but feckless hypocrites barely pay lip service to the tenets of the Law expressed in countless numbers of ways in all of humanity's sacred works. Commandments are ignored and sins are reveled in instead of shunned.

Themis stops to take a breath and calm down.

–Why did I push our guests last night? Because Ge has lost all patience and hope. Don't you feel it, Clea? Haven't you witnessed it? Flood, famine, disease, fire—all of the above?—I don't know what's coming, but it's coming soon. The pandemics, the locust swarms, the earthquakes, the massive hurricanes and unending forest fires—all foreshadowings of what's to come.

Clea hears what her sister is saying but isn't able yet to process it. She asks Themis to give her a moment, and if she wouldn't mind, make her some tea. What she is telling her is not a surprise, as Themis said, but that doesn't make it easier to accept. Since her teens Themis has been talking about the inevitability of Earth having to save itself from the human race.

"There are just too many of us," she would claim. "We have become a pestilence that Ge must deal with."

After Grandpa died, Grandma had told her and her brother that they must trust Themis; they must have faith in her and help her. And since moving to live with her in Hyperborea, they have been preparing for the inevitable. Themis devised her elaborate way to find the right people—people with "like minds"—to survive the cataclysm with them, people predisposed to the Law, people with honor who have respect for life, people with eros in their hearts, not thanatos, and, as Themis bluntly put it, "healthy, intelligent, creative and capable people, people the right age who have few emotional attachments to family. It can't be too difficult for them to say goodbye, and more importantly, when this happens, and if we survive, procreation is no longer a luxury, it's a necessity."

* * *

Sipping the mint tea Themis made, Clea asks, "You're sure?"

–I'm not clear on the details, sister, but I'm sure this is going to happen and happen soon. Mother has been suffering too long, and her human children have proved they just don't care. I mean we've shown that we don't even care about our own brothers and sisters, that we have zero respect for life. Why should we suddenly decide that Mother Earth is something to value? It's just a big ball of dirt to us. She knows it's up to Her to save herself, and She should. She will.

Years ago, Clea gave up trying to imagine the fantastical contents of her sister's consciousness, what she "hears," what she "reads," what she "sees," *what she remembers,* and her sister stopped trying to explain, lamenting, "How can I explain the unexplainable? Everything done, thought, remembered, written, spoken, said, heard is recorded and stored. Where? How about I say everything is stored in the archives of the Aether, which is what? A realm? A dimension? The void? Where is it? Between the Earth and the Sky? Between matter and spirit? And I was blessed—or is it cursed?—with the wings, which is only a metaphor—I don't actually have wings...or do I?—to get me there, that grant me access. They're my passport. There's no there there, no time. Past, present, future have no meaning, they are all one. I remember the past and the future...You see? It's impossible!"

Clea gives her sister an empathetic hug of solidarity. She has complete trust in her. Her faith is unshakeable. She loves her like no other and will never forsake her. "So, I am wondering what happened to Hyperides last night. He actually said you were a bird."

–He saw me. We connected. You should let yourself feel something other than your duty, Clea, especially now. You need to try. Plutarch is here, and he likes you, just as he once did.

–It was platonic. We were colleagues who respected each other's intellect.

–This is a different cycle.

–I feel things besides my duty, Themis, and since you brought it up, if you must know, I'm attracted to Pausanias, not Plutarch. Plutarch is too...

–Cerebral? Chubby?

Clea laughs. "He's too much like me, except for the chubby part. Triptolemos does not give me a chance to build up any fat with all the chores he assigns. Like me, Plutarch gets anxious, he talks too much...but if you're right about what's coming...

–It's not an if, sister, but I can't know exactly when or how. That's not for me to know.

Episode 18

Corinna's Diary

Seems like everybody but me has been writing since they got here. It's not that I don't like writing, though using images and music to express ideas is so obviously superior. Don't try to argue with me on that point. To sit down and apply pen to paper requires motivation that up to now I haven't had. Now I have something to write home about. I'm calling my notes The Hyperborean Diary. Someday, I may transform this diary into an AV piece that truly expresses the beauty of this place.

Dear Diary:

What do I have to write about? How about the mind-blowing gong show put on by Themis, the fabled conductor who pulled a Triptolemos on us last night by appearing out of nowhere. We're out in the middle of fairyland sitting at the dinner table, ready to eat what Trip is cooking, and suddenly she's there talking to us as if she's our server for the night, suggesting we have a little wine, "not much," she said, "don't worry," and when she said "don't worry" it was like, worry, what's that? I'll never have another worry in my life, and I'm looking around at the gang and I can tell they're feeling the same. She's the conductor all right, I thought. We had what started to feel like the last supper. She poured us all a tiny taste of wine and toasted "to health" of all things, not something I ever toasted to, but then again, why not? Health is the most important thing in life. What is more important? So, good toast, Themis! Then we ate Trip's amazing garlic rosemary spinach quiches and before we could digest what was happening we were walking on a moonlit path to grandpa's dome in the woods!

Honestly, this place. Where are we? Who are these people?

Well, we learned a lot about Themis. Her voice is a powerful weapon. There's no way you can resist it. I imagine after a while you might start to depend on it, like, Themis, please tell me something that will make me feel better or please tell my headache to go away. Also, she can play gongs like a madwoman, which I'm pretty sure she is. She's got divine madness, the best kind! The boys have all been talking about how they suspect the Greeks are a cult of some kind, a nice one they hope, and I would say the dome is now Exhibit A in support of their case. That is no yoga studio as advertised by Themis as she lured us to it. It's a church, and the first thing you see and the first thing Clea lectured us on was the omphalos, which symbolizes the center of everything and not coincidentally is smack in the middle of the dome thanks to grandpa the builder.

While Clea was telling us about the omphalos, everyone was looking around, faces were twitching, there were nervous coughs, but Themis cannot be resisted so following her orders we got ourselves pads and blankets from under the laurel bush, which represents a direction—is it north? can't remember—and which is one of four different plants growing in big beautiful iridescent Grecian (of course) urns that are arranged according to the four directions and when you draw lines north/south and east/west the lines cross at the omphalos forming a symbol of the sun, or so says Clea.

We were instructed to lay our yoga pads down around the omphalos to form a human pentagram. Not kidding. Heads toward the gongs (not too close) and feet toward the walls of the dome. We were lying on our backs looking up at the stars through the plastic triangles of the dome. It was like we were in a planetarium and then we found out that the show would be projected in our heads not on the ceiling. Themis started talking, telling us to close our eyes and relax every part of our body, which was easy since she was the one telling us to relax. I was almost asleep when Themis first struck a gong. Then I can't say what I was from then on. The gongs were booming and echoing and the sounds were crashing into each other and into my ears and bouncing around in my head and at times it was so loud that I felt like I completely disappeared only to appear again when Themis slowed down and entered into a mellow, soft phase, and I'd almost be all the way back into existence when she'd start cranking it up again. It was like being in a little sailboat in the middle of a stormy sea, out on the deck, not strapped down. Images were flashing so fast through my mind I didn't have time to process them. It was like watching a movie in my mind on super-fast forward. Then it was over.

When we all managed to sit up and regain some semblance of normal consciousness, Themis was gone. Hypatia had her blanket draped around her like a prayer shawl. Maybe she had been praying. Who knows what everyone was going through or what they were doing while the gongs were pounding us like giant combers crashing over us as we were crossing the Ocean.

Afterwards, Clea and Trip were waiting for us to do or say something. Hypatia finally asked Clea if she could spend the night there. She didn't want to leave. Clea said she was not sure that was a good idea, but then Trip said what if I come back and check on her, and that's when I said, hey, can I stay, too?, because who knows, if Trip comes back, maybe something would happen. I thought probably not, as the dome is a holy place for them, and I think now it's also holy for Hypatia and Hyp from the look of them. Hypatia is zoned out and Hyp is zoned in—on Themis. I don't know about Plutarch and Pausanias. Me? I love this place. I love Trip. I wish we didn't have to leave.

This morning, I'm back at the lodge writing the first entry in this diary. Trip did come back to check on us, but I was asleep, deeply, and he didn't wake me up. He was the first thing I saw when I opened my eyes, sitting cross-legged on the floor close by. He was looking at me and smiling Triptolemos style, which you have to see to understand. I call it the infinity smile. I hope someday to do a piece on that smile to immortalize it. Hypatia was already awake, so we walked back to the lodge. Hypatia didn't say a word until "Thanks for looking after us and walking us back," and going up to her room.

I stood a little awkwardly there in front of the lodge not knowing what to say and waiting for Trip to say something, which he usually does, asking me if I want to tag along for the day. This time he was not saying anything, just looking at me. I had to say something, so I said, "Maybe I'll see you later?" He said, "Why don't you come by in about an hour or so? I'll show you where we hide the chickens and we'll collect eggs." Then he said, "You were snoring so loud last night I couldn't bear to wake you. I was enjoying the music!" He laughed. I guess that's flirting, Triptolemos style.

* * *

Plutarch's Journal

After last night's performance by Themis, it's not entirely clear what our status is anymore. Are we still guests? It doesn't feel like it. After the gongs stopped and we regained awareness, we were looking around at each other slack-jawed and wide-eyed. Themis had asked us if we were "ready for tuning," and I don't think any of us took her literally, but my overwhelming feeling when she was playing the gongs was exactly that: I was being tuned, like a string on a violin. I felt my body and mind, my being, getting stretched tight then released, pulled tight again and released, until it was over, and then I felt in harmony with,

I don't know, with everything. It's not possible to describe without mixing multiple metaphors.

While Themis was playing I remember visualizing the ridge across the river, or maybe it was another ridge across another river, because it was like a dream in which you sense you are in a familiar place but you're not sure. I was sitting on the bank of a river looking intently at the forested rise across from me. The sound of the river got louder and louder, probably corresponding to how Themis was playing, as there were very, very loud crescendos. The rushing of the river became overwhelming and at the same time I saw a crack forming in the hill I was staring at. The crack got wider and wider and a brilliant, unearthly white light was streaming out of it. I felt as if the light and the sound of the river were going to cause me to disintegrate into atomic particles. Then the gongs stopped, and I lost the vision. I remember the story that Clea told us about how Themis got her name in which her mother had a dream with a similar vision. It's possible that I was reenacting that in my mind, but when it was happening, I experienced it as actually happening. I wasn't dreaming. I was there.

If we aren't guests anymore, are we honorary family members? Now that we've met Themis, broke bread with them all, have been welcomed into their homes, and were invited to a ritual performance in their family chapel, how can we not feel closer to the family? Is this the next step toward membership in the cult? Because everything that happened last night feels decidedly cultish, like a stage in our indoctrination. From what I can tell, Hypatia and Hyperides are already enthusiastic members. Corinna as always is unfazed and happy, and why not? She has found a new friend in Triptolemos, maybe even a partner.

Pausanias seemed emotionally moved by the experience in the dome, but not ecstatic. He was somber, introspective, and did not say a word as we walked back to the lodge with Trip. I'd like to talk to them all, but this morning everyone scattered, possibly going to where I plan to go. To visit. I suspect there will be a lot of visiting in our last week here. Time is running out. Themis opened a door and we all want to go in for different reasons.

* * *

Clea finally catches up with Trip at the chicken coop where he's introducing Corinna to the hens and roosters.

"Hi, Corinna. How are you doing?" Clea gasps, out of breath from running around looking for her brother. "Trip, can we talk for a moment...in private?" Then to Corinna: "Sorry, but I really need to pull Trip away and tell him something. It's important."

"OK, sis. Can it wait a minute?" He doesn't like the intrigue. It better be important. "Corinna, sorry, do you mind just hanging out here with the chickens until I get back? Shouldn't be long."

–No problem, Trip. It's fine. Talk to Clea.

She is waiting for him about 100 feet up the trail. "So what's so important?"

"I wouldn't take you away from Corinna unless it were absolutely necessary, brother," Clea says with unnecessary nastiness. She's stressed out.

–Lay off, sister. We're friends. Nothing wrong with that.

–Yes, of course, but after what I have to tell you, your friendship is going to take a turn.

She tells him what Themis told her. Trip doesn't say anything for a while as they stand on the path together. Finally he says, "I told you there was something about this group. We both felt it. No coincidences, right? It makes sense then that Corinna and I would be circling around each other...

–Especially after last night.

–Nothing happened. I didn't wake her up.

–But you were there in the morning, right? I bet you were watching her sleep, waiting for her to wake up, and there you were. That's not nothing.

–Yeah, that's not nothing. Now what? It's up to us to convince them all to stay because Themis says so?

–I'm pretty sure only Plutarch and Pausanias need to be persuaded.

–But even so, the others don't actually know what's going to happen. What it means to stay.

–No. It's up to Themis to work that out with them.

–We have to do everything we can to help her.

–I know, Trip.

Still waiting for Trip to return, Corinna thinks, *Wow, it really must be important. They've been talking for 15 minutes and not a glance at me just sitting here on this stump with the chickens pecking in the dirt around me.*

Clea finally takes off down the trail and Trip comes over to her. "Sorry that took so long."

–Can you tell me what that was all about? You two looked awfully serious.

–It is important and serious, but I can't talk about it right now. Later, though.

–Do you expect me to sleep tonight after dropping this on me? Does it have something to do with us—I mean my friends and me, not us us.

Triptolemos smiles, "I know who you mean. It has to do with all of us. Sorry for the drama, but I just can't talk about it."

–Let's see if I can guess: it's up to Themis.

Trip looks at her and doesn't need to say anything. Corinna can see in his eyes that she's right, and it really is serious. "Let's see if there are any eggs," he says.

Episode 19

Pausanias is looking across the river to where the washed-out dirt road continues. When he woke up, he thought if he occupied himself with the adventure of fording the river and then walking up the road he might be able to shake the haunting images from the night before. It's not working. He doesn't remember walking to where he is now as he was completely preoccupied with trying to replay in his mind what he experienced during Themis's performance.

He is standing at the spot where he, Hyp, and Plutarch had stopped the day before and decided that it was time to go back. *It was only yesterday afternoon when we were here. How is that even possible? It feels like it was at least a week ago. What the hell?* He suspects that whatever it was that Themis was doing when she "tuned" them messed up his, and probably everyone else's, sense of time. *Themis should have warned us about potential serious side effects at least.*

Pausanias does not appreciate having his mind messed with, and Themis messed with more than his mind. He doesn't feel right. Since last night he feels like his body is moving on its own and his consciousness is floating along outside attached by a thin tether. *If I can't shake this by the time I get back, I'm going to talk to Themis. This is not OK.* Standing there, waiting for his autonomous body to move, he continues trying to piece together the bizarre scenes he either dreamed or experienced, but what he remembers doesn't help. If he dreamed what he remembers, it's crazy enough, but if he actually experienced it, then what ? He had a psychotic break? Sometimes he remembers witnessing as in a dream, but other times he remembers experiencing. It's very disorienting.

I'm sorry Pausanias. I should have been more careful. Your visit to the Oracle of Trophonios was traumatic for you, and you remembered it last night. You wrote about it:

First, during the night two citizen boys about 13 years old led me to the river Herkyna and anointed me with oil and bathed me. Then the priests took me to certain springs of water which are close to each other. Here I drank the water of Lethe that I may forget all I have in my mind; next I drank the water of Memory so that I will remember what I see and hear when I enter the oracle down below. Then after the proper worship and prayer, I came to the oracle dressed in a tunic of linen, girded with a fillet, and wearing the boots of the country.

The oracle is shaped like a bread pot and about eight ells deep. I went down by a ladder. There was a hole between the ground and the stonework. Its breadth was about two spans and its height one. I lay on my back holding in my hands barley-cakes mixed with honey and I pushed my feet through the hole first and tried to follow them, squeezing my knees through the hole. Once my knees were through, my body was immediately pulled in and I was shooting along, caught in what seemed like the current of a swift and mighty stream. Then suddenly, I returned back through the hole feet first.

The priests took me and placed me on the throne of Memory which is close to the shrine of the oracle. They asked me what I saw and heard as the future is not revealed to all in the same way. I can't say what I told them. I don't remember now. Then they gave me over to my friends to help me as I was still overwhelmed with fear and unconscious of myself. Later, my wits returned and I was able to laugh again, or so say my friends.

I promise that you will laugh again, Pausanias! Please forgive me.

Pausanias continues to stand by the river waiting for his body to move. The loud rushing of the river brings back last night's vision again, but this time his memory is more coherent. He was lying down on his back in a stream that flowed through a narrow ravine. It was very dark, so dark he wondered if he were in a cave. Then abruptly he was lying on the ground somewhere wondering if he was dreaming or awake.

Suddenly he felt a sharp blow to the top of his head, as if he'd been struck with a hammer, accompanied by a tremendous ringing in his ears. After the hammer blow, he sensed his soul escaping through the wound at the top of his head, and as his soul left it seemed to take a breath, and then another breath, and as his soul breathed in what seemed to be wonderfully pure air, it expanded and became like a sail filled with wind.

Then Themis stopped playing, and the vision of his soul catching the wind quickly faded, but not entirely. It is still there in the back of his mind, and even though he knows he's awake now, he feels like he's dreaming, and when he was in the midst of his vision last night, he felt like he was more than awake, he was hyper aware. It's no wonder that he's not feeling like himself.

Pausanias is startled by a stiff breeze that picks up all at once, shaking the trees and bending the grass on the bank across from him. It almost feels like rain, but there are only a few random cotton-ball clouds. He remembers that he came there to find a way across the river and gathers himself to do that. He feels more like himself setting this familiar goal, to get from one place to the next and from there to the next, and he begins scouting for a promising ford.

* * *

After writing in her journal, feeling worn out, Hypatia lies down in the hammock on the porch. She has one dominant thought: she wants to go back to the dome. Her room in the lodge feels lifeless and claustrophobic to her now, and she wonders if the family would let her sleep in the dome for the week or so they have left. She could lie on her back and look at the stars and watch the moon cross over her at night. She's guessing they have a week left, but if Clea were to show up right now and say it's time to go, she would not be surprised, just depressed.

The main door to the lodge opens and Plutarch is there, journal in hand.

–Hi...how're you doing after last night? That was pretty intense." He's not registering that Hypatia is tired and not looking for a conversation.

–Intense is too mild a word, don't you think?

"I do, but don't know how else to describe it. Insane?" Plutarch is like a dog with a bone. "What do you think it was all about? What was it like for you?"

–I'm not ready to talk about it, Plutarch, if you don't mind.

"Right. OK." He stands there awkwardly not knowing what to say. Hypatia is aware of how uncomfortable Plutarch gets and changes the subject. "Is today our fifth day here? Do you know? I am having trouble keeping track."

–Our fifth full day and our sixth night coming up.

–Thanks, I'm not tracking anything very well right now, especially time. Where are you headed with your journal? You've been writing every day haven't you?

–Everything here in Hyperborea got a lot more interesting after last night, so I think I'm going to be writing more every day. I want to talk to Themis as much as possible for the rest of the time we have here and take notes. She's a fascinating person.

–Fascinating and powerful. So are you headed up to Hobbiton to visit Themis? I'll walk with you. I want to ask her something.

* * *

Back in his room after leaving the dome, Hyperides lay down on his bed and tried to calm his mind. Sleep was not going to be possible for some time, if at all. He had not wanted to come back to the lodge. After the last reverberating note had faded completely away, he had opened his eyes looking for Themis, but she was already gone. He wanted to ask her what had happened to him, what he had seen, what she had done to him, but he thought chasing after her would be too—too what? Extreme? Irrational? Frantic? He wanted to be near her, have her in sight or within hearing, that's all.

When she first spoke, standing there at the table, offering them wine, his thoughts had just stopped. Completely. Then he felt at peace, which is a feeling he can't remember ever having, and if asked to describe it, he would struggle to find the words. He was a lake without a ripple. He had no needs.

Then his thoughts started up again. Still looking at Themis, his first thought was *she is the Good*. Actually, it wasn't a thought, it was a conviction. He was comforted by this conviction as he had lost hope that there was good in the world after the depressing work he'd been doing for years trying to help shield people from the injustices of One America. Intellectually, he believed there must still be good in the world, but Themis convinced him there is good, and it gave him hope that he hadn't had since he was a kid who didn't know any better. He was immensely grateful to Themis for a moment of peace and for giving him hope.

After dinner Themis had told them they were all welcome to visit. She announced it to the group, but he felt she was saying this to him personally. Even though he was sure he knew which house was hers, for some reason he still asked. When he said she is a bird, her smile told him that she was happy he recognized her. He could see her wings, or at least he imagined he saw them.

When Themis started playing the gongs, he resisted falling into the well of sound. He didn't want to forget what he had just experienced at the dinner table. He didn't want the music to wash his memories away, but there was no denying the power of the sound Themis was generating. His defenses fell and he found himself launched into space gaining unimaginable speed. He flew by the moon, then left the solar system, gaining speed constantly. He could see the stars ahead getting closer, then he was passing them, gaining more speed. The stars became blurred reminding him of how speed faster than light is depicted in movies.

Then suddenly he was no longer traveling at warp speed through the universe. He was standing somewhere, on some extra-galactic planet, and near him was a luminous woman dressed in flowing robes. She was the archetype of a benevolent, beautiful goddess, radiating kindness. She had a little baby in her arms, a girl no more than two or three months old. She came closer to him and held the baby up so he could see her face and said *This is your daughter. She wants to go home with you.*

Trying to remember everything that he experienced is like trying to remember a dream, and he wonders if he had fallen asleep in the dome while Themis was playing, however unlikely that seems considering how loud the gongs were. Late into the night, Hyperides finally does fall asleep, and as soon as he wakes to the sun, as he has since arriving, he leaves the lodge to visit Themis. He wants to know what he imagined or dreamed or actually experienced and why, and if any of it was real. He wants her to convince him.

* * *

Plutarch and Hypatia find Themis and Hyperides sitting together at the table where they had dinner the night before. They have been there talking since dawn when Hyperides knocked on her door and Themis suggested they go outside. Being with her and hearing her voice was all he needed to center himself. He forgot about asking her what had happened to him last night, what she had done to him.

"We made a connection is all, Hyp," she said, answering his unasked question. "We both believe in the Law. We believe in the necessity of justice. We want fairness for everyone. I admire you. You accept your duty without complaint."

–But you had wings! Why did I imagine that?

–How many times do we wonder 'was I dreaming?' Or we think, 'I just had déjà vu.' What if I tell you, 'Yes, I am a bird, I really do have wings.' Would you believe me?

–I think I would believe anything you say.

–Do you see wings right now?

Hyperides laughs, "No."

–So I'm not a bird?

–I remember seeing you with wings, but my memory can't be relied on.

–Why not?

–Because it's just a memory. Our memories are not always accurate.

–Why would you have a memory of seeing me with wings. Why would you imagine that?

–That's what I'm asking myself. That's what I just asked you!

–You see me now without wings, right? So now you have a memory of me without wings. Do you doubt that memory?

–No. Why would I?

–Because it's a memory, and memory can't be relied on.

–The two memories aren't comparable. It's apples and oranges. One memory is of something that just happened and the other memory is of something that happened last night, not to mention it's not possible for you to have wings.

–So the only reliable memories are of things that happened recently? What's the cutoff? Five minutes? Ten? What about your memories of this morning before you walked over here? Are they unreliable?

Hyperides laughs. "All right, I give up. I definitely remember seeing your wings last night. I did not just imagine it, so now I have to consider that I may be losing my mind."

–Why? I don't understand.

–Because it's not possible!

"Who says? You? Do you know what is possible and what isn't? Actually, I am a bird and have wings. You said you would believe anything I say. Do you remember?" Themis is smiling fondly at him with laughter in her eyes. Hyperides can feel her affection.

–If you think about it, Hyp, *all we do is remember.*

Plutarch, who has been waiting with Hypatia for the conversation to lag, senses his moment to interrupt, "Is it OK if we join you?" Hypatia had not been listening, lost in nervously rehearsing her question for Themis, but Plutarch had been following the exchange with interest.

He had been struck the night before by how Themis's ability to talk in circles surpassed even Clea, who he had decided was the world champion of circular reasoning. He couldn't imagine anyone managing to say more and mean less than her until meeting Themis, and after listening to the exchange between her and Hyperides just now, he had to concede that Themis was the actual master of doubletalk. This is when he decided what he wanted to do for the rest of his time in Hyperborea: gather material for what he would call 'The Themis Dialogues.' Document and then try to deconstruct all she has to say.

Hyperides doesn't answer Plutarch's rhetorical question or acknowledge that he was obviously interrupting or tell him to leave them alone, but Themis smiles, greeting them. "How are you doing after last night's impromptu concert?"

"I'm doing well, Themis. Last night, your playing, the dome, it was amazing." Hypatia hesitates. "There's something I want to ask. I hope it's not too presumptuous."

Hypatia, relax, it's OK.

Did you just tell me to relax?

Momentarily speechless, trying to decide if she had heard Themis in her head again, Hypatia gathers herself and asks, "I'm wondering if it would be OK for me to sleep in the dome rather than in the lodge. I really like the energy there. Falling asleep in the moonlight under the stars is so magical. I want to experience that as much as I can while I'm still here. I want to feel what I felt last night as much as I can. The first thing I thought of this morning is how much I want to go back." Hypatia is nervous talking to Themis, her words rushed and tumbling out. She is anxious about asking her for anything, not wanting to overstep but wanting so much to get closer, to hear her voice again telling her 'It's OK,' to feel accepted and appreciated, to know she belongs. "If I can't sleep there can I hang out in there during the day?"

–Of course. Sleep there, spend as much time there as you like. You're welcome there and welcome here.

"Thank you! We all appreciate you inviting us to your homes and sharing this wonderful place with us." Hypatia wants to tell Themis about her strong sense of being at home in Hyperborea, of her wish to stay, but not in front of the two men.

Themis gets up from the table, walks over to Hypatia, and gives her a gentle hug. "You have no reason to feel anxious about asking me anything, Hypatia. We're family, sister, and we have been for a long time. I know you feel it."

* * *

Themis turns to Plutarch after Hypatia heads back to the lodge to get her things. She's not going to waste any time moving into the dome. "You've brought your journal, Plutarch. Are you taking notes?"

–Hoping to, Themis. I have a request, too. I want to interview you.

"Do you really want to be so formal? Ask me questions and record my answers? Can't we just talk like friends?" Themis looks at him with an ironic smile. "I don't think my answers to your questions are going to be anything you can let loose in the data stream hoping to get some clicks. What I have to say is not going to be attractive bait. I think the opposite. Your kids might want to read your notes someday, though, so hang onto those."

Themis knowing what he hoped to do with the 'Themis Dialogues' once he returned to the world stuns him. He doesn't know how to respond. He looks over to Hyperides who hasn't said a word since he and Hypatia had shown up.

"I don't think this is going to turn out as you imagine, Plutarch," he says, "as far as who is interviewing whom."

Episode 20

For over an hour Pausanias scouted for a place he could cross the river. He tried a couple of spots where the river did not seem too deep, but it was. The current made swimming too dangerous. He kept working his way up the river farther and farther away from the road until he found what he was looking for: a tree that had fallen over the river forming a bridge. He could slowly make his way across holding onto saplings and shrubs that grew from the rotting log.

Once on the other side of the river he worked his way back to the road. It was slow going. He was scratched up and filthy by the time he finally reached the road and could start walking up the hill, but he felt great. He hadn't thought about the night before at all since starting on his quest. He felt like his normal self, enjoying going somewhere, finding out what there is to see. It was a pleasure to be hiking freely on an old dirt road rather than fighting his way through a dense forest underbrush, and he was excited by the prospect of discovery, of what he might see when he reached the top of the hill.

At the top of the rise, he had something of a vista: there was a range of mountains in the distance, none high enough to still have snow, that was visible under high stratus clouds, and the river was a thin shiny ribbon below him to his left. The road continued on through the forest. He kept walking for another 20 minutes until reaching an opening in the trees. There was a meadow to his right extending up a slope that still had a few wildflowers in bloom. And an old cabin. And smoke rising from a chimney.

The cabin was about 100 yards from where he stood on the road. Pausanias wasn't sure if he should investigate or not and was leaning toward moving on when a woman came out and looked directly at him. He waved, she waved back, and they stood there looking at each other. Finally, Pausanias decided to take his chances. He wanted to hear the woman's story, so he started walking toward her.

She waited until he got closer and said, "Hi, there. You surprised me, son. What are you doing out here?"

–Hi, I'm just exploring up this old road.

–Is that right. Why? Where are you coming from?

He stopped when he was about 10 feet from the woman. He guessed she was in her 50's, wearing overalls, her graying hair covered by a dirty yellow bandana.

–You're maybe the second or third person I've ever seen on this road since I've been living here with my partner. He's out hunting right now. He'll be back any time.

–I think I might have met him a few days ago by the river. He was squirrel hunting.

–Ah, right, he told me about you. Said you were visiting your friends at the hot springs place.

–That's me. I don't think we introduced ourselves then. We were too surprised to see someone. I'm Pau.

–Pa? Like 'father'?

–Exactly.

"Well then that makes me Ma!" She laughs. "But my name is Kate."

"Nice to meet you, Kate." Pausanias smiles. How long have you and..."

–Wyatt.

...Wyatt, been living here?"

–Not too long, a few years. We got tired of scrabbling to survive in the city worried all the time about getting picked up by the VPs. It's pretty easy living here in the warm months, but t gets damn cold in the winter. And sometimes it's lonely, you know.

"You ought to go over and introduce yourselves to the family who live at the hot springs. There's two sisters and a brother. They've got a nice setup there. They're good people." Pausanias regrets his friendly offer immediately, realizing that he's making offers that are not his to make.

–Well, *Pa*, what you say sounds tempting, especially with winter around the corner, but we kinda like our privacy, and from what Wyatt and I have seen, so do they.

Anxious to change subjects, Pau says, "Looks like you have a garden going there. What are you growing?"

–Whatever will grow. It's not much. Some tomatoes, some beans, potatoes, squash, onions. Vegetables we can add to the game.

–So how did you and Wyatt find this place?

–Just luck. We used to camp by the river quite a bit further down the road. We had a tent and built a lean-to shelter over it. Wyatt went quite a bit farther than usual once when hunting and saw it just sitting there waiting for us to find it. It was full of old junk, but the stove worked. Been here ever since.

–How far does that road go anyway? Does it end up anywhere?

–Keep going about 20 more miles or more and you'll hit a two-lane paved road and what used to be a little pit stop town of sorts—gas station, café, little cabins you could stay in. People squat there now, coming and going on that old highway. Wyatt says you can see lights from there sometimes from a high point on the road. We stayed in one of those cabins for a while until it got too dangerous. We have our little pea-shooter rifle, but these guys had automatic weapons, slings of ammo, and bad attitudes.

–People don't come up here looking around like you did?

"And you?" Kate smiles. "Like I said, you're maybe the second or third person I've ever seen since we found this place; we haven't been bothered...yet." She gives a look that's easy to read: You aren't going to be bothering us, are you?

Pausanias looks up at the sky and realizes that it's late afternoon. He's got to start back or he'll be hiking in the dark. "So nice to meet you, Kate, but I've got to get going. It's a rough and slow hike back to the lodge."

–Did you get across the river over that tree that fell?

–Yes I did! And it's not easy.

"Look up there." She points. "See that big rock by the side of the road? There's a trail there down to the river that takes you to where you met Wyatt. It's a much easier way for you, and maybe you'll run into him."

–Hope so, Kate. And this time I'll introduce myself. Thanks!

Pausanias walks up to the rock where the trail starts, turns around and waves to Kate, but she's already gone back into the cabin. He can see that the road continues down from where's he standing and then disappears into another stand of trees. He's surprised to be thinking *escape route.*

* * *

After moving her stuff from the lodge to the dome, which wasn't hard considering all she brought fit into one small backpack, she took the trail from the dome to the wellspring for another afternoon of bliss. The water is hot enough that she can't soak indefinitely, but when overheated, she takes the short walk down to the river and cools off.

Draped over the edge of the tank, she's thinking about Themis and how she seems to know her thoughts and how she "talks" to her sometimes, but she's wary of overthinking as Plutarch compulsively does. She's enjoying the mystery. If she

starts down the road of defining, categorizing, labeling, identi-
fying—of figuring it out—then her experience will lose its shine
and she'll be back in the predictable, dull world she escaped
from only a week ago. Coming to Hyperborea feels like an escape
from an existential prison, and the prospect of returning to
prison is depressing.

"Hey!" Pausanias suddenly emerges from the forest on the
other side of the river. "Mind if I come over to your side?"

"Sure, wade across." Hypatia is surprised at how happy she is
to see Pau.

He sloshes across the river, climbs up the bank to where Hypatia is soaking, and sits on a stump nearby.

"Where have you been? I haven't seen you since last night,"
she asks.

–You know, exploring. You remember we hiked up the river
yesterday to where the road got washed out? I found a way over
to the other side, followed the road for a couple of miles, and
guess what? I found an old cabin...

–Really?

...and I met the squirrel hunter's partner—or wife, I don't
know. Her name is Kate; I found out his name is Wyatt. They've
been living there for several years it seems, refugees from the
city. They've got a small garden that was definitely not thriving.
I think they survive mainly on squirrels and rabbits.

–So, what do they think about their neighbors across the
river?

–Wyatt told me the story about Trip standing on this side of
the river giving him a scary look. They don't feel our hosts are
that friendly.

–That's right. I remember.

–Anyway, Kate showed me a trail from their place to the
river, and here I am. It's lucky she was there; otherwise I'd prob-

ably have been hiking back in the dark and all of you would have been worried and out looking for me.

–Themis would have known where you are.

"Really? And how would she know?" Hypatia's saying that makes Pausanias nervous. Does she believe what she just said?

"She knows things, Pau. She knows what I'm thinking, what I'm feeling. She knows me." Hypatia looks directly at Pau, gaining his attention. "I saw you after Themis was done playing. You were shook up. What happened?"

–I *was* shook up. What I experienced was really disturbing. And this morning, my sense of time was all whacked out...

–Mine, too!

–Really? What about the others?

–I didn't talk to them, but Plutarch was very excited to talk to Themis today. We walked up to Hobbiton together from the lodge. He had his journal and was going to talk to Themis and take notes.

–Sounds like Plutarch.

–Hyperides was already there sitting at the table with Themis. He must have come as soon as he woke up. He's totally changed. You were there. You saw.

–Yeah, that was strange. We all were affected by her voice, but Hyperides...he's not the same guy we met a few days ago.

–I think he's either in love or is now a disciple of Themis or both. I get the feeling he doesn't want to let her out of his sight.

–Doesn't that scare you? I mean wasn't last night basically a pagan ceremony of some sort? Is Themis a witch or something like that? And for what reason? Why did Themis take us there and do that? Does anyone doubt now that they're some sort of cult?

"I get what you're saying, but I'm not scared. I don't know what I am. I think I'm hooked." She looks at Pausanias for his reaction. "That's probably not what you want to hear..."

–What are you hooked on?

Though worried about what Pau might think, Hypatia tells him that Hyperborea feels like home, that she dreads having to leave and wants to stay, that Themis talks to her... "I can't explain it. I hear her say things, but it's not like her voice is in my head, it's more like I remember her saying it. I'm replaying what she says, as if remembering something from a dream."

Listening to Hypatia's confession, Pausanias can't help feeling affection for her. She is trusting him, and her trust inspires him to trust her, and he's grateful, since he's been feeling paranoid all day. "You hearing Themis in your head is nothing compared to what I experienced last night. I didn't think I'd be able to tell anyone, or want to, but now I think I need to talk about it."

He describes in detail the bizarre trip down the hole into the fast-running stream, washing up on the bank, getting hit on the head, the loud ringing in his ears, and the vision of his soul leaving through the hole in his head and filling up with ethereal air as if it were a sail.

"Then today, I was remembering the hike yesterday with Plutarch and Hyp, but it seemed as if it had happened weeks ago, and I had the strange sensation that my body and my mind were not connected. My body moved on its own without direction from me, like it was a robot controlled by an unseen operator, and my consciousness was floating along beside my body attached to it with a cord. It wasn't until I found a way across the river and started walking up the road that I felt normal again." He takes a deep breath and sighs. "Thanks for listening. I really needed to tell someone, and here you were."

–And you think that's just an accident?

–I don't think Themis orchestrated our meeting if that's what you mean.

Hypatia thinks, *that's exactly what I mean*, but doesn't say it.

"You're OK now?" She briefly puts her hand on his arm and lightly rubs it.

–I thought my vision was out there, but yours....No wonder you were upset. What I remember from last night while the gongs were going is being in some kind of plaza, like an Italian piazza from the distant past, but what time period I don't know. I couldn't tell because my awareness was not focused on my surroundings, it was focused on the dozens of people surrounding me, listening to me speak. I don't know what I was saying, but these people looked up to me, I was important to them, even loved by them, and their admiration and love were for what I had to say. I felt so proud, so fulfilled like I've never felt before. I guess it was a fantastic wish-fulfillment dream. Maybe I'm hooked on that. Hyperborea, Themis, this experience has been the fulfillment of a wish I never knew I had.

They sit in silence for a while appreciating the glow of intimacy they share. Pausanias breaks the silence by pointing to the sun, which is disappearing below the treetops. "Guess we should head back."

"I didn't tell you. I've moved into the dome. I asked Themis and she said it's OK. She said anyone who wants to join me is welcome."

I can't believe I just said that!

They walk back together past the dome and then on to the clearing. Plutarch, Themis, and Hyperides are still at the table talking . Clea is with them, but not sitting or talking, seeming to preside over the scene. Triptolemos and Corinna are busy making dinner, bustling around the oven.

–Looks like everyone's staying in Hobbiton now, Hypatia.

Episode 21

Every current resident and guest of Hyperborea was sitting at the table near the cob oven. They had finished the shepherd's pie concocted by Triptolemos and Corinna and were drinking herbal tea provided by Clea. Pausanias protested half seriously, "Clea, is this the same tea you served last night? I'm afraid to drink it after what happened." Clea smiled, "Don't blame the tea Pau."

Over dinner, Hypatia told everyone that Themis said it was fine if she stayed in the dome until they had to leave; then she confessed that she didn't want to leave at all, a desire she found out is shared by Corinna, who asked if she could join her in the dome. "It will be the women's dorm! Leave the lodge to the men."

After talking with Pausanias earlier, Hypatia felt safe enough to tell the group about the strong connection to Hyperborea she had felt from the moment she was invited to come, and how the feeling that this is where she belongs is just getting stronger. "It must be true then," said Themis, who didn't add anything else.

After his talk with Hypatia at the wellspring, Pausanias felt more at ease with what seemed to be happening, which was his new friends being pulled into a cult. He listened with a bemused smile to Hypatia and Corinna expressing their desire to stay in Hyperborea. He was still troubled by last night's vision and to-day's unsettling mind-body split, but Hypatia's trust in Themis convinced him to at least keep on open mind. As they were finishing their tea and preparing to call it a night, Themis jolted him to attention by saying to Plutarch, "You should tell everyone what we were talking about today. I think Pausanias would be interested."

Plutarch was surprised. "It won't be easy to summarize. I was just going to start writing about it tonight."

—Wouldn't it be helpful to collect your thoughts before writing?

Their conversation had been long and complicated by many twists and turns instigated by Themis. That morning, as soon as he sat down at the table, the first thing she said to him was "All you men are worried we're a cult. So, tell me: what exactly is a cult? and why are you worried?"

Hyp said, "See? I warned you."

Trying to satisfy Themis's request, he explained to the group they had talked about the concept of "cult" and why people are afraid of cults. Themis had suggested start by trying to answer the question, "What is the opposite of a cult?" Plutarch had thought about that for quite a while before admitting he was stumped. The only thing he could think of was "a group of free individuals." Themis had countered with "What do you mean by 'free'?"

"This is ridiculous. We'll be here all night," Plutarch sputtered in frustration. "I can't do our conversation justice right now. There are too many nuances. If anyone's interested, I'm going to be writing it all up, and you can read about what we discussed. I can't think of a way to quickly summarize what we talked about. All I can say is I'm looking forward to our next meeting, Themis." Plutarch was praying that she would let him off the hook.

"So am I, Plutarch, there's never a shortage of things to talk about, especially with you, but please, I know you can sketch it out for everyone." Themis was not going to let him off so easily. She had a point to make. Hyperides gave Plutarch a told-you-so look.

Exasperated and tired, Plutarch sighed dramatically. "I'll try, but I have the right to give up. OK, in a nutshell then, we agreed on the basic premise that humans naturally form groups and that every group of humans could be considered a 'cult' in the sense that members of a group invariably have a leader or leaders to whom individual group members relinquish control to some degree, which is the central feature of what we think of as a cult. Sometimes the members of a group choose their leader, sometimes the leader is imposed, but for the sake of the argument this is not important: if you are a member of a group, you have a leader, and therefore you do not have absolute freedom to do as you wish. So, we decided that it is the degree of control that individuals in a group surrender that is the key: If the leader of a group demands, or takes, a high degree of—if not absolute—control over the individuals in a group, that group is considered a cult and this is the reason people worry about cults. Giving up some control is OK, but giving up all control is not. So groups with leaders who demand absolute obedience from their members are considered 'cults' and are feared, because people value their liberty and autonomy. Often those cult leaders claim their entitlement to absolute authority is from God, or from some sort of divine right, or for some supernatural, metaphysical reason." Plutarch stopped and looked at Themis "Good enough?"

"That's the gist Plutarch. You are truly a master summarizer!" Themis gave Plutarch a warm smile. Everyone else was amused by her enthusiasm, but what Themis said next sobered them.

–So, according to this argument, we are a cult of some sort, since we're a group, and I think it's fair to say that everyone considers me to be the leader if for no other reason than this Hyperborean retreat center is my idea. Before last night you had not even met me, and I had not imposed any authority as the leader or taken control away from anyone in the group. However, as you all experienced, I did take some control away from you last night, and for that I apologize.

Themis looked around to each of her guests. She did have sincere regrets, but at the same time she knew what she had done was necessary to protect them all. "Some of you are concerned, even afraid that I was able to take control of you like that, and I understand. You have every reason to be worried, even fearful. All I can say in my defense is that I have what I honestly believe is a legitimate reason for what I did. I can't explain what the reason is at this moment, but I promise you I will explain very soon. I hope you trust me, and if not, I hope you will trust me—or at least forgive me—once I've explained."

No one knew what to say, and no one wanted to say anything when Themis was through. They sat together in the deepening twilight trying to understand what they were feeling about the convoluted argument Themis had made, but especially they were concerned about the mysterious *reason* that the tuning in the dome had been "necessary" as she put it.

Plutarch's mind had overheated trying to explain what he and Themis had talked about. Pausanias was physically and emotionally exhausted. He had been called out by Themis, and this was not how he had wanted the day to end, especially after it had made such a pleasant turn. As Hypatia had said, she knows things.

Hyperides, who no longer talks very much, had the last word. "We should trust Themis. She is looking out for us."

PART III. MESSENGER

Io, Kouros most Great, I give thee hail, Kronian, Lord of all that is wet and gleaming, thou art come at the head of thy Daimones.

To Dike for the Year, Oh march, and rejoice in the dance and song that we make to thee with harps and pipes mingled together, and sing as we come to a stand at thy well-fenced altar.

Io, Kouros most Great, I give thee hail, Kronian, Lord of all that is wet and gleaming, thou art come at the head of thy Daimones.

And the Horai began to be fruitful year by year and Dike to possess mankind, and all living things were held about by wealth-loving Peace.

Io, Kouros most Great, I give thee hail, Kronian, Lord of all that is wet and gleaming, thou art come at the head of thy Daimones.

To us also leap for full jars, and leap for fleecy flocks, and leap for fields of fruit, and for hives to bring increase.

Io, Kouros most Great, I give thee hail, Kronian, Lord of all that is wet and gleaming, thou art come at the head of thy Daimones.

Leap for our cities, and leap for our sea-borne ships, and leap for our young citizens and for goodly Themis.

HYMN OF THE KOURETES

Episode 22

Corinna's Diary

I knew something was up because of Clea whisking Trip away from me and the chickens to confer with him privately about something important that he couldn't talk about now but would explain later. Themis coming out with it, though, telling all of us with her weaponized voice that she took us on a wild gong ride for a mysterious reason to be explained later was still a surprise. Now we're all consumed with "the reason." The question is in my head first thing in the morning while I'm brushing my teeth, during the day it pops up whenever I'm not focused on doing something, which here in Hyperborea is often (well, not for me, since I'm with Trip who never stops working, but when he gives me a break), and there it is again, the last thing I'm thinking about before trying to fall asleep and not succeeding because I'm thinking about the reason! It's annoying, Themis! Enough drama. Let's get on with whatever it is.

The most annoying thing about the reason is no one has a clue about what could possibly be the reason for Themis to hijack our minds with her voice and then whale on gongs to send us all on journeys to the scary depths of our unconscious, or was it to the memory banks of the universe? Do I believe that's possible? How can I believe something is possible or not if I have no way of imagining what it could be? This whole situation is bizarre, especially bizarre for me since Trip and I have a relationship—undefined and maybe undefinable, but it's a relationship. I am emotionally involved, and I believe he is too. What if it turns out that the Greek nature worshippers really are an evil cult with a reason we are not going to accept as reasonable at all? With a reason we are going to reject utterly and completely? This is a terrifying possibility considering the power of

Themis. There's no denying that she has power, and her power may be simply that we can't deny her. We were all nervous when we first got here (I can't believe it was only a few days ago; it seems like a lifetime) but I don't think any of us (except maybe Hyp—and look what happened to him!) imagined just how nervous we should have been.

We all got together (except for Hyp who is always with Themis now) and shared notes about our dome experience, and there's no doubt I got off easy, especially compared to Pausanias. Who can blame him for some resentment and distrust after what he experienced? He's pissed at Themis. He feels what she did was a violation of our rights. It's a tricky question since she didn't exactly hold a gun to our heads or anything, but her voice could be considered a gun if you can accept that it has some supernatural power. I don't think this kind of thing is admissible in court. Hyp would know, if we could talk to him, but now he seems to be like her palace guard or something. After Pau told us what he had gone through while Themis was playing the gongs, I gave him a hug, and so did Hypatia. (Is something going on there? I sensed something.)

Hypatia and I are sharing the dome now, but we don't talk much. I asked her why she was crying after Themis admitted "Yes we're a cult, but don't worry about it, even though I messed with you. Sorry. I had my reasons, which I can't tell you about now but trust me." Hypatia said she didn't know why she cried. She was just feeling a lot of stuff. So am I. Even though I'm impatient to hear what the reason is, I'm happy. I'm happy that stuff is out in the open even if we don't know what the reason is yet. I'm happy that Hypatia got permission to stay in the dome and that I can too. I'm happy that she and I have both confessed that we'd like to stay here indefinitely and that that idea didn't immediately get slapped down by the cult leader. Then again, if we are a cult, wouldn't the leader want us to stay?

I don't care what we are called or how anyone wants to categorize us. I choose to stay here if I can and be a devoted cult member (Just so long as they are not evil. I draw the line at sacrificing animals, which includes humans. I hope I don't have to think about where I draw the line. I really do hope that does not become an issue. Please Themis, don't be an evil sorceress.) which I believe I already am since I work every day with Triptolemos tending the gardens, turning the compost, harvesting the crops, gathering the eggs, repairing and maintaining the tools, preparing meals, etc., etc., but I'm not complaining. This is the happiest I've ever been, and I think Trip is happy to have my company and my help.

It's nice being in the family compound now, no longer a guest, and I'm not the only one who feels this way. Hypatia is also a cult member in good standing even though she doesn't help out much, spending her time in the dome spacing out or at the wellspring zoning out or joining Plutarch and Themis in their daily deep conversations concerning philosophical questions. Hypatia says we're not a cult, we're a school, which according to Plutarch and Themis is just another name for a cult, but maybe Hypatia was not listening closely. Honestly, I'd rather be a cult cult than a school cult. If they make attendance at their meetings mandatory, I will have something to say about that.

Hyperides is also here at Hobbiton all the time, following Themis around like a puppy, like he has since Themis introduced herself and used her voice, but who am I to talk? Hypatia and I assume he's sleeping in the men's dorm with Plutarch and Pau, but we're both suspicious since he's always around early in the morning and stays late into the night. So we wonder. I'm pretty sure he is a cult member who hasn't come out of the closet yet, though saying to Themis, "You're a bird" would seem to qualify as coming out.

Plutarch may not be an actual cult member, but he's going to be a cult groupie for as long as Themis agrees to keep talking with him, because if there's one thing Plutarch loves it's talking.

That leaves dear Pau who is someone who does not like groups in general and cults in particular. He's a loner, not a joiner. It's ironic that his "vision" was the must cultish of all—his soul leaving his body and all—but I'm pretty sure he's not interested in staying past the due date. If the vibes around here continue to get more intense, I think he'll be out of here. He does have his car waiting at the old gas station. Hope it's still there.

Episode 23

Themis Dialogues

You made a toast 'to health" and then asked if we were 'ready for tuning.' Is there a connection?

A tuned violin is a healthy musical instrument, right? All the strings vibrating exactly as they should to produce a harmonious sound. Same for us. If we're in tune, we're in good health.

We're like a musical instrument?

You are a musical instrument. You vibrate and make music along with every other body in the universe.

So how did you decide we needed tuning?

You can tell if someone is out of tune just as you can tell when a violin or a piano is out of tune. With a musical instrument you can hear when it's unhealthy, with a person you feel it.

I can infer something about a person's health by how they look and sound, but I don't know what you mean by feeling it.

You could feel if someone is in tune and healthy, but you have to be open to feeling the vibrations. If you're deaf, you can't hear if a violin is in tune or not.

That's about as solipsistic as you can get.

That's a big word you're using, but if you're saying you want me to explain how you can feel someone's health, I can't in the terms you're used to. I can feel the vibrations from your three strings and how they're harmonizing and tell if they are all in tune. If you're in tune you resonate health. You could feel what I can feel if you allowed yourself to feel.

Solipsism is the belief that the only way to actually know something is through your own experience.

How else can you know something?

Hypatia: Plutarch, can we get back to vibrations, please? I remember from physics classes that at the quantum level everything in the universe is composed of vibrating strings, so your metaphor is the same one used by physicists.

'Vibrating strings,' is a good metaphor, because we are vibrating, every tiny bit of us is moving at various frequencies, as if we we're made of trillions of strings being plucked by an invisible musician. When we stop vibrating, we're dead, and the music stops. And when your vibrating is impeded somehow there's friction, heat, inflammation. The music is dissonant, the rhythm chaotic...you're unhealthy....Where were we, Plutarch? I'm getting carried away by metaphoring.

How about talking about the 'three strings' you just mentioned. What are they?

People usually use the words body, mind, and spirit. Your health in spirit, which depends on your health in body and mind, is what I wanted to check on. Think of your experience in the dome as a checkup during which I took your frequencies, checked your beat...see Plutarch, this is why describing reality with language is so inferior to knowing reality. You have to rely on metaphors. This is like this which is like this which is like this...Yes, I am a solipsist. I confess. Reality can only be known by experiencing it, not talking about it.

I give.

Hyperides: What do you mean by "health in spirit"?

What is your spirit?...I'm asking you, Hyp.

Hyperides: I know what my spirit is, but I'm having trouble putting it into words.

See, more solipsism, Plutarch! [Themis laughs] We know what we know. Why is it so important to explain away in words?

I think of my 'spirit' as my will. Without spirit, I would have no will. I would be an automaton. I guess that could mean that I think of my spirit as my soul.

Hyperides: I agree. I'm thinking of the expression "if the spirit moves me." I will do something if the spirit moves me; otherwise I won't. The spirit, my spirit is the inner force that moves me; without it, I wouldn't move.

Hypatia: There are a lot of people who don't believe in spirit, or the spirit as a vital force that moves us. They believe we are just animals with big spiritless brains who are motivated by instinct, that our behavior is entirely the result of genetic coding and environmental conditioning. Our instinct is to survive, which basically means to pursue pleasure and avoid pain. That's it. There's no 'spirit' that 'moves' us anywhere. There's just operant conditioning from which we learn how best to stay in the pleasure zone and avoid the pain zone.

Those are people who for emotional reasons don't want to know who they are. Knowing their spirit, knowing themselves, is frightening, painful, so they refuse to know. They work hard to rationalize their fear of self-knowledge by insisting that unless the spirit can be perceived by the senses, unless it is 'proven,' it cannot be real. Seeing is believing, so the spirit cannot and does not exist, even though if for a moment they allowed themselves to know their spirit, they would not be able to deny its existence.

I take it these people are not 'healthy in spirit.'

All three strings are interdependent, and one string out of tune affects the others. If you're trying to play a violin concerto but one of your strings is not tuned correctly, you can't play it. If the body string is out of tune, it affects the mind and spirit strings; if the mind string is out of tune, it affects the body and spirit strings, and so on.

You said that you were interested in the health of our spirit. Why? And what's your assessment? How healthy in spirit are we?

I felt you were all very healthy in body and mind compared to most people, so I knew you must have pretty robust spirits, which you do. Your overall health is actually not the issue. I needed to tune all your strings together to a higher frequency to accelerate you. It's a blessing to have health in this age of dis-ease, and you're going to need it.

How did you know we were healthy?

Like I said, I could feel your health; otherwise you would not have been invited. I can feel your health right now that you're here. We're not a healing center for human beings...yet. Maybe down the road. Like I said, I needed to tune you up to a higher pitch.

What kind of a center then are you?

I'm not sure I can answer that. I think Hypatia might have it right. She says we're a school, a center for learning about Nature, how's that?

You haven't said why you were interested in the health of our spirit, especially since you claim you knew we were healthy already, with 'robust' spirits.

Such a taskmaster, Plutarch! You're not going to like my answer. The vitality of your spirit is important for the reason I invited you to the dome, the reason I promised to explain, and that's why I needed to check on it and tune you up to a higher pitch. I needed to accelerate you to prepare you for what's to come. I promise to explain. Please understand that it is not an easy thing to tell you what I need to tell you—not easy for me, not easy for you, not easy for anyone.

You know, Themis, the circles you and Clea run around us have worn a deep groove. There's a metaphor for you.

Apologies, Plutarch, but you will forgive me in time.

Episode 24

For the last couple of days Clea has been working with her brother and Corinna. There is a lot to get done in the fall around the gardens in preparation for winter—harvesting, canning, dehydrating, mulching—there is maintenance to be done on the pools, the plumbing, the solar system, and the backup methane gas system. As a younger man, her grandpa had visited the Museum of Toilets in New Delhi and had learned how methane gas from composting outdoor toilets could be captured, pressurized, and used to create electricity, so he designed and built his own system to be used in case of solar power collapse. He wasn't worried about losing power so much as he just liked DIY projects. All of the normal seasonal preparation is fraught with a tremendous urgency since Themis had told her and Triptolemos what is coming.

Before long she will be helping Trip and his girlfriend make dinner for the second night in a row. She reminds herself, *Tomorrow I'm calling a meeting and insisting that if we are all going to live together in a commune then communal duties need to be assigned.* How many days has it been since the orientation in the gazebo? A week, just a week. It seems as if it's been longer, maybe because she's anticipating it being much, much longer. She hasn't come to terms with that prospect, not remotely close to terms. Not even one term yet. She's already missing being only the mysterious host. She doesn't have an idea yet of what her role may be in the new world. Themis was trying to goad her with her crack about procreation, but she knows there is truth in it if she is right about what's coming, and she has no doubt that her sister is right. *So my fate is to be a breeder then?*

* * *

162 ~ DW HOHLBEIN

Pausanias, lying on his back on the sand of what he thinks of as Hypatia's beach, is daydreaming. *How long have we been here now, anyway? I have no idea anymore. No phone, no clocks, just the sun coming up and going down. I can't remember when I used to know what day it is, and not just the day of the week, but the day of the month.* When did he tell the others about the "lake?" Did he even tell them at all? He doesn't remember. Hypatia is lying next to him in the warm sand. She had walked down to her favorite place after leaving Themis, Hyperides, and Plutarch to their Q&A session, and there was Pau.

–Did you learn anything this time?

–Not really, but I enjoyed listening to Themis interrogate Plutarch.

–I thought the idea was Plutarch would interrogate her.

–That may have been his original plan, but I'm pretty sure he understands now that it's his ideas that are going to be challenged, not hers. He's a good sport. He just likes ideas; I don't think he cares whose they are or even how much validity they have. We talked about the spirit, trying to define it, and how everything in the universe vibrates, all of which had to do with what happened in the dome.

–What about the spirit?

–What it is, does it exist, why we need it for our health. You might have been interested since you experienced your soul leaving your body.

Oh shit! Hypatia smiles nervously, wishing she hadn't said that, hoping she isn't triggering a reaction.

–I don't know what I imagined I experienced, and I don't understand why I would imagine that experience whatever it was. I don't even believe in the soul, so why would I imagine my soul coming out of the top of my head? Why did I even think, *Oh, that's my soul?*

-Maybe it would help if you talked about it with Themis.

Reaction triggered. "Hypatia, I know that you trust Themis and believe she has 'powers' if that's the right word, but I'm not there with you. Maybe she's psychic. Some people are psychic. That's a fact. I'm waiting to hear her explanation for doing whatever she did to us in the dome, and after that I am pretty sure I'll be leaving since I don't have much hope that her explanation is going to convince me to stick around. I think she hypnotized us somehow. Just like some people are psychic, some people are hypnotists. Maybe she's both. I don't think it's right that she wasn't straight up with us. I can forgive her, but I have lost a lot of respect for her."

"I'm sorry, Pau. I shouldn't have said anything. I know that vision you had was really disturbing." *Why did I bring it up? Stupid!* She feels bad that she upset him, but she also doesn't want him to leave.

-Have we actually been here longer than two weeks? Feels like it.

* * *

"Hyperides, why don't you just come in? You can sleep on the bench in here. It's more comfortable than that chair." Themis is standing in the doorway of her hut. She can see Hyperides nodding off in the Adirondack chair that he took from the porch of the lodge. This is his second night of vigil outside of her cob house.

Hyperides hasn't tried to figure out what he's feeling because he knows it's impossible to figure out. There's nothing to compare what he's feeling to unless he remembers being a child and what he felt as a child, which he doesn't. He has no memories of his childhood, but he imagines that what he's feeling must be what a child who needs to be near his mother would feel. With her voice Themis took away a pain he hadn't known he was carrying until the weight of it was gone, and then how much lighter he was!

What was it that had oppressed him? What was the burden she had lifted? He didn't know if he needed to stay near her to keep the pain from returning, to keep the burden from weighing him down again, but he didn't want to risk it, now that he knew how it felt to have it gone. Maybe this is what converts mean when they say they've been saved. I feel saved. I don't know from what, but it feels like salvation...or is it absolution? What did I need saving from or forgiveness for?

"Come in, Hyp. It's OK." Themis remembers this is what happens, but she can't help worrying about him. She's worried about them all. She worries that what she's doing is not entirely Themis, and she must be entirely Themis or what's supposed to happen will change, and she's sure it won't be for the better. What's supposed to happen is why she is here, now, as Themis, which means whatever she does needs to be entirely Themis.

"I don't know, it feels wrong." Above all, Hyperides fears offending her. He has placed her on a very high pedestal and can't imagine her coming all the way down from it just so he can get a good night's sleep.

"Really, my friend, it's fine. I may be a bird to you, but I'm not a delicate one. You shouldn't worry about offending or hurting me." Hyperides sits up in the chair and looks at her directly for the first time since she opened her door. "Are you really inviting me in for the night? To sleep?"

"I am. Why is that so crazy? This is the second night in a row you were going to sleep outside in that chair you lugged all the way here. Shouldn't you be worried that I might be upset about your taking that chair from the lodge?" She smiles and looks back at him. He is able to hold her gaze long enough for her eyes to convince him.

* * *

"How are you feeling, Hyp?" Themis has made tea and they are facing each other on the long cob bench that curves in a semicircle around the wall. "Still nervous about being here?"

–Of course I am, terrified and excited more like it, but thanks for letting me in. It's getting cold at night.

–Are you willing to tell me why you're sleeping outside my door?

–Don't you know?

–I don't know everything, Hyp! I'd like to hear from you rather than guess.

–I'm afraid that if I'm apart from you that whatever it is you did that makes me...happy, I guess is the word...will wear off.

–I didn't do anything to you. You had a revelation. It happens.

–It was your voice that caused the revelation.

–My voice doesn't cause anything except sound waves. You were ready for a revelation, and the revelation came.

Hyperides laughs. "I'm not fooled by your mumbo-jumbo like Plutarch."

–I don't think Plutarch is fooled, he just enjoys mumbo-jumbo. Themis laughs along with Hyperides.

They stop talking for a while and sip on the tea. Hyperides looks around the circular hut which inside is one large room except for a partition which creates a private space where he assumes Themis sleeps. There is no furniture besides the bench, a small table with a couple of wicker chairs similar to what they have in the lodge, and a padded chair with an end table and a lamp for reading. The walls have numerous cavities and shelves molded into them that hold books and bric-a-brac. There are tall mature plants in large ceramic pots scattered around.

–Not much to see, I know. I don't spend much time here.

–Where do you spend time?

"Lately, talking with Plutarch and you! If Trip or Clea don't need my help, I guess I commune with nature, as they say. But they usually need my help with something or other." Themis isn't entirely sure this is the moment to say what she wants to say or is supposed to say or has said—she's not remembering clearly—but there's no way of knowing the precise right moment for anything. The right moment for anything just happens as it has always happened, as it always will happen, so she says it.

"Hyp, just so you know. I'm not a goddess or anything like that. I don't need to be worshipped, and I definitely don't want to be. Please don't worship me! How can we be friends then? I'm a woman just like you're a man..."

At this, Hyperides noticeably flinches. "Oh stop, there's nothing to be afraid of...what I'm trying to say is that it makes me uncomfortable when you treat me as if I'm some precious work of art that you must protect at all costs. I'm a human being, like you, but as you saw, I'm also Themis, which means I have no choice but to represent the Law. I think this may be the revelation you had: you heard my voice and understood that I am an avatar for the Law, and this makes you happy. You fight for the poor and powerless with no real hope for justice, begging for crumbs of fairness, absorbing daily humiliation, and yet you persevere, and here in the middle of nowhere you find a powerful ally who you know in your heart will never let you down. We both stand for the Law as it is found in the scriptures of all religions, as is found in the Christian Bible: "He who oppresses the poor taunts their Maker, but whoever is kind to the needy honors Him." The rich and powerful who control this world taunt the Creator daily with their cruelty. They despoil and desecrate their Mother with impunity, and this is painful for you and for me. Knowing I'm someone who will share that pain with you may be the great relief you feel. But this is no reason to worship me; it's a reason to join with me."

While Themis talked, Hyperides heard her words in his ears, but he *felt* her words in his heart. There may have still been some of his pain buried deep in his heart of hearts, and when she finishes talking, that pain is also gone. He is crying. How long has he been crying?

Themis slides over on the bench, puts her arm around his shoulders, and draws his head down to her. He continues to cry, and she keeps holding him. The joy of fellowship is almost unbearable.

Episode 25

"Oh, Hyperides. Sorry, I didn't know you were here." Clea had given her sister's door a cursory knock before letting herself in. She had come to talk with her about how the new society that already seems to be forming should be organized. She wants it known that she is not going to be a head cook. Hyperborean politics was not something they had discussed in their preparation for the Omega event, as they have been focused on how they would find the right people to be with them when the time came. The time has come and the right people seem to be here, so now what?

When Themis had first proposed her scheme, the thought she and Trip both had was "WTF?" But the word-of-mouth invitations for two weeks at a remote rustic lodge—with hot springs! Pay what you can!—had brought the right people, who after visiting brought more of the right people, and now miraculously the best people they could have hoped for. *I suppose this must be what Themis remembers, she just didn't tell us.*

Are they going to be a little democracy or will everyone assume Themis is the queen and the rest of them either drones or workers? She is in a mood after cooking for eight again the night before, though she has to admit the new family members are nothing but helpful, Corinna especially, who has been working side by side with Triptolemos every day. Her bright energy and enthusiasm never falters, but her most endearing quality has to be her unquestioning embrace of whatever the moment brings. No entitlement and no complaints. She understands her sacred duty to life. *I approve, Trip. She's a great addition to the family.*

I agree. I hope it works out with the Bee Maiden.

Hyperides is here! Where are you? This is embarrassing.

I'm coming now. Relax.

I can tell he's as uncomfortable as I am.

–I came to talk to my sister, Hyperides. Do you know where she went?" (*Awkward!*)

–I don't know. I was just leaving. (*Stop blushing, there's no reason to be embarrassed.*) Will you tell Themis thanks? (*I'll just wait over at the table. Plutarch will be showing up soon.*)

–Sure. (*Thanks for what? Please just go. This is too weird for me.*)

Themis arrives soon after Hyp leaves.

–Sorry, sis, Hyperides and I were talking until very late, and he was sound asleep when I got up. He needed the sleep. I just talked with your brother, and I was out looking for you, but here you are.

–You were up late?

–Honestly, sometimes you're just so prim.

–Does 'prim' mean 'responsible?'

–Ha, ha, funny....I had to do something didn't I? You think it better for him to sleep in a chair outside my door every night?

–No, better would be to send him back to the lodge to sleep with the other men, his friends. It's they who need to be bonding right now, not you and Hyp.

–We were already bonded before he came here. We are always bonded. He's bonded to me as a principle, as Themis. He follows the Law. He accepts his duty. We don't always have a personal emotional bond, but it seems we do this time. He saw our connection in his own strange way the other night. He realized that Themis is on the side of *the Good*. I guess that's why he saw me with wings, like I was an angel."

–He said you are a bird, not an angel.

–He saw wings...he was making connections without knowing it. Birds are omens, and I'm an omen of sorts, a living, breathing omen. And soon what I'm an omen for is going to happen, which is what I want to talk about.

–I'm listening.

–It's time to tell them everything. I asked Trip to be ready to take anyone who wants to talk to their family up with him to the Eagle's Nest if they can't get cell service down here, which they probably can't. You've kept their phones charged haven't you?

–Yes.

–Plutarch is coming again today for more talk therapy with me. I'm sure Hyperides will be there and Hypatia. I asked Triptolemos to bring Corinna once we start talking. That leaves Pausanias, who may refuse to come if I ask him. I'm hoping you can persuade him.

–I think Hypatia can persuade him. They've been spending a lot of time together in the last few days. I think they're getting close. I'll ask her.

–Please make sure Hypatia knows how important it is that he hear me out.

–She'll know without my telling her. She's on your wavelength, sister. She can hear the trees talking to her.

–And me.

–You're kidding, right?

–She's receptive, just like you, sister! I remember Pausanias leaving, but he needs to be there tonight, so please talk to Hypatia about convincing him.

Episode 26

Themis Dialogues

Can you explain why your voice had such a strong effect on us when we first met you? Everyone felt it.

What effect?

Your voice commanded us. Especially when you were offering us the wine. It was so unexpected. We had all assumed no meat, no drugs, no alcohol in Hyperborea, just as we were told in the welcome letter from Clea. You seemed to sense our confusion and said, 'don't worry,' and we instantly relaxed, but it was actually more than that: we weren't worried about anything at all. It was like you got inside our heads and turned off the worry switch.

I don't know, Plutarch. It's possible my voice had a little extra resonance that prompted you to feel the way you wanted to feel. You were all overly excited about meeting the mysterious Themis on top of the anxiety you've been feeling since you got here. I gave you permission to let that all go. To release it. And you were happy to do so. Like auto suggestion.

We didn't imagine it. Your voice had a powerful 'resonance' as you put it that affected us dramatically.

Maybe because I'm tuned to this place, which vibrates rapidly, so my voice gets a boost...It's true that I wanted you to be in a 'no-worry' frame of mind so you would be open to following me to the dome. Since you've arrived, your frequencies have been accelerating, but I needed to tune you up higher so we could all be humming along together, healthy and strong....

Why was that so important and why didn't you tell us?

Imagine my telling you about vibrations and frequencies and all that before suggesting we go to the dome for a 'tuning,' do you think you would have come?

Maybe, if you had explained it.

I'd still be explaining it, like I'm trying to do now. Always having to explain the unexplainable. It's exhausting. It's so much easier just to know.

So why was it so important to get us 'tuned' up?

I'll explain just as soon as everyone else is here.

Hypatia: I talked to Pausanias. He'll be here.

Good, I expect Corinna and Triptolemos to show up any minute.

Hyperides: Why did we all have such strange experiences while you were playing the gongs? Was that part of the tuning?

Think of my playing the gongs as an app that connected you to the universal data stream. Our minds normally prevent us from connecting as it is confusing, frightening, sometimes enlightening, but as far as our brain is concerned, not serving a purpose, not functional, so there's no reason to make the connection. The gongs override the brain's security software and allow you to connect.

Hypatia: So we accessed our unconscious? Like a waking dream?

That's right as far as it goes, but it's not just your personal unconscious, it's everyone's and everything's unconscious. It's the universe's memory, and it contains everything. Obviously, it is extremely difficult to navigate, especially the first time! There are no useful menus dropping down for you. It's chaotic, incoherent, and extremely weird, but with practice and experience, you may be able to remember.

Remember what?

Who you are. What is real.

I'm not even going to ask about what you just said. I *know* better. You knew this was going to happen to us?

I knew you would have an experience, but I had no idea what it would be. Every soul is a unique iteration, so your experiences would be uniquely your own.

Hyperides: We were dreaming?

You were remembering.

* * *

It took almost an hour due to interruptions, questions and answers, and having to repeat important points several times for Themis to explain why she hoped they would all stay, why they needed to stay.

Once she stopped talking, and before anyone else spoke, Pausanias, who had been angrily fidgeting the whole time, vented his pent-up frustration: "So you did this tuning knowing we would have potentially frightening experiences, even traumatic ones, so that we would be prepared for an end-of-the-world event that you know is going to happen soon, but you can't say what it is and when it will happen?" Pausanias glares at Themis. "Do I have it right?"

Themis nods. She knows not to smile.

–Clea, Trip, you're her family. You know Themis, we don't. We just met her a few days ago. You grew up together, and you've been living here with her for years, and she claims you've been prepping for doomsday with her this whole time. Do you really believe this is going to happen? That we need to stay here for our safety, and ultimately, if all goes to plan, to start building a new society based on the 'law' as she puts it?

Trip replies, "If Themis says it, I believe it. She's never given me any reason to doubt her."

–What about you, Clea? I have a hard time believing you don't have doubts. You're a no-nonsense person. At least I thought you were.

–I have no doubts, Pau, no doubts at all. I have complete faith in my sister, and as you say, I know her a lot better than you do. But I completely understand why you have doubts. Who wouldn't? It's not only your serious doubts about Themis knowing the things she says she knows, which any rational person would have, but it's your inability to accept the unacceptable, that there is going to be a catastrophe that will be if not an exinction event for humanity, something close to it. Who can get his or her mind around that? Who wants to? While I believe Themis, honestly, Pau, I still can't accept that it's actually going to happen, and I sincerely hope she's wrong. But I definitely would not bet on it.

Clea's speech calms Pausanias. What she said is so reasonable that he doesn't feel like everyone has lost her mind. He's looking at the ground. "OK, I know you're feeling like family now, and it feels good, I know, and Hypatia and Corinna, you already said you want to stay, so I don't imagine what Themis said is going to change your mind. You're probably relieved in some way..."

Hypatia quickly responds, "That's not fair, Pau." And Corinna, genuinely irritated for the first time since she arrived says, "The prophesized death of the human race does not relieve me, Pausanias. Reserve your outrage for Themis, though I don't think that's fair either."

Hyperides says, "I'm staying, and if the world ends, I'll be glad I'm here when it happens. What is there to go back to but a shit world ruled by shit people?"

"Pausanias, I think you're angry about being manipulated, and so am I." Plutarch isn't really angry, but he wants to make a point. "We've been manipulated from the start. Themis just explained how the entire scheme is an elaborate manipulation. There is no way to characterize it as anything else but a con. That said, we chose to come and agreed to the inherent risk. Remember how nervous we were on that first day? But it's not like we're being forced to stay. Clea said she'll drive us out to the highway, and your car is still there. Themis has come clean, and whether or not we can accept her prophecy, we are free to go. Clea even offered to drive us to where we can get transportation if your car has been stolen or vandalized."

–No, Plutarch, I definitely don't appreciate feeling manipulated, but what's really getting to me is how you all are so easily sucked into the end-of-the-world scam. It's such a cliché. How many dystopian novels and movies have been based on this plot? Just about all of them one way or another. All of the shows and books about the horrible future in store for us center on some end-of-the-world scenario, and the plot turns on who believes and who doesn't. And historically, in real life, how many cult leaders have explained to their brainwashed disciples why they must follow them to a remote place where they will be saved from certain disaster...and then what happens? No doomsday except actual days of doom enacted by the murderously insane messianic leaders of the cults. I have been imagining all the things Themis might say, but one thing I rejected as completely implausible is that she would pull the end-times card from the bottom of the deck. And here we are in the middle of nowhere without our phones, no communication with the outside world, being told we must stay, because it's not safe to leave. I mean, don't you all know this story? This is what upsets me the most. I thought you all were pretty intelligent, savvy people, but look at you!

No one says anything for quite a while. Pausanias's reaction is not a surprise, and his friends want to respect his anger, but still, they feel attacked and insulted. Finally Hypatia, speaking slowly and firmly, says "I believe Themis, Pau. I believe she knows things, as I told you before. I'm hurt that you consider me a fool for believing, but I understand why you would think that, because I happen to be an intelligent, savvy person."

Corinna adds, "I don't worry about believing or not believing. I just want to stay here. I like it here. I feel appreciated. I feel like I am part of something good. I'm hoping the world doesn't end,

but if it does, I'm with Hyperides, I'd rather be here than anywhere else."

Themis looks at Pausanias with an expression of sincere concern. Everyone is literally holding their breath. "Pau, the world
is not going to end. What's going to happen is going to save the
world. That's what I remember, at least. And that's supposed to
be the reason that I'm Themis, here on earth at this particular
time."

"You 'remember' the future then? How does that work?"
Pausanias sputters angrily.

–Everything in the memory of the universe has happened,
is happening, will happen every moment. The distinctions are
meaningless, so that's how I remember the future and the
past...or try to.

–So why can't you remember the important details about
doomsday, like what will it be and when will it happen?

There are too many variables. An infinite number, actually.
Too many things may change at any moment. The universe is
creative and responsive, not deterministic. I remember the forest, not the trees. Something like this event is so momentous,
though, that I remember it without any doubt whatsoever. The
emotional charge is far too great to forget. It's like how we
vividly remember a traumatic event from early childhood.

By now Pausanias has calmed down enough that he's actually
listening to Themis and grasping what she says, even though
he's resisting at the same time. "Plutarch, what about you? Will
you come with me? I'm taking Clea up on her offer."

–No, I'm not coming. I want to keep talking to Themis. I don't
think the catastrophe is going to happen, and since we've been
invited to stay, I will leave when I'm ready. Like Hyp said, what's
the point of returning to our shit world before we have to?

Episode 27

Hypatia follows Pausanias back to the lodge trying to calm him down and convince him to stay, pointing out that they were not the true believers he accused them of being, and doesn't it make sense to stay whether or not her dire prophecy comes true? Why return to their crumbling world just to make the point that he's no fool?

"There is no chance it's going to happen," he says.

–You know we're not completely clueless and understand what you're feeling, right?

–Of course, and I apologize for calling you fools. I understand your wanting to stay for your reasons, but this scenario is not for me. Waiting around for the apocalypse and joining a commune in the meantime. The Greeks had slaves, you know. Look at Corinna. Triptolemos is a strict overseer.

–That's not what's going on. If you're jealous, own it.

Hypatia is behind Pausanias as he walks up the stairs to his room, talking at his back. At the top of the stairs, he turns suddenly, facing her, and gives her a warm hug. She hugs him back.

They break their embrace and Pau says, "I'm going to miss you, and the others, too. I'm going to miss the Greeks. I like them all, including Themis, believe it or not. And I promise to come back to see how it's going as soon as the world doesn't end.

Hypatia says in a whisper, "Please stay. I really don't think you should go. I'm worried."

Hypatia waits at the door to Pau's room watching him pack his bag. He stops to scribble in his journal, tears out a page and hands it to her. "Here's my address and phone number. We don't live that far apart."

–Thanks. I'm going to wait downstairs for Clea.

"Don't tag team me, OK?" Hypatia is making this way harder than it's supposed to be.

Pausanias is packed in just a few minutes, but he sits down in the chair by the window and takes in the view for the last time—the familiar trees, the river steaming where the mineral water dribbles into it after its serpentine journey down the bank. Despite what he told Hypatia to make her feel better, he won't come back. Maybe she really will look me up once she leaves here. If she leaves here.

He's lost track of time since the night in the dome. He's pretty sure he hasn't been here the full two weeks, but it feels like he's been here for months. He's interested to find out what his experience of time will be once he's plugged back into the ubiquitous devices with their batteries that keep track of time without fail, as relentlessly as time moves forward without fail. Will the compulsion to check devices for messages come back? To browse for some obscure factoid? To see what new shows are streaming and on what platform? To forward something, anything? To tweet or retweet? Like or dislike?

He actually doesn't need to have compulsions, the devices are designed to compel him all on their own with alerts, pings, and subtle sirens of all kinds that lure him to the shoals of the data stream. Once there he will sit for hours, his consciousness stranded, with nothing to do but follow another link. The ultimate purpose of the unending chain of links is always the same: to get him to buy something. To take whatever money he has and then move on to the next target. All that's required of him to keep the capitalist waste machine operating and help kill the planet is to click. So easy. And so convenient. It is a shit world I'm running back to...why? To prove I'm no fool? Only a fool gets trapped by pride.

He hears Clea pull up and Hypatia greet her. *No turning back now, fool.*

* * *

The reality of what Themis told them has broken through Corinna's defenses, the same defenses everyone put up to shield themselves from the unimaginable prospect of the death of billions of human beings. A prospect that includes their own imminent deaths as Themis made it clear that she could not remember if they would survive or not. I don't have access to that is how she put it. No one except Clea and Trip could allow themselves to believe that it would happen, and that is only because they've been preparing for it for years.

"Do you really think it's going to happen Trip?" Corinna is with him in his hut, which has the same semicircular bench as Themis's. They're sitting next to each other shoulder to shoulder, unsure how to proceed. How do you proceed when the world may end at any moment?

Triptolemos takes Corinna's hand. It's the first time they've touched. "I'm sorry. I want to comfort you, but it is going to happen. Themis has been talking about this since she could form complete sentences. She could not handle the OAP and the Dominionists taking political control of this country. She was so angry all the time, and she was only 12 years old! We thought she was having a psychotic break. She would rant about how Mother was going to have to save herself now. America becoming One America was the end of hope. She'd chant their creepy slogan—Liberty plus Fealty equals Prosperity—with disgust and mockingly rant as she marched around the living room as if walking in a protest march: Whose liberty? THEIRS! Whose fealty? OURS! Whose prosperity? THEIRS! She ranted about a lot of things in her teens. She dropped out of school and came here to live with grandma and grandpa who somehow, amazingly, knew what was going on with her. They helped her to understand who she is. They helped her become Themis, not just carry the name. Without them, without this place, she probably would have been institutionalized and heavily medicated her entire life. I can tell you, though, Corinna, she knows what she says she knows, don't ask me how."

"Trip, believe me, you are a huge comfort. You're comforting me. Don't kick me out, OK? I want to stay here to face the fire and brimstone or whatever it is that the Earth is going to kill us with. I don't want to be alone." Corinna squeezes Trip's massive, calloused hand with her blistered one, and he squeezes back. This is how they proceeded.

* * *

Plutarch's Journal

Today Themis gathered us all at the table in the middle of the family's complex, sending out Hypatia to make sure Pausanias would come. Since I began taking notes for the Themis Dialogues, the oven and the table nearby, the omphalos of Hobbiton, has become our meeting place, our agora. Hyperides and Hypatia have been regular participants with Clea often standing by, monitoring the proceedings, but rarely commenting. She seems to have adopted the role of executive assistant to Themis, or is it more accurate to say she's her consort? Clea often shows with her body language disapproval of something Themis is saying, just as a lady of the court might express disapproval of what her queen says, believing that it's beneath her royal highness or perhaps politically dangerous. Triptolemos and Corinna are always busy. They wave when they pass by. Lately Trip has been talking about building a shelter over the agora since we're all congregating there now. "The weather isn't going to hold forever," he warns, "there will be rain, then snow. The oven will keep us warm if there is a roof and some walls to trap the heat."

Pausanias has been scarce, as he has been since we arrived, but today he joined us and listened to what Themis had to say. He blames Themis for his disturbing experience in the dome. He feels she crossed a line she shouldn't have, and he wouldn't have come to hear her explanation at all if Hypatia had not convinced him to give her a chance to defend herself. He was not happy with what she had to say. He thought her prophesizing a cosmic cataclysm that could mean the end of humankind was a cheap trick, a 'cult cliché' he called it, and he berated us for giving her prophecy the slightest credence.

He said he was disappointed in us for being so gullible. He accused Themis of hypnotizing us and manipulating us into staying there indefinitely with the family while we all waited for the end of the world which would obviously never come. Pausanias came to the meeting feeling hurt and vulnerable by what had happened to him in the dome. He was in a reactive state as it was, and what Themis had to say triggered a pretty harsh and unforgiving reaction. He basically called Themis a charlatan and the rest of us fools.

All of us—the former guests, that is—defended our choosing to stay for essentially the same reason. We all hoped Themis was wrong. We didn't necessarily believe that her prophecy was going to come to pass (the degree of belief being on a sliding scale depending on the person), and whether or not the 'event' does happen, we all would rather be in Hyperborea than back in the world we were happy to escape for two weeks. Now that our vacation has been extended for an undetermined longer time, why leave? I believe Pausanias would have been feeling the same if not for how unsettled be became after his near-death experience in the dome when he saw his soul leaving his body. After chastising and insulting everyone, I suppose he felt he had no choice but to leave.

Clea drove him to the old gas station where he had left his car, and when she returned, she reported that the old, trusty Honda was where we had left it, and it started right up. She said he was relieved, but she thought he was also feeling some regret. She said, "We didn't talk much at all in the car. I didn't want to bring anything up, and neither did he. Once he got his car started, he got out, looked back at me, and waved. It was a sad wave, not a happy one."

* * *

Hypatia's Journal

I'm not surprised that Pau left. He's not someone who is comfortable with social obligations, which if he stayed he'd have to accept. We are all going to be family now if what Themis predicts comes true. "Family" in a loose sense of course, not the blood relative sense. He likes to take responsibility for himself and no one else. He wants to be in control of his daily agenda, which he's shown since he's been here, going off on his own most days to explore and coming back just as it's getting dark.

After we had our chance (was it?) meeting at the wellspring and talked about our visions in the dome, I think we both felt a connection, and it felt nice. I was surprised by how nice it felt, how I welcomed feeling close to someone. How long has it been since I felt this? I was hoping that whatever Themis had to say would help him let go of his resentment, but that's definitely not what happened. As soon as she finished talking—after at least an hour—he went off on her, calling her just another fake prophet in a long line of con artists, actual and fictional, and calling us idiots for believing her. He was pissed.

I followed him back to the lodge and tried to calm him down. I did not want him to leave for his own safety, because I do believe Themis when she says that if we leave now we may be in great danger, but also because I just don't want him to leave. I thought we were on our way to a relationship of some kind, though it's impossible now to imagine what kind of relationship, but still, it was pleasant fantasizing about all the possibilities. I could use a friend here besides Corinna and Plutarch, whom I'm friendly with and feel friendly toward, but neither of them feels like a friend.

Pausanias feels like a friend. I asked him why he thought he had to leave when we don't necessarily believe that what Themis says is going to happen will happen, that we want to stay because we like it here and are happy to be allowed to stay past the two weeks. His reasoning is that the entire scheme is going according to design, that we're now caught up in the con as planned, like fish in a net, and that today was just another step toward the ultimate goal, and it was an important step: "Don't you see? This is her way of weeding out the nonbelievers. She wants me gone so I don't infect you with doubt. That's why she insisted I come to 'hear her out.' She knew that what she said would actually drive me away."

I said, "But to what end? What goal? Why?"

"To be determined," he said. "TBD."

I told him his paranoia was an overreaction. "What do you imagine she and her siblings have planned for us?"

He said, "I imagine a lot of things, none of them good." And I said, "Like what? What do you imagine?"

And that's when he stopped responding, and it's easy to guess why: he doesn't imagine anything. He has no idea what the grand goal of their nefarious scheme may be. He's too embarrassed to admit that he's the one who's caught in his own defensive, angry net.

I followed behind him up the stairs to his room. At the top, he startled me by turning around to face me. We were literally nose-to-nose looking at each other. Then he hugged me, and I hugged him back. He said he would miss me and gave me his address and phone number. He said he'd come back after the world doesn't end to see how we're doing.

I don't believe him, not because I don't think he might want to, but because I believe Themis. He won't be able to make it back. He will probably die. I went downstairs to wait for Clea.

I was crying.

Episode 28

Hyperides and Themis are still sitting at the table when Clea gets back from her trip to the highway. She reports that all went well—the car was there and had started up with no problem. Hyperides asks Themis "Are you upset that he's gone?"

–Yes, but I knew he was leaving. It's just that I was sure he was coming back, but now I'm not sure." Themis looks concerned. "I'm not upset that he wanted to leave or by the things he said, I'm worried about him, that he may suffer, that he may die, and I feel responsible for his paranoia. Pausanias was not prepared for what I did in the dome that night. I meant well, but I should have known. I should have taken more care.

–How so?

–Play differently. Sing differently. Not push as much as I did. Pausanias was too vulnerable.

–We weren't vulnerable?

–Not so much as Pausanias. He has an unresolved trauma that he carries with him. What I did in the dome basically tore the scab off his wound, and he remembered the trauma. He wasn't prepared for that. After, he was confused, hurt, angry...all of the above.

"You shouldn't be too hard on yourself, Themis. You were doing what you believed needed to be done. Your intentions were good, which is all that matters." Hyperides looks Themis in the eyes, "You don't believe you're infallible do you?

Themis smiles. "Thanks for reminding me, Hyp. I need reminding. I am definitely not infallible. There is a lot hidden from me, and I hide a lot from myself. And you know what? I could be wrong about Ge's final solution for dealing with humanity's obstinate lawlessness."

–I'm counting on your being wrong.

* * *

Are you home? Can I come over?

Yes, I'm here. Are you OK?

Not really.

Clea has just finished making tea when Themis comes in. "Here," Clea hands her a mug, and they sit down on the bench. "Rough day, huh? Saying goodbye to Pau was really hard. I was hoping his car had been stolen or the gas siphoned out of his tank. I'm going to miss him. I like his spirit."

–I feel responsible, but Hyp reminded me to forgive myself. Sometimes I forget that even Themis deserves forgiveness.

–Good for Hyperides!

–I think he's living with me now.

–Is that what you want? Is that wise?

–Yes and yes. And since you ask about the wisdom of suddenly cohabitating with Hyperides, this is a good time to tell you something about us. I know you don't appreciate being blindsided.

Themis told Clea what Hyp had experienced while she was playing the gongs. How he had traveled through space at speeds faster than light (or so it seemed to him) to what he thought was another planet and met a beautiful woman holding a baby. "He said she was 'luminous,' dressed in a long flowing robe. He thought she was a goddess or something like a goddess. The baby was very young, just a few months. The woman held the baby up so he could see her..."

–So a boy or a girl?'

–A girl. Now listen to what she said: This is your daughter; she needs to go home with you.

–Really? That's what he told you? Hyperides told you all this? That's intense! At least he didn't flip out like Pau. He should have told Pausanias, give him some perspective.

–Honestly, Clea, sometimes not only are you prim and proper, but you're a little dense. Why do you think I'm sharing with you what he told me?

Clea was not in the mood for her big sister's condescension. "And sometimes—no, often—you are just rude. What is your problem? I know you're upset about Pausanias, but why take it out on me? Aren't you the one who needed to talk? I was about to go to bed. I made you tea. I'm listening. I'm sympathetic, and you call me dense!

–I'm sorry. I guess I'm a little on edge.

–Understandable, but still...so why did you tell me what Hyp saw?

–So you will be prepared and not judge...

...The woman is me...the baby is ours. It's our daughter.

Clea is staring at her sister trying to decide if she is pranking her. She doesn't think Themis would joke about this, but she needs to be sure. "OK, this may be the strangest thing you've ever told me, and that is saying a lot. You know this? How is this possible?"

–I know it as much as I know anything. I remember. When Hyp told me the other night about the woman and the baby, I knew immediately.

–Are you trying to tell me you're pregnant?

Themis laughs. "Not yet, but I'm going to be. It's just a matter of time. Hyperides needs to get more comfortable with our arrangement. Right now he considers me untouchable. He would not dream of defiling me, which is how he would feel if we kissed, much less had sex, so there's work to do."

After Themis leaves and Clea gets into bed, she can't sleep. What is she feeling? It's not anxiety. The dire reckoning for the human race is something she's accepted as a given for as long as she can remember. Her crazy sister kept her up on school nights talking about the 'Law' and how Ge was going to punish the law-breakers. How she would rise up and wipe them all out. How old was Themis then? Twelve? So she was ten and Trip only seven. Now that adult Themis twenty some years later is predicting that it's actually going to happen, and happen soon, it's not anxiety she feels, it's more like relief. Finally. Let's get it over with. At least she can move on from endless anticipation to...what? But it's not worrying about the 'what' that's keeping her up, either. She really doesn't care anymore about the what? That's what happens when you devote years to speculation about the what? At some point, you don't care anymore, and she doesn't.

Trying to understand what's disturbing her, she goes over what Themis told her. She imagines her pregnant, visualizing her and the proud father walking around, everyone putting their hands on her belly to feel the baby kick. She can see her sister, glowing with motherhood in a post-apocalyptic world in which her baby is the most precious thing possible. Themis has harped on it for years: if the human race is decimated by some unimaginable disaster, then mothers and daughters suddenly become highly valued. Men are needed only for work and their sperm; mothers and their daughters are needed to keep humanity from going extinct. It will be the blessed end of patriarchy.

She will be Aunt Clea to a star child.

She goes outside to look at the stars. Did Hyperides actually travel there? She'll never be able to comprehend the dimensions of space/time that her sister has access to.

Oh, God. I know what it is. I know what I'm feeling. It's obvious. My sister has a partner and is going to be a mother. My brother has a partner and is probably going to be a father. I said goodbye to Pausanias who I will never see again.

I'm lonely.

Dig deeper.

I don't want to die alone.

Faith, sister. Get some sleep.

PART IV. THEOPHANY

When the spirits return many years later, the oracles, like musical instruments, become articulate, since those who can put them to use are present and in charge of them.

PLUTARCH

The best of seers is she who guesses well.

EURIPIDES

Episode 29

Themis Dialogues

When you were telling us of your premonition you said that Ge, the earth, is going to save itself...

Herself.

...herself from the "devastating effects of a 'lawless human race'"...

I've had this premonition my entire life, and it didn't start with me. It started with my mom, who had a prophetic dream and named me Themis. I was born with the premonition. It's in my genes.

I appreciate how important the premonition is to you, but what I want to understand is what you mean by 'lawless.'

Start with my name. 'Themis' is a name but it's also a principle. If you follow Themis, you live in a lawful way. If you don't follow the Law, you're not living according to 'Themis.' You're lawless if you're not following the way of Themis.

So the 'law,' the 'way,' and 'Themis' are the same thing?

It's all one. Follow the Law and you are following Themis; follow Themis and you are following the Law.

Hyperides: Now I understand what you meant when you told me that as 'Themis' you have to represent the Law.

I don't have a choice. It's my duty. I am a bird, like you said, Hyperides. Birds are omens, and my being here is an omen. So-called civilization is a lawless town without a sheriff. Greedy, evil people terrorize the town, taking what they want, killing on a whim. But I'm not the sheriff, I'm an omen of the sheriff's arrival.

Hypatia: What is the Law then? How do we follow Themis?

Follow the examples of Nature. Nature expresses the Law. Why is Nature beautiful? Why does all of Nature work together in harmony? It's not a miracle. The beauty and harmony of Nature follow from the Law. Everything is needed for the whole and all must do their duty. The only creatures in nature who refuse their duty are humans, because they are the only ones who have a choice. Acting in opposition to Nature is blatant lawlessness. What should we expect will be the result of our opposing Nature? Of abusing her, of shitting on her with the waste we generate? This is our Mother we disrespect and assault.

So we're to be punished?

We already punish ourselves with compulsive self-destruction. We're destroying our home and then salting the ground. Ge has to save herself and her children from our insanity. It's not punishment, not revenge, it's survival. It's a mother protecting her children and herself. Should we expect her not to protect her children?

But we're her children, too!

She's not willing to sacrifice herself and her children to our madness, and why should she?

[Themis takes a breath. She is extremely agitated.]

Hypatia: So how do we learn to follow the Law? How do we know we're following it?

First, stop believing that you are somehow not a part of nature, that you are a superior being apart from nature who has no responsibility to any life except your own. A basic principle of the Law is that all life is sacred, and yours is no more sacred than any other. 'Thou shalt not kill' is a commandment in every religion, because it is fundamental to the Law, but human beings not only kill animals for food, they kill each other. The height of our insanity is killing each other in the name of God! It's our calling card.

[Themis, still agitated, pauses for a while before continuing.]

Such an animal could care less about poisoning bees with pesticides, but look at the consequences: there aren't enough bees to pollinate the plants that we depend on for our survival, so not only are we killers, we're suicidal! You want to know how to follow the Law? Observe the bees. See how they do their duty without hesitation, without question, because their work is so important, just like the work of the worm who creates the soil in which we grow the food that we need to survive, the soil that grows all of the plants who do their duty every year, coming up in the spring then dying in the winter, year after year, being born and dying again and again for us and for all of the living creatures who depend on them. And

we in our delusional pride believe we are superior to these beings who do their duty selflessly so that we may survive. We
consider them lowly compared to us. Calling someone a worm
is an insult. Everything in Nature does its duty without complaint, working together for the good of all, except for human
beings who believe they have no duty, and if they are confronted with their duty they shun it, they make excuses, they
say later, maybe someday when if I feel like it, and that day
never comes.

[Themis stops talking again, and Clea gives her a concerned
look. Even in the bright sunlight we can see what look like lines
of electricity, tiny lightning bursts, crisscrossing her face. Clea
gets us all a glass of water. In about 10 minutes Themis starts
talking again.]

Human beings were blessed with self-consciousness to be
aware of and appreciate the wonder of the Creation—to know
ourselves—but instead of gratitude for our incredible gift, we
turn our blessing into a curse upon our Mother and all life.

Hyperides: Pausanias was so excited the other day to see a
Monarch butterfly. He was overjoyed to know that they were
not extinct. We watched the butterfly pollinating the wildflowers on the riverbank for a long time. He would have watched it
as long as it was there, but we needed to go...actually, the truth
is I wanted to go.

He appreciates Nature. That is how to follow the Law: respect
and appreciate every one of Nature's creations, including
yourself, including your fellow human beings. Show your

gratitude every day for what Nature has made for you, what Nature does for you.

Do unto others...

Yes! That is the Law and our moral duty. But who follows it? We do unto others what benefits or gratifies us, and if our selfishness causes suffering, we make excuses. We rationalize. Anything but take responsibility. Our hypocrisy is limitless. Everyone knows what the Law is. It's not a secret. Everyone knows what is right. Everyone has a conscience, the Creation built that into the system. But how many listen to their conscience? They listen when it's convenient, when it's telling them what they want to hear. The thing is that voice that tells them what they want to hear is not their conscience.

* * *

Corinna's Diary

Everyone has noticed the change in Themis. She's getting serious. She hasn't been around much since giving us the terrible news and Pausanias throwing a tantrum and bugging out. The only time I see her is at the table talking to Plutarch, Hyperides, and usually Hypatia. I've listened in a few times but honestly, I don't see the point. Plutarch loves it, though. Who am I to begrudge him enjoying a few more moments of pleasure before everyone—except us, fingers crossed—dies. I'm counting on the goddess, the almighty Themis, saving us, not to mention we're here with her brother and sister. She won't let them die will she?

I'm not sure, but I think it's possible that Triptolemos has some powers of his own, though he hasn't yet demonstrated them. If he does have powers, I will find out, since we're living together now. I feel bad leaving Hypatia alone in the dome, but I think she's actually happy that I left. Pausanias was angry at Themis, and it's easy to understand why, but he was really stupid to leave what may turn out to be the safest place on earth, and if it turns out Themis is wrong, then what has he lost? Oh, yeah, the foolish pride of a silly man. He blasted Themis for being a false prophet and then he blasted us for being taken in by her, but nobody took offense and everybody wishes he were still here. I hope you make it back Pau!

Themis hasn't even been joining us for meals or tea. I miss her. I miss her old attitude which was way more playful than it is now. Now she's got stuff on her mind. Funny, yeah, stuff on her mind. That phrase is meaningless when it comes to Themis since everything is on her mind all the time, or so she says. No one can possibly imagine what's on her mind or if she even has something that resembles what we consider to be a mind. I know what's on my mind most of the time, and what's on my mind does not seem in any way to correspond with what's on hers. She said that by playing the gongs in the dome she got us access to the "universal database," which is, supposedly, the "memory of the universe." I might have been in those memory banks while she was playing, but I don't know what I saw or heard. It all zipped by so fast I couldn't actually focus on anything. If what I experienced is like her mind, it's nothing like mine, and she's welcome to hers.

I try not to bug Trip too much with questions...What's going on with Themis? How's Clea doing? Do you think today is the day? We have plenty to do to prepare for the worst while my friends are sitting around the table drinking tea and talking. That's OK. I'm with Trip, which is where I want to be, and he never says a snarky word about how we're the ones busting our asses to get ready for the apocalypse. Since we have no idea what's coming, we're trying to prepare for everything, which means the work never ends. Maybe our work and all work will be ending soon, forever. If that happens, I hope I'm going to heaven with Triptolemos because I can't imagine wanting to spend eternity with anyone else. Sappy, I know, but true. When someone like Themis says the human race is facing possible extinction, I'm allowed sentimental thoughts.

Episode 30

After dinner, as has become custom, the new family is sitting around the table drinking tea. *Our first ritual, Clea thinks, and a good one. Hopefully, we will develop more good ones and few bad ones.* This is the second day since Themis made her announcement of impending doom and Pausanias left in a fit of pique. His pride was insulted. He believes Themis and her siblings are playing him and everyone else for fools. After expressing his anger at being manipulated and taken for a ride and then venting his frustration at his fellow guests for not sharing his self-righteous anger, he felt he had no choice but to leave. Of course he had a choice, only not according to his ego. Not an unusual conundrum for men, and once they've made fateful decisions based on their damaged pride, they almost always have regrets.

Everyone is at the table except for Themis who had not been joining them for dinner since her announcement. The only time anyone had seen her was when she had joined Plutarch, Hyperides, and Hypatia for another one of Plutarch's interviews.

"This might be a good time to talk about what's happened and how everyone's feeling about it," Clea says. "Themis dropped a bomb a couple of days ago and there was significant collateral damage."

"You mean Pau leaving?" Hypatia says.

–Yes, of course, but I'm sure there is more than that to talk about.

–Pausanias leaving is distressing, but I'm not surprised. I wish I felt free to share what happened to him in the dome so you could understand why he reacted the way he did. His vision was traumatic for him. He was angry and ready to leave before Themis told us her prophecy. I convinced him to stay and hear what she had to say...well what she said was not what he wanted to hear. At all.

–What she said is not what anyone would want to hear.

–Of course, Plutarch, that goes without saying.

–I suppose so.

–I'm sorry, you're right. It's upsetting for everyone, but none of us went off like Pau.

I probably would have left with Pausanias if I weren't so interested in what's going on here. I share his disgruntlement with our hosts not being straight with us.

"'Disgruntlement' Plutarch? Really? You're going to use that word?" Corinna says, irritated.

–Why not? It's what I feel.

–Why not use the 'A' word? Don't you really mean you're angry, like Pausanias? At least he owned it. 'Disgruntlement'...I mean, what is that?

–I didn't say I was angry because I'm not angry. What is there to be angry about? I chose to come here, and I choose to stay. We all could have left with Pausanias, crammed ourselves in his car, and gone back to resume our former lives. But we didn't. I was surprised by what Themis said and disgruntled by it, but I'm not angry about it. I am interested, though. This Hyperborean vacation is turning out to be more interesting than I ever imagined. Clea talked about expectations and fantasies on that first morning, which now seems so long ago, and I had expectations and fantasies before coming just like everyone else, but I don't believe any of you imagined being here at this table, the 'omphalos of Hobbiton' of all things, talking about our feelings concerning our host's prediction that the human race may soon be meeting its demise at the hands of Mother Earth.

–OK, Plutarch, enough. Stop, please. I'm sorry. It's just that sometimes your way with words is...

–Pretentious? ...Condescending? ....Annoying?

Corinna grins, "I guess that covers it."

–By the way, 'gruntled' is a word that means pleased or contented, so I was definitely disgruntled by what Themis said, as I'm sure we all were to some degree, but I don't believe any of us were actually angry, except for Pausanias, and Hypatia explained why he was on edge.

Clea, waiting for an opening, interrupts. "We're all on edge—who wouldn't be, if we believe what Themis predicts is actually going to happen? I am wondering about your trust, though, being one of your hosts. Pausanias obviously didn't feel like he could trust Themis or us [looks over to Triptolemos] anymore. How about the rest of you?"

Hypatia speaks first. "I know that Themis is being honest about what she believes and that you and Trip are being honest about believing her, so I don't mistrust you or her. What I don't trust is what Themis says is going to happen. I know she's sincere, and I don't for a moment believe she's lying to us, but I can't get my mind around it. I don't think I can or want to."

–That makes sense. Thanks for your trust, which I don't actually think we've earned, especially after what Themis did in the dome. I did not approve, even though Themis insisted it was necessary.

"If Themis believes it was necessary, then it was necessary," Triptolemos says sharply. "I'm sorry that Pausanias was traumatized and wish he hadn't left, but that's no reason for doubting her."

–I didn't say I doubted, I said I didn't approve.

–Now you're twisting words like Plutarch.

Plutarch is used to snide remarks, as he's generated plenty in his life, but Trip's dig is too much. "Can someone tell me why today is dump on Plutarch day?"

"I am wondering that myself, Plutarch" Clea says. "I think everyone is stressed out, and when stressed, you look for a target to relieve the stress."

–I get that, and I'm happy to take one for the team and all, but I'm getting the strong impression that you all wish I would just shut up. Which I can do, believe it or not.

Nobody says anything for a while. Then with perfect timing, Corinna says, "Prove it!" Plutarch laughs along with her and everyone else. The air is cleared.

Clea thinks to herself how Plutarch has the rare gift of an almost complete lack of self-consciousness, a peculiar innocence which can make normal self-conscious people anxious and defensive. It's as if instead of a judgmental ego always trying to feel superior he has an indiscriminate data collector. Instead of evaluating with the usual polarities like/dislike, approve/disapprove, good/bad, painful/pleasurable, he sorts with the simple rubric of 'interesting/not interesting.' Since Plutarch finds Themis exceptionally interesting, he'll stick around and keep asking questions as long as Themis is willing to answer them.

The laughter dies down and Plutarch says, "OK, do I have permission to talk some more?"

"I want to hear what you have to say," Clea says, smiling warmly at him. She is feeling like it's time for everyone—including herself—to start appreciating Plutarch, someone who doesn't judge, as Pausanias had judged, on the basis of wounded pride.

–For me, trust isn't an issue—yet. I don't feel I need to trust any of you, which is a way, I suppose, of saying that I'm not afraid. I don't believe you have any nefarious designs, but I also don't believe Themis's premonition is going to happen, at least as she describes it. I think it's more likely that she has psychic abilities and has a strong intuition of a terrible catastrophe. The end of the world has been predicted countless times throughout history and has never happened, but there have been many horrendous events that have killed large numbers of people, and there have been people who had intuitions of these events. It's not that hard to believe that another one is coming, like a volcanic eruption or a huge earthquake…I'm sorry. I'm doing it again.

–What are you doing?

–I just can't seem to stop talking. I go on and on. My point is…

–You can do it, Plutarch, you can make your point!" Hypatia says affectionately.

…my point is I trust that you are sincere and believe what you say you believe, but trust isn't an issue for me unless what Themis predicts actually happens. Then we're all going to need to trust each other without question.

* * *

"Do you think it's a good idea to tell them you didn't approve of what Themis did?" Trip asks Clea after the rest of the group gets up from the table and goes off in different directions. "Isn't that going to cause more uncertainty and confusion? Seems like we need to be a united front of confident good will and reassurance."

–I think the most important thing for us, especially now, is complete honesty. Always. And I was honest. Our sister's not being completely honest is the reason Pausanias left. So where is she? Do you know?

–She and Hyperides went to the grotto. I think she's trying to access more details on what's going to happen and when, however it is that she does that. Do you think she would let Hyp in there with her?

–I'm pretty sure Hyp would insist. He doesn't like to let her out of his sight.

–Is he in love or is it something else?

–What would something else be?

–I don't know. You would know if anyone. You're the one who shares your mind with her.

–It's not sharing...it's an invasion, and I have no army to fight her off....I don't know if you can call what Hyperides is feeling 'love,' but what would I know? I'm not someone who has any experience with being in love. Is Themis in love? That's another question. I do know they share a strong bond. A very strong bond, but it's not what you would call romantic. It's more like hyper-romantic, or meta-romantic. It's cosmic love! That's what it is.

–You've lost me Clea.

–You should ask Themis about their bond, then you'll understand.

* * *

"Where are we going?" Hyperides asks as they take a trail from the wellspring that leads them farther up the ravine. "If Pausanias had not left, he would have already been up and back on this trail and then reported back to us."

"He does like to wander," Themis says, distracted. "We're going to what we call the "grotto" where I try to remember. I feel so uncertain knowing so little about what's going to happen, but I have no uncertainty about it happening and happening soon. I'm so worried about Pausanias. He must return safely. He's supposed to be here. I remember him being here. We need him. That much I know.

–You're certain he's going to come back?

–That's what I remember. If he doesn't, if he dies, I don't know what the effects will be, but there will be effects. We all need to be here, and we all need to live.

"What if I had left?" Hyperides realizes after he says this that he's actually jealous of the attention Pausanias is getting from Themis. "Sorry, that's a stupid question. I know you said we all need to be here."

"Oh dear, you must know how important you are to me. Don't you feel it?" And while she's speaking, Hyperides is feeling just that. Feeling this loved by someone is not familiar to him. With her, he often feels like a child, but the love he feels is not just the love of a child for his mother, and the love he feels from her is not motherly love. It's a direct current of unadulterated love that seems to flow between them.

–You would never have left, Hyp. You and I have important work to do together.

After walking for about 10 minutes, slowly descending from the top of the bluff to the river, they are standing on the riverbank in front of what appears to be a cave, a large opening in the tall rock face of the ravine. Water is flowing out, creating a channel that empties into the river. The water is not deep, maybe two or three inches, but it's a steady stream of warm mineral water about four feet across. The opening in the rock is large, maybe 20 feet across and 15 feet high. Looking inside, Hyperides can't make out how far back it goes, but he can see that the height of the ceiling gets slightly lower as it extends into the rock. "Is there a spring inside?"

"Yes. Follow me." Water from the spring which has been flowing for however many thousands of years has created an impressive work of art out of the rock it has been flowing over and through, sculpting the walls of the grotto into different shapes and patterns. There is iridescent white sand on either side of the shallow stream. The sand sparkles from the light that reaches into the darkness which grows deeper the farther back they walk. Ferns are growing in hundreds of clefts and crannies in the walls, dripping into the slowly moving stream creating small circles that spread out and overlap. Countless circles within overlapping circles. "It's so beautiful," Hyperides whispers, and his whisper echoes back to him, reverberating in the closed, quiet space where the only sound is the random staccato of water drops from the ferns.

About 100 feet from the entrance, the grotto widens and the ceiling, which had been getting lower, suddenly gets higher. Past the spacious amphitheater carved out of the stone Hyperides can see that the ceiling gets lower, and if they go much farther they will have to stoop. There is a waterfall formed from water forced out of fissures in the back wall—the source of the stream.

Themis stops and motions to the sand. "Please, Hyp, make yourself comfortable. I'm going to be here for a while, and I have to warn you that I may make some strange sounds, say words you don't understand, my appearance may change. I can't predict how this will go."

–Like it did during the last session with Plutarch? You were really worked up. Your face looked electrified.

–It may be like that, but I don't think so. I'm going to sit over here and concentrate, so please be quiet and don't ask questions. And don't be worried if I get agitated.

It's cold enough in the grotto for the stream to be steaming slightly, so there's a warm mist in the air. The entire scene is a dreamlike image of a magical place, but it's not a dream. Hyperides feels safe with Themis, but he's nervous. He's wondering if she's somehow going to send him off on another galactic journey. He's not sure if he can handle that again, and he is sure he doesn't want to have to handle it. When he met Themis that first night, since hearing her voice, his consciousness has been transformed. He doesn't think like he used to; he doesn't react emotionally as he used to; he doesn't perceive as he used to—there is nothing left of what he's used to. He can barely remember how he used to be, what he was like, who he was, and he doesn't care to remember. He has no idea who he is supposed to be or if that even is a consideration anymore. What he knows is he wants to be near Themis and so far she doesn't seem to mind.

Episode 31

Hypatia's Journal

Clea came to see me tonight. She was wondering how I was getting along now that it's just me here in the dome. She wanted to make sure that I was OK with being alone after what Themis told us. I told her I'm fine, which I am. It's not as if it's that far to Hobbiton from here. It only takes about five minutes to walk, and it would take only a minute or two if I were running.

I'm not surprised Corinna is shacking up with Trip. No one is, and I'm happy for her. She really does seem to be in love with him, and it's easy to understand. He's pretty lovable. Sometimes I have to admit I wish Corinna were still sleeping here keeping me company, but there are more times when I'm glad for the privacy.

Plutarch is by himself now, too, in the lodge. I asked him if he was lonely, and he said he was. It was just a week ago—scratch that, I shouldn't even try to approximate time anymore. I have lost all sense of it, at least the sense I used to have, which was oppressive. I knew what hour it was of what day of what week of what month of what year. Most of the time (funny) I had a fairly accurate sense of what quarter hour of the hour it was. This unerring ability had nothing to do with a well-developed time sense, it had everything to do with wearing a watch, carrying a phone, opening a laptop, seeing an electronic display in a store window and any other of the countless ways the exact minute of any hour of any day of any month of any year was in my face nagging at me, reminding me that I have something to do, or that I have forgotten something I'm supposed to be doing, and how many minutes I have missed of doing that thing.

Time is the source of all anxiety. The source of our ultimate anxiety, death, so I am glad to have rid myself of all the sources of anxiety that I used to carry around with me, that I used to power up and log into, reminding me minute by minute that I am a minute closer to death.

Was it a week ago we were all still sleeping in the lodge, each to her little room? I really can't say. Maybe. I'm thinking it's 50/50. I can say what it feels like, which is it was a lifetime ago, and now I am living another life, a life in which time does not have a stranglehold on me. In my new life time passes in broad, cyclical strokes instead of short discrete units arbitrarily chopping up and defining each day, like the 'prime time' that Plutarch brought up back in that other time when we were all still together in the lodge.

In my past life there was the minute that the alarm goes off, the 30 minutes to get ready for work, the 40-minute commute to work, the 120 minutes of work, the 15-minute break, the 120 minutes of work, the 45-minute lunch, the 120 minutes of work, the 40-minute commute back home...and, after several more minutes of time, there was the time to go to bed—right after the 5 minutes to brush teeth—the 480 minutes of sleep, and then the minute the alarm goes off.

It's a revelation to be free to live a natural rhythm rather than endure the lash of digital time slapping every last hope for joy out of me. I resigned myself like most people to the exchange of my precious time for the sad reward of money.

I remember when Clea took our phones. That first morning in the gazebo she started with what seemed to be a warm-up joke, "Having phone anxiety yet?" It wasn't a joke, it was a message, a clue. She knew what was going to happen to us living according to the sun and the moon, day and night, lengthening shadows, animal sounds, the season, which already I feel is changing each day, the temperature getting just a little cooler, the days getting a little shorter and the nights a little longer, the air feeling a little more moist, more and more clouds forming. She knew we were not going to feel anxious at all—well, Hyperides said he missed his phone, now look at him now! Themis's bodyguard or suitor or both. None of us knows. She knew we would feel liberated. Not one of us has missed her phone. Not one of us has even thought about her phone. Thinking about having it in my pocket again is what makes me anxious.

Earlier in the day, while Plutarch and I were waiting for Themis and Hyperides to come over to the table for another interview session, I told him I thought of these conversations as 'classes,' since I had had the epiphany that Hyperborea is a school and Themis is the head teacher. He said he thought that made sense since we were all learning in various ways.

"I had an epiphany, too," he said. "This table we congregate at is an agora, which in ancient Athens was a marketplace where people would gather to buy and sell not just material goods but their ideas, back when philosophical ideas had value."

"So that's why it's called 'agoraphobia." I said.

"You're right! I never made the connection!" Plutarch's eyes lit up with the excitement that only he would feel. There's nothing Plutarch enjoys more than making connections, seeing relationships and correspondences, how everything fits together. I bet he is a good teacher.

* * *

Corinna had asked Trip that morning if he could show her the 'tank' sometime after they got the chores done; now in the late afternoon they are walking along the trail that leads there from the dome.

–The boys call it 'the tank.' That or the 'wellspring.' What do you call it anyway?

–Themis calls it the 'tholos,' because it's circular and she considers it a sanctuary. That's what the Greeks called their circular temples or tombs. She and grandpa designed and built it together not long before he had his accident. Themis knew he was going to die and for her the tholos is like a symbolic tomb to honor him. It's a special place. You'll feel it.

–Tholos...that's so much better than the tank. I feel bad that we called it that. I'll let everyone know. We should have the right attitude when we go there.

–Hypatia has spent a lot of time there. I'm sure she's been respectful.

Coming out from the forest trail into a clearing on the edge of a ravine, Corinna sees the tholos and understands why the boys call it the tank, so she forgives them their sacrilege. "It's built over another hot spring, right?" Corinna is bent over the walls of the tholos testing the water with her hand. "Definitely hot! So nice to have the tholos perched here overlooking the river."

–Do you want to take a soak? I'd join you, but there's only room for one.

"Sure...it does look a little tight for two." As Corinna starts to take off her clothes, she notices him looking away. "Really, Trip, are you not comfortable with seeing me naked? We sleep together now!" She's having a hard time not laughing.

"Go ahead and laugh. I don't know why, but it doesn't feel right to see you naked...yet." Trip is openly blushing now, and Corinna can't process how much love she feels for him at that moment.

"Yet?" ...That's progress.

–I can't explain why I'm feeling so shy. I just am. I'm not used to feeling like this. It's not like I've had a lot of opportunities to experience these feelings, so cut me some slack.

"Experience what feelings exactly?" Corinna looks at Trip, but he's too embarrassed to look up and meet her gaze. "Don't worry Trip, you get all the slack you need, and when you want me to pull you back in, just tell me, and I'll pull with all my tiny might."

Corinna finishes undressing and lowers herself into the tholos. They aren't talking, just enjoying their sweet moment when they hear someone in the woods. Hyperides is first to emerge into the clearing from the opposite side, followed by Themis, who looks worn out.

"Oh, hey, I'm glad you're both here," Hyperides says, looking worried. "We were in the grotto for several hours and Themis is really tired. I'm not sure she can walk all the way back."

"I'm fine, Hyp. I told you I'm fine." Themis says, obviously tired. "It's no problem walking."

"We were wondering where you've been," Triptolemos says, looking at Themis with concern. "Are you really OK?"

"The grotto?" Corinna looks around at all three of them.

"It's a place Themis goes to..." Trip is glancing at Themis wondering what to say.

"To meditate, among other things," Themis says, rescuing her brother.

"Please, Themis, I'm all in with everything Hyperborean," Corinna says smiling, "I'm working every day keeping the place up, and I've moved in with your brother. You don't have to hide things from me. Don't you mean you were trying to hook up with the universal data stream or whatever it is you do when you remember?"

–It's silly to pretend with you, I apologize.

–It's silly to pretend with any of us. We all stayed didn't we? And maybe it's none of my business, but isn't Hyp staying at your place now? Plutarch says he's not sleeping in the lodge anymore. He's there by himself.

"It's hard to break habits, Corinna, we've never been close with our guests. Never welcomed anyone into our family. We're used to keeping up a façade to keep guests comfortable. Most people are not as open minded and open hearted as you all. That's why it was so difficult to tell you about my premonition. We're in the habit of shielding our guests from things that might make them uncomfortable, and hearing that a terrible calamity is on its way is not something people want to hear, obviously. Most people would react just as Pausanias did to what I said. So what's going on with the rest of you that you're still hanging around?" Themis is perking up and smiling now. She should have realized what Corinna told her. Everything has changed. Defaulting to old habits is another indication of how uncertain and off-balance she is feeling, and her time in the grotto had not helped.

"We're people of like mind, remember?" says Corinna. She is happy to have ironic Themis back for at least a moment. "In other words, we're crazy!" Everyone laughs.

–I'm frustrated. I thought time in the grotto would help me remember at least something so we can be prepared, but it's not coming to me. All I know is that everything is vibrating more rapidly.

"Like you were?" Hyperides says. "Your entire body was vibrating really fast, like hummingbird wings."

"You're a poet now, Hyp," Corinna says, sincerely impressed.

"That's exactly how I felt, like a hummingbird flapping its wings a million times a second, hanging in the air getting nowhere." Themis sighs. "I'm sorry. I wish I knew more. What am I supposed to call it? There are so many words but they are never the thing...I think I called it the Aether the other day, or was it the Astral realm? The Aether is a useful metaphor. The Aethernet is having connection problems. Something is causing interference, and I suppose it has to do with whatever is coming. The Creation doesn't seem to know either, or at least it's not willing to share with me. Maybe the Creation is in the dark, too."

She sighs again and takes a deep breath. Suddenly she's loudly pleading, *Do you understand that I'm struggling?!* They can see Themis vibrating just as Hyperides had described. "Do you understand that I am responsible for your safety?! That I want to know more and all I'm getting is static?! That I can't remember?! It's just dark. All I remember is darkness."

Themis's anguish, the power of her voice, is overwhelming all of them. They feel themselves vibrating inside and out in sympathy with her—it's not just their bodies shaking; their minds are trembling, too. Hyperides, standing next to Themis, instinctively puts his arms around her and holds her tight enough to stop her body from shaking. She loosens his bear hug enough to be able to clasp her arms around him.

They don't break their hug until the vibrating stops and everyone stops shaking.

Episode 32

Themis Dialogues

Hypatia: I wrote in my journal about time. Not having a phone or any other device to keep track of time, and not having any reason to keep track, has changed my consciousness.

How so?

Hypatia: Well, everything seems to have slowed down. Like every moment is extended.

Why, do you think?

Hypatia: Umm, because back in the world we carry a device in our pocket or wear a watch on our wrist that is constantly reminding us that time is passing. Then, because we have these devices, we compulsively check on the time, and as if that isn't enough, the devices beep alerts which remind us to look. But that's not the end of it: there's the laptop we just opened up that reminds us, or there's an electronic display on the car's dashboard, or one in a store window, or a clock mounted on a building. There's no escaping having an incessant awareness of time ticking away, so having awareness of a moment becomes impossible. We don't actually experience a moment, we monitor it as if we are clocks ourselves. We're hamsters on the time wheel trying to reach some actual moment of experience but never getting there. My consciousness has been dominated by the tracking of time and now that it's not, I have a completely different experience of life, of living.

Is it an enjoyable experience of living?

Hypatia: Very enjoyable, but what has there been not to enjoy since we arrived?

You mean besides hearing that the human race is facing possible extinction?

Hypatia [smiling]: You know what I mean. We have no obligations, here, no agenda. We're on vacation.

But haven't you been on vacation before and still been tracking time?

Hypatia: Yes, exactly. I have, and now I understand why you impose the strict no phone, no laptop, no device rule here. We have nothing to track time with except the sun and the moon. Time becomes simple—sunrise/sunset, day/night, birds singing/birds quiet, insects active/insects inactive, frogs croaking/frogs not croaking—but also much broader, more expansive, measured in the phases of the moon, the rising of planets and constellations and their path through the night sky. If I want to know the time, I look at where the sun or the moon is in the sky. I'm no longer trapped on the face of a clock.

Nature's time is simple. And undemanding. It doesn't nag. It goes round and round in a circle, just like it does on a clock or a watch, but there's a big difference between clock time and nature's time that you just mentioned.

Hypatia: I did?

And very poetically—you said that you're no longer 'trapped on the face of the clock.' Nature doesn't have hands pointing to numbers ticking off arbitrary units of time, reminding us without ever taking a break that another unit of time has just passed, and another, and another. One, two, three, four up to 12 and back again. Why must we live constantly reminded of the passing of every little increment of time? How about just a couple of times a day? The sun is rising, let there be light! A joyful time every day. The sun is setting, my work is done—another happy time. Life is good.

Clea: One of grandpa's favorite old rock songs is going through my head right now. He'd always quote it when he was disgusted by another OAP atrocity...

Same as it ever was...

Clea: Yeah, how many times did we hear that? Grandpa never could let go of his cynicism and anger about politics in One America. 'Same as it ever was' is all he'd say, and he'd always say it with intense bitterness.

Hard to blame him. In his teens he was a hippie with fantasies of a new age just around the corner. Then the 21st century arrived. The age of Aquarius! But it was just the same old age, only worse. Same as it ever was. Our so-called civilization is supposed to be superior to all the civilizations that came before. What progress we have made! We have laid waste to our home and forced our Mother to turn on us in order to survive. The only progress we've made is in more efficient and powerful modes of self-destruction.

Clea: Grandma kept him sane. She's the one who convinced him they needed to live here and leave One America behind. He said if it weren't for grandma he would have probably died of a drug overdose. She definitely kept him busy! Anyway, listening to you, what's going through my head is another line from that song: 'Time isn't holding us; time isn't after us.'

Except the clocks with their hands mercilessly pointing to each passing second convincing us that time is definitely after us.

Can we get back to Hypatia's feeling that time has slowed, that moments are extended?

Hypatia: Sure. Where was I?...I just don't pay attention to the passing of time anymore. There's nothing reminding me or alerting me. I don't think 'what time is it?' a hundred times a day. I don't check to see what time it is, so I'm able to stay in moments of time—moments of experience—longer, and then longer still, and then sometimes it seems as if time isn't passing at all, which is why I have no idea how long we've been here.

Who's to say time isn't actually slower, that your 'moments' aren't in reality extending and getting closer and closer to timelessness? Imagine how humans before the tyranny of clocks experienced time. It was probably pretty close to what you describe. They lived in slow time, extended moments, standing motionless for long periods while hunting, building temples that would be in use for thousands of years, the people using them performing the same rites and rituals, singing the same songs, chanting the same prayers for thousands of years. And it wasn't just when worshipping—people were basically doing the same things over and over again in all aspects of their lives for thousands of years because that is what was always done and always had been done. It was what had to be done for plants to grow, animals to live, rains to come, the sun to rise, for babies to be born, for life to continue. They weren't living in seconds and minutes. Their lives weren't organized around the clock. Time was not historical. It wasn't linear and terminal. It was nature's time—cyclical and eternal. Now people believe that their fate is on the clock. They believe we are born once in history and die once in history. No do-overs. Better live it up while you can, but more importantly, better be good or else. What I will never understand is that billions of people believe they live in historical time, that their one story of this one lifetime is all they will ever have. Believing this they are forced to confront their mortality, face the terror of death, the fact that their one precious life is going to end, so most of them are eager to believe in the salvation offered by religion—that if they are good people, when they die they will live in eternal bliss, but if they are bad they will suffer eternal torment. Billions of people believe this and yet most of them aren't good. It doesn't seem as if they even try to be good. It makes no sense. It's not that hard to be good. All the religions spell out how to be good in easy-to-understand maxims and commandments that are not that hard to follow, but only a small percentage of alleged believers follow the prescriptions that will get them to heaven. I don't get it.

I think you'd get an argument from a lot of people about how easy it is to be good according to the prescriptions of religion.

No doubt, anything to avoid responsibility, but that's not an argument, that's just the usual hypocrisy. It's not hard to follow the golden rule, unless breaking it gives you pleasure, which for too many people is true. Too many people, especially men, feel gratified when they dominate and intimidate others. It makes them feel powerful. One America operates on the premise that if hurting people and destroying ecosystems is the price of doing business and making a profit, then it's not only acceptable, it's to be commended! That's not an ethos, that's thanatos, that's death dealing for money. It's not hard to be kind and generous, to sacrifice for the common good. It's only hard if you don't want to make the effort, if you don't want to delay your personal gratification. The reason people aren't good is because they are taught to be bad and they are told that it's good. This is what we learn in One America: dominating others and winning by any means necessary is the definition of success; pursuing selfish goals at the expense of others is the definition of freedom; considering ourselves superior to all beings and entitled to anything we desire is the definition of liberty. All the people doing bad things parade around self-righteously crowing about all the good they're doing and mock the people who are actually doing good. They laugh at the 'do-gooders' because in their eyes doing good is for losers and fools.

We've ventured pretty far from the theme of time, now, Themis. Before we stop, since we were on the topic, I was hoping to ask you about your personal experience of time since you've talked about it a lot in ways that aren't really comprehensible to us—or at least to me.

For example?

You say that when you access what you call the universal data stream or the universal memory...

I have to use words and these are fairly useful metaphors, but for me, rather than 'accessing' something, like going to a website, the experience is more like entering the Creation itself rather than being on the outside witnessing.

Right, but back to time. You say past, present, and future have no meaning there, in the Creation, and you often say you are trying to 'remember the future,' especially in regard to your premonition, since you want to remember more details. Can you explain what you mean by 'remember the future'?

I'll try, but I won't succeed. As you said, it's incomprehensible to you, and no matter what I say, it will remain incomprehensible to you until you actually experience it, which is not at all the same as understanding an explanation in words. I think we talked about this in our first conversation.

Clea: He accused you of being solipsistic.

I remember. Still, Themis, thank you for trying.

When do you experience something?
   Plutarch?

I don't follow.

Do you experience something in the past or the future?

No.

Right, you experience in the present. You can't experience the past or the future. They are both fictions, despite your memories of the past. Like a novelist we create our character and the story of our life using our memories as source material. I use the expression 'remembering the future' because that's what I'm doing...or trying to do. It's no different than remembering the past or trying to. Everyone knows what it's like trying to remember something. You know there's a memory there, you're trying to make it appear, but you just can't quite see it. That's what it's like trying to remember the future.

But that's absurd. How can you have a memory of something that hasn't happened?

When do things happen?

In the present.

Exactly. As I said I enter the Creation in which everything is present, always. Everything is happening as it always will, as it must. The space/time coordinates we rely on for our bearings here on the outside are meaningless.

You say 'everything is happening as it always will, as it must,' so everything in the universe is pre-determined?

No, everything is being created always, simultaneously. It's not like there's a box of parts with instructions from which the universe is assembled. The parts are being created and instructions are being written...world without end, amen.

I'm not able to grasp what you're saying.

Because I can't explain. I warned you. I'll take one more stab at it for you Plutarch, since you're my brother now. You've had déjà vu, right?

Of course.

When I'm in the Creation, it's like constant déjà vu. It's quite disorienting. Sometimes the déjà vu is crystal clear, as if it's happening now. Sometimes it's like the usual déjà vu we have when we think we remember experiencing something that we have already experienced but we just aren't sure. I've been frustrated by how clearly I remember the magnitude of the event that's coming, but the details are not accessible. I guess this is just how it is, and I should accept it.

But how can you have déjà vu of the future?

When you're inside the Creation, there is only the present. Past and future are meaningless. I've put it in a lot of different ways, and if I think of another way, you'll be the first to know. I'm sorry, Plutarch, but it may be helpful—and terrifying—for you to realize that eternity itself is a solipsism.

Episode 33

Clea can't decide if she should pay a visit to Plutarch or not. Her inner voice is telling her it's the right thing to do, and imagining it makes her feel good, but still, she hesitates. Is it right? What are her true motives? Is she being honest with herself? Just like Plutarch, she thinks, weighing all the options, going over every scenario, interrogating my motives, meanwhile, unable to act, paralyzed.

It's getting late, past twilight, and visiting after dark has symbolic implications. *Oh my God girl, get over yourself! Just do it. You know Plutarch will be touched. After all, you've always known him, and he's always been your friend, it's time to acknowledge that.*

* * *

"Hey, Plutarch! It's Clea." She's at the foot of the stairs trying to get his attention. "How about some tea?"

"Clea?" Plutarch has been transcribing another Themis dialogue, which is how he occupies his evenings now. He opens the door to his room and sees her standing at the bottom of the stairs. "What are you doing here?"

–I've come by to visit you. I'm worried about you being here all alone every night. It doesn't feel right that we're all up at Hobbiton while you're down here by yourself. Take a break and have some tea with me on the porch.

"So nice of you to think about me. Sure." Plutarch is touched, especially after having his feelings bruised the other day. He wouldn't admit it to himself or to the others then, putting on a brave, good-natured face, but Clea's gesture opens him up to realizing it now.

Clea heads into the kitchen to boil water and Plutarch meets her there. "How's Themis doing? She seems pretty distraught."

–She's frustrated, that's for sure. I'm glad she has Hyperides now, otherwise, she'd be leaning on me.

–I imagine Themis leaning on you can be pretty intense.

Clea laughs. "Very perceptive, Plutarch."

With mint tea in hand they go out to the porch and settle into the Adirondack chairs. "I see Hyperides returned the chair," Clea says.

–I hadn't noticed it missing.

You wouldn't, would you? "Yeah, after he left the dome that night, Hyp came down here, carried one of these chairs back, and parked it outside Themis's hut. He slept in it that night and the following night and was going to sleep in it again until Themis came out and invited him in. Since then, well, I guess they're engaged in a way." *Oops, went too far there. Guess I really want to tell someone. Maybe this is the reason I came to visit.*

–Engaged in a way, Clea? What are you saying?

–I shouldn't have said anything. I have a big mouth.

–Do you really think I'm going to let you get away with not telling me what you mean? Aren't we siblings now?

–Well, only figuratively. Technically we're both single adults. *What is with me?*

"True." Plutarch gives her a look that says *what exactly is going on right now?* "Don't try to distract me. I appreciate your coming to visit poor lonely me...really, I do...but now I'm thinking that beyond your altruism there may be a hidden agenda, as in you really want to tell someone about what's going on with those two, and believe me, we all want to know."

"I think maybe you're too perceptive, Plutarch," Clea says, stalling. "I need you to understand that whatever I tell you, Themis will know, and she's not going to appreciate it. And I also want you to know that I really did come to see you because I care about you and was worried about you. No one likes to feel lonely." *Who is saying these things?*

"No, no one likes to feel lonely Clea." Plutarch smiles. His flirting back is not lost on her.

"Uh, Plutarch, if you want me to tell you anything more, then stop imagining things," Clea says with unconvincing seriousness, mainly because she's turning slightly red and nervously changing positions in her chair.

"I'm just making conversation. Isn't that what we're doing?" Plutarch smiles again, and Clea can't help smiling, too, though she tries to hide it by looking down. They stop talking for a moment and sip their tea, which is getting cold.

"What do you mean by 'Themis will know'? How will she know?" Plutarch is not going to relent.

–She can get into my mind. She'll know.

–That sounds scary.

–It was in the beginning. I'm used to it now, and we've established boundaries. If I tell you about her and Hyp, I'm definitely violating a boundary.

"I understand." He thinks, *she actually meant what she said about Themis reading her mind.* "You don't have to say anything more."

"You know, Plutarch, we were talking about trust the other day, and guess what? Out of all the guests, I trust you the most, because I feel like I know you somehow even though this is the first time we've actually had a personal conversation. I hope you trust me, even though you said that trust isn't an issue unless the apocalypse actually happens and we're depending on each other for survival—which, by the way, I call bullshit on. Trust is always an issue—the issue." Clea realizes just how much she really does want to talk to someone besides her siblings. The only question now is how much she's going to tell him.

"Of course I trust you, Clea. I don't think you're capable of lying. I can't say why I believe this, but I do. It's an example of what Themis means by *knowing*, I suppose."

–The feeling's mutual, Plutarch.

Both of them are enjoying the warmth they've generated. They've forgotten how nice it is to feel close to someone. Their tea is cold, and the last light of the day is gone. It's dark enough for bats to start their evening insect hunt, and they can see them flitting around. Soon the moon, almost full, will be up. It won't be long before the harvest moon rises at sunset.

–OK, I'll tell you the story Themis told me. It will be the craziest story you've ever been asked to believe.

Clea already feels some relief. For some reason the story of the cosmic child has been a burden for her. It brings up feelings about being a mother, about having children, feelings that she doesn't allow herself, thoughts that she doesn't let herself have. She has been preparing for the cataclysm that Themis is so sure is coming her entire adult life. She and Trip have felt obligated to help, not just because Themis is their sister but because their grandmother ordered them from her deathbed to listen to Themis, believe what she says, and help her. Since then, Clea never allows herself to think beyond her duty. Maybe her confiding in Plutarch is a first step toward considering herself for once, for once in her life indulging herself. She turns in her chair to face Plutarch and begins to tell the story. Once she starts unburdening herself, the relief she feels is so welcome she tells him far more than just the story of the star daughter to be born to Themis and Hyperides.

By the time Clea finishes talking—surprisingly without interruption by Plutarch—it is much later. The moon has already traveled quite a way overhead. The resident great horned owl is hoo, hoo, hoohooing.

"Wow, Clea, I'm ready to believe just about anything at this point, but the daughter on another planet who wants to return to earth is not really something believable, it's something out of a fantasy novel." Plutarch feels compassion for Clea. She had clearly been holding a lot in.

"Thank you for listening, Plutarch." Clea is leaning closer to him and at that moment wants to kiss him on the cheek, but the chairs keep them too far apart. "I guess it's pretty obvious that I needed to talk, huh?"

"I always want to talk," Plutarch says laughing, "and I'm happy to listen. I don't know what to think about the story of the divine child, but what you told me about the night we met Themis and went to the dome is pretty outrageous."

–Like I said, I didn't know, and I didn't—I don't—approve. I was angry and confronted Themis. She believed and still believes it was necessary to prepare you for what's to come.

–That's the thing about belief, there's nothing to appeal to. You either believe or you don't.

–More solipsism...

–Exactly. You know what you know, believe what you believe, have faith or not. Actually, I've taken mushrooms several times, and what I experienced in the dome was nothing like that. What I experienced in the dome was far more real, hyper-real.

–What was in the little bit of wine you drank was just enough to enhance the effects of the vibrations Themis created. It was a first step.

–Toward what?

–A first step toward knowledge, I guess. Toward knowing.

–Now you're scaring me. Are you saying there are more steps to come?

–You said you believe I'm incapable of lying, and you know what, I think you're right. Nothing bothers me more than dishonesty, which is why I was so mad at Themis. Yes, there's another step, and another, and another, and there's nothing to be afraid of except not taking the steps and not knowing, and that's the truth, Plutarch.

They sit together in silence for a while. They don't want to move and break the bond of confidence they've created, but it is going to have to be broken. They are getting chilled by the night air.

"A lot to think about, Clea," Plutarch ventures. "Are you worried about how Themis is going to react? You said she'd know what we talked about."

–Talking to you somehow makes me less concerned about how Themis will react.

–Is that good?

–I think it's good. It feels good at least.

They are both smiling in the dark. Clea had not known exactly why she felt the need to visit Plutarch that night, but now she knew—she wanted to be friends again with an old friend. She needed someone to talk to besides her siblings.

Plutarch is grateful that she came, and he doesn't want her to leave. He is lonely in the lodge by himself at night. "So, Clea, listen. I'm not getting ideas, but I do have an idea: why don't you sleep in one of the empty rooms tonight? You wouldn't have to walk back in the dark, and it would be nice for me to have some company tonight in the lodge. Maybe we could have coffee together in the morning..."

–That's just what I was going to ask you. Thanks for making it easy.

Episode 34

"So were you spying on me last night?" Clea asks abruptly. She is sitting at the table in the middle of Hobbiton with Themis. It's early morning. Feeling self-conscious about the night before, she had purposely left the lodge before Plutarch woke up, not wanting to deal with the awkwardness of encountering each other in the morning.

–No, why would I? Is there something you want to tell me? You're acting strange.

–I visited Plutarch last night at the lodge. I was feeling sorry for him being alone there while we're all cohabitating up here. Well, everyone but me. I guess it was one lonely person visiting another.

–And?

–And we had a good talk. It was nice. I got some stuff out that was bothering me. It turns out he's taken mushrooms before, and he has a very hard time believing in your divine child.

Themis looks her in the eyes but respectfully stays out of her mind. "I see...You and he had quite a conversation then. Well I hope you're feeling better. It's all going to have to come out anyway, so I'm glad Plutarch knows. You're in the mood to confess—first to Plutarch, now to me—why?

"I don't know. Good question." Clea thinks about it for a while. "I'm looking for attention, I guess. I want to be noticed. I wanted Plutarch to notice me, and I want you to notice me, so I act out, like a child."

"You know how much Trip and I love you, but I don't think you know how much our new family members admire you." Themis has scooted over next to Clea and has her arm around her. She can see Clea is holding back tears.

"I've kept the faith for so long, sister. I've done my duty without question. Now that you've announced the end is actually near, I just want to let it all go." Tears are coming now. "I'm tired of being responsible, of being the main 'host,' the liaison, I want to lean on someone and have someone carry me for a while."

Clea catches her breath between quiet sobs. "If it's Plutarch, I'm happy with that. He's a good man. We're friends. I remember that now. And the way everyone is pairing up, it seems we're destined to be together again in this eternal game of musical chairs, but I don't want to be relied on to keep our mystery play going or the game of musical chairs going or to keep anything going. I'd like to sit out for once. I want someone else to keep it going. I just want this cycle to end and get on with whatever comes."

Just then, Plutarch arrives. Clea wipes her face with her sleeve and takes a deep breath to calm down. Themis is smiling broadly with genuine joy. Pausanias is with him.

Episode 35

Pausanias had arrived late the night before. Clea was asleep in Hypatia's old room, but Plutarch was still awake finishing up the transcription of a Themis Dialog. He saw headlights and was getting worried until he recognized the little Honda Civic. Plutarch came down and waited for him on the front porch.

–You're back.

–I should never have left.

–I'm exhausted. Would you mind getting caught up in the morning?

"Of course not. I don't think you have any idea how happy everyone is going to be to see you, especially Themis. Your leaving really put her in a funk." Plutarch gave Pausanias a hug. "I'm so glad you're back. I missed you. I'm the only one sleeping in the lodge anymore. Actually, Clea is sleeping here tonight, but only because..."

"It's OK, Plutarch, you can tell me tomorrow. I'm about to pass out." Pausanias grabbed his pack and headed up to his old room to crash. Luckily, his was not the room Clea had chosen to sleep in.

In the morning when Plutarch woke, he saw that Clea had already left. He wasn't surprised. He knew, like him, that first thing in the morning she hadn't wanted to go through trying to figure out what their relationship is now. They had made some kind of a connection, but neither of them knew what it meant or even if they wanted to know what it meant. Pausanias was motionless, deeply asleep. Plutarch continued on the transcription that Pausanias had interrupted and waited for him to wake up.

* * *

"Hey, Plutarch, so how've you been?" Pau is standing in the door to his room. He had slept until late morning.

–I've been fine, great. Everybody is doing fine, except Themis who is obsessing about her prophecy. She can't *remember* the details, as you know, and it's really bothering her. She's going to be glad to see you; she feels guilty about what happened to you in the dome.

–Well maybe she should feel some guilt, but I'm going to try to make up with her. I was stupid to leave.

–Not so stupid. I would have gone with you for the same reasons you left except I'm too interested in Themis and how this is all going to play out. Especially after what Clea told me.

–Still, it was stupid, and you would have been stupid if you'd left with me. I was pretty upset after the gong trip into the depths of my unconscious mind, but I'm over that now...I think. I guess we'll find out. I made sure that no matter what happens, doomsday or not, I can't leave. I bartered and sold everything I own, which wasn't much, and I got winter clothes for everyone. It's going to get cold around here pretty soon. There will be snow, and we're not going to be able to stay in the hot springs 24/7 to keep warm. I did stock up on gas in case we have to make a getaway. Come out to the car. I'll show you the stuff I picked out for you.

The Honda is full of coats, boots, wool shirts, and stocking caps along with what appears to be the last of what Pausanius could call his own: books, pictures, tools, and a guitar. "I didn't know you were a musician," Plutarch says, pulling the guitar out from under a pile of clothes.

"Hardly, but I know a few chords. It's by far the most valuable thing I still own. I thought if we're the last of the human race, having a guitar might make me the wealthiest man on earth. Not that it would matter, and not that I care, and not that I think that's going to happen." Pau smiles and pulls out a blue down jacket with a hood. "This is for you. I hope it fits."

It fit perfectly as did the leather boots and the Pendleton wool shirt. "Thanks so much, Pau! This stuff must have cost a fortune."

–Actually, not that bad. My favorite thrift store had everything I was looking for, and I had some credit left with them. Plus, they're friends of mine, so they gave me a great deal, especially after I told them why I was buying all this stuff. They thought I was joking, and they were so impressed by how I was able to keep a straight face while telling them about the coming apocalypse they gave me an even bigger discount. It pays to be honest, huh?

–That's funny. That's what Clea and I were talking about last night. Honesty.

–Important thing to talk about considering.

–It was the first time we had any kind of conversation at all. It felt like our having a personal conversation was a confession of love. This whole experience has been so strange.

–Uh, you think? Is there something going on with you two?

Plutarch sighs and takes a breath. "It felt like something last night, but who knows if and when we'll talk again like that in private? I do know that when I met her that first night I had déjà vu. I 'remembered' her."

Plutarch is laughing to himself. Just an hour ago he had finished transcribing Themis talking about how her 'remembering' is like having déjà vu. Everything is a synchronicity here; nothing is a coincidence.

* * *

"Look who's back!" Plutarch says redundantly as Clea and Themis are both crowding around Pausanias and giving him heartfelt hugs. All anyone can do for a while is smile. Eventually Pau says, "I'm sorry for blowing up like that, Themis. By the time Clea got me to my car, I wanted to come back, but you know how men are about admitting mistakes."

–I could tell when you were waving goodbye that you were regretting it. I told everyone that you looked sad.

"Well you were right, Clea." Pau looks relieved. "I've been worried about how everyone would feel if I came back. Thanks for being so welcoming." Pausanias is choking up. His pride in retreat and his defenses down, for the first time he's allowing himself to fully realize that everyone in Hyperborea really is a family now and that he is part of the family. He's realizing that this is why he left and why he had to come back. There is love here, which he craves, but so much love also makes him want to run away.

"You had to come back, Pausanias," Themis says, still smiling, "you just had to, and you did, so don't doubt that you and we have grace, brother!"

Pausanias doesn't register what she's saying, but he can feel her affection showering him, and while he feels welcomed back to the family like the prodigal son, he's not ready to let her affection in. He's not ready to be overpowered by her emotion, or by any emotion. He's still on guard.

"I come bearing gifts," Pau says brightly, "they're in the car. Winter clothes for everyone. I thought we could use them."

"That's so thoughtful, Pau!" Clea says genuinely impressed. "We never thought about how you all aren't prepared to spend more than two weeks here in the mellow September sunshine. We should have thought of that, Themis." But Themis isn't listening, and Clea thinks, "I guess you remembered that Pau would bring these clothes, huh?"

Curious about the commotion, Hyperides comes out of Themis's hut, trailing Triptolemos and Corinna who are also heading to the center of the clearing. Pausanias whispers to Plutarch, "You really are alone in the lodge now aren't you?"

Clea says in a co-conspirator tone, "That's why I came over to see Plutarch last night, I was worried he was lonely." She thought Pausanias had seen her the night before and wanted to preempt any suspicions he had, not knowing that Plutarch had already explained and raised suspicions.

Triptolemos in his uncanny silent way is suddenly upon them giving Pau a huge hug, lifting him off the ground. "Welcome back, brother! We knew you'd come back."

–You knew, huh? Was it that obvious?

–Well, Themis knew. I was hoping.

Hyperides says, "Themis knew you'd be back, like Trip said. I'm glad. You belong here."

"C'mon, Hyp, give me a hug like everyone else." Which he does, squeezing the wind out of him.

"Hey, Pau, it's about time you got back here." Corinna moves in and hugs him. "You do realize you're an idiot, right?"

"Absolutely. No need to remind me or anyone else, Corinna." Pau smiles and gives her another hug.

–Well you really disrupted the vibrations that Themis tuned us up to, you know. You set things back. She's been sulking since you left.

"I'm getting that. I'm sorry. I've already pled guilty to being stupid. Do you want to add more charges?" Pausanias does look chagrined, and Corinna takes pity on him.

"No, you've suffered enough just by leaving. Now you're back, and all is well." Corinna gives him another hug. "You know we love you, brother."

"I'm feeling the love. It's overwhelming, actually, so can everyone tone it down before I start crying?" It's too late for that. Pausanias sniffles and takes a few shallow breaths. "I want you all to see what I brought you, but we have to go down to the lodge. Do you think Hypatia will be up and around by now?"

"Probably. You should go find out. She definitely won't mind," Corinna says smiling.

Hypatia is in the midst of her morning yoga stretches when she sees Pausanias walking around the dome. It takes her a few moments to register that it really is him, enough time for him to reach the door and knock. She opens the door—or rather, she flings open the door—and before he has a chance to say something, grabs him, hugging him hard. Pausanias, already tenderized by his reception from the rest of the family, breaks down and starts crying again.

"Pau, it's OK. I'm so happy you're back. I was so worried." They are still hugging and Hypatia is talking directly into his ear, and Pausanias says directly into her ear, sniffling, "I've already seen everyone else. They're all waiting. Everyone has been so nice. It's not what I expected at all."

Hypatia breaks the hug and pushes him away playfully, "What did you expect? That we would reject you? That's ridiculous." Then she gives him another quick hug.

–Not that. I guess I didn't expect to feel so much. I didn't expect to feel love from everyone. What I really wasn't ready for was my feeling so much love for everyone. I was pretty checked out when I left.

–Are you checked back in? Are you feeling less anxious about what happened?

–I am definitely checked back in. I made sure that I can't leave, or at least can't leave without you all if it comes to that. I sold almost everything I own and bought winter clothes for everyone. According to Themis, we're all going to be wintering over, possibly the last remaining tribe of human beings, so we're going to need to keep warm.

–That is so nice of you, Pau. It's so great you're back.

–I missed you, Hypatia.

"I missed you, too." Hypatia looks down not wanting him to see in her eyes just how much she missed him and how glad she is that he's back. "You said they're all waiting for us; maybe we should head over to Hobbiton."

Episode 36

Rather than everyone walking down to the lodge to pick up their new clothes, Pausanias, Triptolemos, and Plutarch retrieve them from the Honda, bringing them back in the large garbage bags in which Pau had stuffed them. The coats, boots, hats, sweaters and shirts are strewn on the agora table, piled high. Pausanias distributes what he brought for Triptolemos and Hyperides but asks the women to decide for themselves what they want. "Where's Themis?" he asks. "Shouldn't she get first pick?"

"That doesn't matter to her, Pau," Hyperides says.

–Right, of course, but where is she?

–She went to the tholos. She needed to have some time alone. Thanks for reminding me; I'm supposed to tell everyone not to come there today...please, she said.

–The tholos?

–What we used to call 'the tank.' The family calls it the tholos. It's a sanctuary, a place to remember their grandpa. He and Themis built it right before he died in his accident.

"'Tholos' is what the Greeks used to call their circular temples," Corinna adds.

–I never liked calling it the 'tank.'

"I've gone there every day since you told us about it," Hypatia says, "it's my favorite place."

Everyone is sitting around the table while Hypatia, Corinna, and Clea negotiate about which coat, which boots, which hat. It's fun, but it also brings to mind the prophecy. Pausanias was right to think about winter and what that means. Hyperborea is situated in a river valley nearly 1,000 feet above sea level. They have no idea what's going to happen, if anything, but regardless it's going to get cold for months. There may be snow on the ground for long periods. His gifts prompt thoughts of what they're preparing for.

Hypatia asks, "What was it like to go back? To be in the world again?"

–It was loud. The noise was unbearable really, after being here for however long it was—a week? Only a week or so, but I was totally used to hearing nothing but rushing water, clattering rocks, bird songs, and the wind in the trees. There were no pleasant sounds there in the city. None. Only jarring, painful noise. Constant noise from traffic, from people crammed together in sidewalk cafes eating, drinking, and talking—loudly. People shouting at each other. Sirens. So many sirens. I actually went to a bar for a beer when I first got back, thinking I might as well get back to normal life, but I immediately left. It was so loud in there with all the drunk people yelling at each other over the background music in their obnoxious drunk voices dialed up to maximum volume, and the smell was awful. There were hamburgers getting cooked, and I gagged. The vibrations of the place assaulted me. It felt like there were invisible little demons attacking me. I was literally choking on the air whenever I was outside. My only thought the whole time was why the hell did I come back here? I did not miss the irony of feeling like a complete fool for leaving after I accused you all of being fools for not leaving. On the first day back, I made my plans for returning to Hyperborea as soon as possible and started selling all of my stuff, then closed out my bank account and went to this thrift shop where I got good deals on all these clothes. I am completely broke. I wanted to make sure that I could never go back.

While Pau's evocative description amuses them, they are also aware that what he describes is what they imagine it would be like to return. They came expecting to leave after a pleasant

wo-week vacation and now they can't imagine ever leaving. No
)ne wants to go back to hell.

–There's something else I need to tell you. Before selling my
aptop I Googled who we are named after to find out if there's
;ome kind of connection with who we are now. Well, there are
a lot of connections, and since we're all here, this seems like a
;ood time to tell you what I learned.

"Themis isn't here," Hyperides says.

"That's OK, everyone is going to want to talk to Themis when
;he gets back about what I found out." Turning to Clea and
Triptolemos, Pausanias asks, "Is it OK? You know all about your
1ames and ours, right?"

Clea says, "Sure, of course. Actually, I'm interested to hear
1ow you feel about the names."

Triptolemos assures him that it's fine.

"I'm ready," Corinna says, "Who was I?"

"I have to get my notes out. Just a minute." Pausanias checks
:he pockets of his jeans and finds the crumpled pages. "OK,
'll basically be quoting from what I found in the data
stream...Corinna...you were a Greek lyric poet who lived in the
3rd century BC, which would be about 2,300 years ago. Supposedly she was popular back then, but not much of what she wrote
s still around. She was famous back in the day and still is—at
east famous enough to have a Wiki page. All of us are famous
:hat way, some more than others.

Hyperides asks, "So who's the most famous, Pau? I know it's
1ot me."

–I think it has to be Hypatia and Plutarch, in that order.
There's even a movie that came out in 2009 about Hypatia's life,
and I streamed it. She was an amazing woman for her time—or
any time. Plutarch is still famous, too, but only with academic
:ypes. I tried to read some of what he wrote back then but it was

so incredibly wordy and hard to follow because of all the ancient references that I gave up.

"Of course it would be wordy to you or to any of us," Plutarch says, "that was the style back then, and everyone reading it would recognize his references." Everyone is smiling, amused by the absurdity of Plutarch defending his ancient self. "Well, it's true."

–So getting back to not-as-famous Corinna. She was a woman artist like me. Did you know about this Trip? It's a little creepy.

–Not in so much detail. Clea knows more about the names and how and why Themis picks them.

"C'mon...you know as much as I do, Trip. I know you're used to being close-mouthed with the guests, but we're not with guests anymore. We're family now. We're preparing for a horrible calamity that together we hope to survive." Clea looks around the table, clearly distraught. "I'm sorry everyone, please forgive us for our habit of keeping secrets."

"It's not that, Clea," Triptolemos says, looking sheepish. "I'm embarrassed. When Pausanias brings out his notes and starts talking about everyone's names and where they came from, and then Corinna jumps right in as she always does, it's just embarrassing. Pausanias reporting on what he found out makes what we're doing here seem like a silly game of pretend."

–You know it's not a silly game, brother. Why don't we get to what's really bothering you? I'm sure Corinna doesn't think you're silly, either.

"He's only silly when he gets embarrassed. I've seen it before," Corinna puts her arm around him. "You're silly, but really charming, Trip, don't you know?"

"So, Clea, you know about the names then?" Plutarch asks. "How Themis chooses them and why?"

–Yes.

–Will you tell us what you know?

–Yes, but we should hear what Pausanias has found out first. I'm sure everyone is anxious to find out who they are.

Plutarch looks at Clea and says, "You mean who they're named after, right?

–I meant what I said, Plutarch. Like you, I choose my words carefully.

"All right," Pausanias says, "I'm sure we all agree with Clea. I'll just go through what I've got here; try not to interrupt until I get through these notes. Hyperides, you lived in the 4th century BC, so you're more ancient than Corinna [everyone laughs]. You were a famous orator, a speech writer, the ancient Greek version of an attorney. Your claim to fame is that you were a militant defender of Athenian democracy and especially its constitution. You hated the Macedonians who under Alexander the Great ruled the city state of Athens. You actually led a rebellion against the Macedonian king after Alexander died, but your rebellion failed and you were captured and executed. Hypatia, you are the youngest of us. You lived in the 4th century and were a legendary philosopher, mathematician, and astronomer in Alexandria, Egypt. I'm quoting here: 'a renowned teacher who was greatly admired for her intellect, moral character, and beauty.' But you suffered a gruesome fate. Christian fanatics whipped up by the local bishop accused you of being a witch and a mob of them tore you to pieces and then burned those pieces."

Pausanias looks up: "That's pretty intense. Should I go on?"

"It's fine, Pau," says Hypatia. "Please keep going."

"Jesus, Pau, what about you? I hope you had a better end," Corinna says.

–I was a Greek geographer and historian who lived in the 2nd century. I traveled all over the ancient world and wrote about all the places I saw. Let me tell you I went to a lot of places and wrote a lot. I think I must have always been traveling.

"Just like you wish you could do now," Hyperides observes.

"Like I said, this is getting really creepy," Corinna says nervously. "The connections are so obvious. Trip, I'm going to ask you again: did you know all this?"

"Yes, this is how it is. There are many connections, sometimes more than others. Clea or Themis will be able to explain a lot better than I can." Triptolemos looks longingly in the direction of the gardens.

–That leaves Plutarch. I saved him for last because the parallels are so interesting. He lived in the 1st and 2nd century and was a Greek philosopher and writer who later became a Roman citizen. He was famous for writing biographies of famous characters of the classical world...

"Like the profile of Themis he's working on here," interjects Clea.

...but here's the really interesting part: for the last 30 years of his life he was the head priest at the Oracle of Delphi in Greece. There were a lot of oracles back then, places you could go to ask questions about the future, but the Oracle of Delphi was the most famous by far, and supposedly in operation since mythological times. It was actually considered the omphalos of the world. Anyway, Plutarch here was the head priest in charge of the women who worked as oracles. The oracle would sit on this three-legged stool which was placed over a steaming spring—I swear I'm not making any of this up—and people would come into the chamber and ask her questions. The oracle would sit on the stool over the spring inhaling the fumes, looking like she was possessed by some spirit, and then give her answer in cryptic verses that the priest would interpret...

"I'm actually starting to freak out now, Pausanias" Corinna says.

–I know. Reading this out loud to you all makes it real, but I'm coming to the best part—actually, parts. First, the original Oracle at Delphi was Ge, Mother Earth. And who do you think was her daughter?"

–Themis.

–Right, Hyp.

–Too easy. Who else could it be?

–Fine. I was surprised when I found out. Themis was a titan whose parents were the Earth and the Sky, and in prehistoric, mythical times, besides serving as the arbiter of human morality and the voice of Divine Law, Themis inherited the role of the Oracle at Delphi from her mother, Ge, the original Oracle, until she turned it over to Apollo who eventually left it in the hands of mortal priests like Plutarch. There's more: Delphi is located on the slope of a mountain, and it gets really cold in the winter. Apollo would leave every winter to escape the cold, shutting down the Oracle. And guess where he went?

"Must be Hyperborea," Hyp says, smiling.

"Right! Where the sun always shines. The playground of the immortals. I guess that was the second kicker; now the third one: Clea was actually one of the Oracles at Delphi when Plutarch was the head priest. They worked together for a long time and were good friends. Plutarch was Clea's boss!" Pausanias is excited to get to the punchline. The irony is priceless.

Everyone looks at Clea to see her reaction, but she disappoints them by having no reaction except to face Plutarch and say, "Yes, it's true. Funny, I know. Ha, ha. Actually kind of creepy like Corinna says. At first I thought Themis was playing a joke on me when I found out she gave you the name 'Plutarch,' but after getting to know you, it is obviously true. You are Plutarch, through and through."

Plutarch is looking at Clea with wide eyes. "You're talking as if you believe I really am Plutarch and you really are Clea. Silly or not, this is just some kind of elaborate LARP."

–I suppose it is a game of sorts, a game the Creation plays with itself, and we're all pieces, but I think of it more along the lines of an eternal play in which each of us has a role but we have to improvise all of our lines.

Hypatia, who hasn't said anything while listening to Pausanias, even after learning of her namesake's horrible death, says: "I don't think anyone should be surprised by what Pau's telling us, except for the Plutarch/Clea connection—that's pretty crazy! I can't imagine how Clea has been feeling since he got here."

"Uncomfortable," Clea looks over at Plutarch hoping to see a smile, but he's not paying attention. He's trying to figure out how to argue with her.

"We shouldn't be surprised at all that our names are personally meaningful and have a direct connection to us, to who we are," Hypatia continues earnestly. "Of course they do! Since we got our invitations everything has been personally meaningful. Clea said on that first day that each of us was called and each of us responded. We all wondered what that meant. She said we would work that out on our own—or not. Isn't that what we're doing? I'm sure if we thought deeply enough about our experiences in the dome, if we were emotionally open enough, we would discover just how personally meaningful they were. Remember what Clea said when she answered Plutarch's question about what matters? She said 'everything matters,' and every moment of our time here has mattered, does matter, and will matter. Clea is right that what we're doing here is not a silly game. We're here for a reason, which is what Themis has been

elling us one way or another since we met her. We are supposed to be here. We have to be here. We can't be anywhere
else. This is what I've known since getting the invitation. Look at
Pau—he's back, and I bet he thinks it's because he realized that
the world out there is hell and he wanted to be back in paradise,
but that's not why. He's back because he had to be back, just like
Themis said. He was called, he responded, and he's working it
out in his own way. We need to take the next step, the step Clea
and Trip took when they were teenagers, which is to have faith
in Themis. Our hosts, our new family has never done us harm.
They are doing everything they can to follow the Law, to listen
to the Earth and help us follow too. Why should we doubt their
good intentions? Look at where we are now. Look at our trans-
formation. Look at Pau's reaction to going back to the world.
Even if there were no prophecy none of us would want to go
back. Can't you feel how the vibrations have been accelerating
since we've been here? Don't you notice the change in your consciousness? Themis thought it was necessary to gives us a boost,
to tune us up to the next level. Who are we to doubt her? Pau
said he was overwhelmed by the love he felt from everyone today. It was so strong all he could do was cry. Right, Pau?"

–Yes.

–We all feel it. Suddenly we're all saying we're a family. Isn't
that because we feel love for each other? Have faith in that love
even if you resist having faith in what Themis says is going to
happen. Is that such a sacrifice? Is that a burden? Why do we
resist at all? We resist because we've been programmed by our
fucked-up culture to reject love, to reject life. Stop rejecting.
Stop resisting. Have faith in what you know in your hearts is
true.

Amazing, Hypatia, thank you.

Can you hear me?

Yes.

I feel like it was you speaking through me. I am overflowing right now.

Not me. That was the Creation speaking. You were an open channel.

Episode 37

While everyone at the table had been listening with eager attention to what Pausanias was telling them and then transfixed by Hypatia's passionate speech, Themis had been close by, unobserved, listening to it all, waiting to make her presence known. She didn't want to burden Clea with explaining the names, especially after her breakdown earlier, so when Hypatia was spent, and while everyone was still speechless, stunned by her intensity, she made her presence known.

"Good, everyone's here." Hypatia is the only one not surprised to see Themis suddenly standing there talking to them. "There's something important we need to talk about at dinner tonight, so please, everyone, be there."

"We've been talking about the names, Themis," Clea said. "Pausanias looked them all up while he was away. He was interested to know if there were personal connections, and so on. Do you mind answering their questions?"

"What about Triptolemos?" Corinna blurts out. "Pausanias didn't say anything about him."

"He's from my era, Corinna," Themis replies, "prehistory, from mythology. Demeter, the goddess of grain, took care of Trip when he was a baby, nursed him on her divine milk, and when he was a grown man she made a one-wheel chariot for him that was pulled by dragons. He flew around the world on that chariot sowing wheat everywhere and brought the art of agriculture to the world.

"So he was a god?" Corinna asks.

–Not exactly. He was born a man, but Demeter gave him some godlike power to help humanity. She also taught him the secrets of her initiation rites. He was the first high priest of her sanctuary at Eleusis, which is where Greeks came for thousands of years to be initiated and learn the mysteries of life and death.

"I always suspected you had godlike powers, Trip. This explains how you move without actually moving—you're riding on your magical chariot." Corinna is looking at him with wide eyes.

–Stop it, will you! I'm not a god or godlike. Themis, tell them. I'm just a guy who loves to garden.

"He's just a guy who loves to garden," Themis says, smiling.

"Right, and I'm just an AV artist who used to be a poet. Got it." Corinna grabs Trip's hand and says, "I don't care what you say. Everyone has wondered about how you move since we got here. Now we know."

–Think what you want. I'm just light on my feet is all. Some people are.

"Can we get to the real question?" asks Plutarch whose patience has evaporated. "Are we reincarnations of these people?"

"Well, that depends," says Themis. "on what you mean by reincarnation."

–It's irrelevant what I mean. I'm simply asking are you saying we are reincarnations of these people?

Clea, exasperated, says sharply, "Will you two just stop with this nonsense? Nobody cares about your sophistry. Sister, just answer the question or I will try myself, and then you'll have to correct me."

You're in a mood aren't you? That talk with Plutarch riled up some feelings.

Will you please just get on with it? And I hope you're going to tell them everything. Don't forget to explain about the spiking of the wine. If you care so much about Pausanias, then you'll do that.

Everything is going to be out in the open by tonight.

–Clea, you're right. Plutarch, what I mean is I don't think you're reincarnated in the sense that most people have of it.

"Which is what?" Plutarch asks.

–That when you die you reincarnate as the same person in another body, that you carry on through eternity as a recognizable, indivisible, and permanent "me." The problem with that is your soul is not a personality. It's not a 'someone' with memories. We are one with the Creation, not separate personalities who have coexisted throughout eternity. Personalities are fabrications, transitory, ephemeral. Only the Creation is eternal. Each soul is a unique aspect of the Creation, but the soul is not an ego, it's a seed. Within eternity, the seed grows expressing its unique aspect in an infinite number of ways. Like a plant that dies in the winter and comes back in the spring, we die and come back, sometimes sickly, sometimes healthy; sometimes with flowers, sometimes barren; sometimes tall and spindly, sometimes a dense bush. A plant expresses itself in countless ways, year after year, but it's always the same plant grown from a single, unique seed. You are that eternal seed of the Creation, not the personality you create whenever you are reborn again into another body. To really understand reincarnation is to understand the relationship of eternity and infinity. Each soul is an eternal aspect of Creation expressing itself in an infinite number of ways. That's all I've got, Plutarch. Please don't ask me to explain it in another way.

Pausanias chimes in, "I get the seed and plant metaphor. Plants die every winter and come back every spring. It's the same plant, but it comes back in different ways, but how is it that you knew each of us was an "iteration" of the eternal soul of these people you named us after?"

"Good question," Plutarch says.

–Honestly, I'm not playing with you when I say it's like I do a deep search of the universal database. I have a lot of access—not as many firewalls in my brain as you have—so I'm able to make pretty accurate guesses once I locate your archives. From the archives I can make solid inferences as to who is an iteration of whom. Is that grammatical, Plutarch? It's definitely possible for me to be wrong. I'm not infallible, but I'm sure I'm right about all of you. Just from what Pausanias reported you can see how easy it is to make the inferences.

Pausanias faces Themis and asks earnestly, "Do you really believe you are Themis? The Themis? Do you really believe you are a titan who is the daughter of the Earth and the Sky, the original judge and jury of humanity?" This is the only question he cares about. He wants to know if Themis is so far gone as to believe she really is a mythological titan. He's been wondering that since he looked up the names.

Themis doesn't answer right away. Instead, she looks into the eyes of each of the former guests, now family, slowly, one by one, trying to gauge how they feel about this question. She knows how she answers is critical.

Finally she says, "My answer is what you expect to base your faith on, right Pausanias? Ironically, you will have faith in me if I say, 'No, of course I don't believe I am the mythological titan,' and you will lose faith if I say, 'Yes, I believe I am that Themis from Greek mythology.' I understand what is behind your question and don't blame you for testing me with it, but my belief or your belief is meaningless, because belief is not eternal. Belief is not true or false, good or bad, or anything else—it's just belief, which is easy to gain and easy to lose. The truth is I don't believe I'm Themis. I know I'm Themis, but I don't expect anyone without an experience of knowing to understand the difference. Undoubtedly Plutarch is right now in his head accusing me of my usual solipsistic BS. But you heard Hypatia: she was expressing her faith, which is knowing, not believing, and I dare any of you to say she wasn't speaking the truth. You felt the truth of what she said in your hearts, because her heart was speaking directly to your hearts. That's knowing, not believing. Tonight I'm going to be talking to you about taking a necessary step, which is not just having faith in me as Hypatia talked about, it's about preparation for what's to come, because it's coming soon. In fact, I believe it will be tomorrow night, the first night of the harvest moon. Everyone should take time today to think about and talk about how they feel about that.

"How we feel about what?" asks Plutarch.

–About taking the next step toward faith in me and what I know and preparing to cope with the coming reckoning for humanity.

Plutarch's not disgruntled this time, he's frustrated and resentful. While he's been fascinated up to now with Themis and her Hyperborean Shangri-la, he's not interested in taking a "next step" toward anything. "Next step" sounds too permanent, irreversible. For the first time since he arrived he's feeling unsure about the motives of Themis and the family. "Next step" sounds ominous. The next step could be over a cliff, or losing a mind, or worse.

–First off, you just said you 'believe' the apocalypse is scheduled for tomorrow night. The night of the harvest moon for God's sake! Have you ever seen any horror movies? Probably not. Talk about a cliché. But aside from that, you said you believe whatever's coming is coming tomorrow night. What happened to knowing? Now you're asking us to believe what you believe right after you just tried to persuade us that believing is meaningless—'ephemeral' you said...

Themis interrupts Plutarch's rant: "Plutarch, I get it, but I've also said this is something I can't know. I can't remember. I don't have access. I don't expect you to understand, but I have no way of helping you understand. I do strongly believe, though, that the reckoning—we have to call it something—is going to happen tomorrow night. I feel it, but I can't say that I know it.....Sorry."

"Fine, whatever," Plutarch says dismissively. "How can I think about how I feel about something when I have no idea what that something is? The 'next step?' What is that? I have no idea, but you suggest we think about it and talk about and see how we feel about it. So, what is 'it'? You always talk in circles. You can only know if you know. If you knew you'd know. I didn't know until I knew. Really, what are you asking us to do now?!" Plutarch is beside himself. He's raging. Everyone is concerned, looking around at each other, saying with their eyes, 'What is going on? Plutarch is losing it.' Themis, though, seems unconcerned about Plutarch's petulant, nasty tone.

–I'm asking you all to do what you, Plutarch, are doing right now. Open up, feel, process. I suggest getting with your partners and trying to come to terms with whatever you need to come to terms with: trust, faith, belief, love, fear, resistance. Pausanias is back, so it's time. We'll see how everyone is doing at dinner tonight. I'll have a lot more to say then.

"Partners?!" Plutarch calls out to Themis who is up from the table and walking away with Hyperides.

"Relax, Plutarch, really, calm down now, please." Clea says, taking his hand. "Please try to relax. It should be obvious who the partners are. Look: there go Hypatia and Pau back to the dome. Who does that leave? Will you come with me to my place? Wouldn't you like to see my little home?"

Episode 38

Corinna and Triptolemos

As usual, Triptolemos and Corinna are tasked with making something for dinner. Corinna has never complained, until now. Everyone, including her, is ramped up, which is not surprising considering all that has happened in the last day or so, and faced with meal prep again, she is resenting her objectification as a family laborer: all the heavy and light lifting, such as cooking, that she and Trip do every day being taken for granted. She is a noticing a not-so-subtle stratification of their new society in which they occupy the lowest strata, apparently tagged as the group's intellectual inferiors, fit only for manual work.

–They're all talking every day about what? Does it matter? No, it doesn't, but it's a lot easier than working on the farm. And look at Hyperides. All he does is follow Themis around like a little puppy. Then there's Queen Themis who goes off to her cave to make contact with what? Herself?

"You know, just a few days ago you held a pitchfork in your hands for the first time, and you were happy working with me," Trip says. "What is it that's really bothering you?"

–You, that's what's bothering me. It's time to be straight up with me, your alleged 'partner' according to the Queen, and why don't you start with this 'get with your partners' directive. That came out of nowhere.

–What do you want me to say?

–Explain. Tell me what's going on. How about that?

–Um, OK. I don't like talking about the whole scheme because it sounds so ridiculous. Why would I have ever agreed to help Themis with her plan? But I did. I do.

–Stop stalling. Do you really think I'm going to judge you?

–Fine. But remember this is my sister's thing. I just agreed to help.

–But you believe her, right?

–Of course I believe her. Now more than ever because you and your friends being here at this time is exactly as she remembers. The partners thing is what she remembers. There's the five guests—that's you—three men and two women, and when there were guests in the past there was always three men and two women, and there's us—two women and one man—and according to Themis, when the time comes we all partner up before disaster strikes. Having a partner helps everyone cope, gets us through the night, and after the human race is decimated, it's important for us to repopulate the world with people who know the Law. We need to build a new and better world, one in which human beings live in harmony with Nature instead of at odds with Her. Anyway, 'partnering up" is a main piece of the grand plan, which is why it was important for Pausanias to come back which Themis knew would happen, but still even she has doubts just like us.

–She sure doesn't talk like she has doubts. She knows this knows that.

–Well, the thing is, she does know. I've been with her my whole life and have no doubts about what she 'knows.' She knew how we all would 'get with a partner' didn't she? I mean, look at how everyone fell in together. How did she orchestrate that? It just happened as she remembers, starting with you and me.

–You're saying you and I are partners as if this is something already established. I don't remember ever talking about it.

–Aren't we?

"I wouldn't mind finding out, Trip," Corinna says. "When do we start? I know: let's start with you telling me everything. If you want to be partners..."

–I do.

"…then what you know, I know and vice versa. That's being honest with each other, the basis of any partnership."

–Then I want to show you something.

Corinna follows Trip as he walks to the edge of the clearing and takes the trail that leads to the chicken coop and on to the dome. After just a minute or two of walking he veers left through the trees onto a faint trail that she's never noticed before.

–Where are we headed, Trip?

–It's a secret, so I'm going to show you. No more secrets, right?

Before long they reach a spot in the forest where the canopy is not as dense and sunlight slivers through branches revealing what is clearly a cultivated patch of something. It's spread out on a small rise where it is exposed to thin shafts of light coming through the trees.

"Are those what I think they are?" Corinna asks.

–If you think they're mushrooms, then yes.

–Oh my God, Trip, you really have a hard time with your habit, don't you? Let's try again.

–Yes, those are psilocybin mushrooms.

–Magic mushrooms?

–Yes.

–And you're growing them?

–Yes. Well, not really—trying to be ultra-truthful now—they grow themselves, but at one time grandpa started this mushroom patch.

Triptolemos stands by while Corinna inspects the mushrooms blanketing the area. He asks, "Have you ever taken them before? Do you recognize them?"

–Yes and yes. What else do I need to know, Trip?

"Follow me." Trip leads her back through Hobbiton to his hut and then around it to a cob shed nearby. It's small, but big enough to hold both of them. Inside, there are shelves lining both sides of the shed, and there is one window opposite the door to let in light and air.

"You remember the mysterious bottle of wine on the table that night?" Trip pulls down one of the jars lining the shelves and brings it into the light. A Mason jar filled with what looks like blue honey infused with little brown particles. "There was some of this in that wine you drank."

"I remember. That swallow I had was very sweet." Corinna understands everything now. "This honey is blue from the mushrooms, right? Themis got us high that night."

"It was a very small dose. If you hadn't gone to the dome, you wouldn't have even felt it, beyond maybe a slight buzz of well-being. Themis wanted to make sure everyone would be receptive to the gongs."

–How thoughtful.

* * *

Hyperides and Themis

Themis hasn't told Hyperides what she plans to talk about at dinner, and he hasn't asked. He never questions her, except to ask if she's feeling OK, how is she doing. His unquestioning devotion to her is welcome since she questions herself constantly.

While she's confident in what she knows, she's not nearly as confident about playing her part in the drama of life on earth, especially now. Her duty is clear enough: prepare the extended family for their initiation, guide them on their journeys to self-knowledge, raise their vibrational level to help them to cope with the reckoning, and above all keep them safe. Nothing to it.

Pausanias returning signaled that the reckoning is imminent. She still doesn't know what will happen, but tonight at dinner she has to convince everyone to have faith in her. In order to prepare for what's to come, she will ask them to take a stronger dose of grandpa's blue honey than what was in their little thimbleful of wine on the night they went to the dome. She will ask them to follow her and Trip through the forest lit by a harvest moon to the tholos where they will take part in an initiation rite and from there walk to the grotto to wait for an unimaginable catastrophe. *It's not like I volunteered for this responsibility,* she cries out to the Creation, *but I have accepted it and never complained. Please help me.* She's been praying a lot in the last few days.

Hyperides is next to her with his arm around her saying something, "Themis, hey Themis, are you asleep? You're mumbling something. Are you talking in your sleep?"

–Oh, Hyp. Sorry. I'm fine, just daydreaming. I'm tired.

–Why don't you lie down then?

–Why don't you lie down with me?

They lie together on the bed in their usual chaste way—Hyp with his arm around her and she snuggled up in the crook. There's not yet been a hint of desire for anything more than that from either of them. They instinctively know that now is not the time.

Lying there she remembers this is the moment to tell him what his vision of the goddess and her child is all about. Everything changes tomorrow night, changes that may be totally devasting. There is a chance they won't survive after all. Hyp should know what it is that he saw.

"Hyperides," Themis starts, "I want to tell you something." There, she's done it, no turning back.

–OK.

–I know the meaning of your trip to the stars.

Hyperides slips his arm out from under her head and sits up in the bed. "Why haven't you told me until now? You know I've been obsessing about it."

–I've been afraid of your reaction. What you experienced and what it means is just so unbelievable, I thought if I told you, you would reject me, think I'm a lunatic, which, who knows? I may be.

–That's not possible. How can you think that?

–Because I'm not an immortal divine being without human emotions. I'm a human being, a woman, and I have fears of being rejected just like you do. And once you hear what your vision means, you're going to understand why I was worried about telling you.

–It's OK, Themis, I understand, but you should know by now that no matter what, I'm not going anywhere. Where would I go? I don't even know who or what I am anymore except when we're together, and then I don't care. Then everything is exactly how it's supposed to be. I'm content. I've never been content before, I mean actually content for real. I don't want to lose that.

–All right then. Here goes. This is a story that the poet Aratus wrote down long ago, around the time that Corinna was writing poetry 2,000 years ago. It will explain a lot about what you experienced:

She dwelt on earth and met men face to face, never in olden times disdaining the tribes of men and women, but mingling with them, she took her seat, immortal though she was. Her men called her Dike, meaning Justice, and she, assembling the elders in the marketplace or in the wide-wayed streets, spoke, ever urging on them judgements that were kind to the people. Not yet in that age had men knowledge of hateful strife, or carping contention, or din of battle, but a simple life they lived.

Far from them was the cruel sea and not yet from afar did ships bring their livelihood, but the oxen and the plough and Dike herself, queen of the peoples, giver of things just, abundantly supplied their every need. So long as the earth still nurtured the Golden Race, she had her dwelling on earth.

But with the Silver Race only a little and no longer with utter readiness did she mingle, for she yearned for the ways of the men of old. Yet in that Silver Age she was still upon the earth; from the echoing hills at eventide she came along but no longer spake to any man in gentle words. When she had filled the great heights with gathering crowds, then would she with threats rebuke their evil ways, and declare that never more at their prayer would she reveal her face to man. 'Behold what manner of race the fathers of the Golden Age left behind them! Far meaner than themselves! But ye will breed a viler progeny! Verily wars and cruel bloodshed shall be unto men and grievous woe shall be laid upon them.' Even so she spake and sought the hills and left the people all gazing towards her still.

But when they, too, were dead, and when, more ruinous than they which went before, the Race of Bronze was born, who were the first to forge the sword of the highwayman, and the first to eat of the flesh of the ploughing ox, then verily did Dike loathe that race of men and fly heavenward and took up that abode, where even now in the night time the Maiden is seen of men.

"Did you follow the story?" Themis asks.

"Well enough, I think," Hyp says. "Dike was the goddess of justice who used to live on earth during a golden age of peace and prosperity, but the human race degenerated and she became disgusted with their evil ways and stopped advising and helping them. Peace and prosperity vanished and there was nothing but war and suffering. Eventually Dike couldn't bear to live on earth anymore with the violent, meat-eating men of the latest degenerate human race and flew off to heaven to live."

–You must be a good lawyer, Hyp! That was an excellent summation.

–The story describes exactly what's happening now. Our race of men couldn't get much more degenerate, and here you are. Are you trying to tell me you're this Dike and have come back to dispense justice? Are you the one who is going to cause the reckoning?

"No, Hyp, that's not what I'm trying to tell you, but what I am going to tell you is just as unbelievable, so try to listen with an open mind and heart. The 'Maiden' Aratus refers to at the end of his story is the constellation Virgo, which is where you traveled to that night in the dome, and which is where you *met your daughter......Dike......*"

Themis stops to check on how Hyperides is taking this. He is sitting up, fully attentive now, and glances down at her.

–Go on, I think I know who the woman is.

–Yes, that was me, her mother, holding her. Our daughter Dike needs to return to earth after the reckoning. It's up to us to bring her here, and it won't be by magic.

Themis looks up at her partner's face and is relieved to see he's smiling.

"I can't wait," he says.

* * *

Hypatia and Pausanias

Pausanias didn't think about what he was doing after Themis left them all to "partner up," he just instinctively followed Hypatia as she took the trail back to the dome. Right before he catches up to her, she stops and turns to face him.

"So we're partners, then? Good! I have one request, and it's a big one considering what Themis just said: don't leave me without a partner, partner, and since I'm not leaving here, and since I'm going to follow what Themis says we need to do, that means you're going to have to do the same. Can you agree to that?" Hypatia looks at him expectantly, waiting for his answer.

"Can we wait to talk until we get to the dome?" Pausanias pleads, out of breath. "I just got back here. We were going through the winter clothes I brought back and then suddenly we were partners to ride out the apocalypse together."

Hypatia laughs, leans into him, and whispers, "OK, you've got five minutes."

The great relief Pausanias had felt a few hours earlier after his warm reception from everyone he had called gullible fools is gone, replaced by anxiety and confusion. If it weren't for Hypatia's sincerity when talking about her faith in Themis and her clear invitation to him just now, he might be back at the lodge thinking again about leaving. He suspects she knows that and is trying to preempt his instinct to bolt. He had no idea that he was actually important to whatever plan Themis has, but it's clear now that he is important, if for nothing else than to make the family an even number, four men and four women. *Are we having an orgy under the harvest moon tomorrow night, is that it? Is that the "initiation" at the tholos Themis talked about?*

In his research into the names, he had read about Dionysus and his maniacal cult. He was the god who occupied Delphi when Apollo was wintering over in Hyperborea. Themis may be using Dionysus as inspiration. That night they met, the first thing she did was offer them wine, which the followers of Dionysus would drink to excess and then in a drunken frenzy proceed to tear woodland animals apart. He can't bring himself to believe that this is what she has planned.

Themis was right that his faith in her depended on her answer to his question. She had had a chance to say, "Hey, guys, here's the thing: it's been fun, but obviously I'm not the Themis. I'm just someone my parents decided to name Themis, and I guess I can get a little carried away. From now on let's just enjoy our time here together. You're all welcome to stay as long as you want. People of like mind enjoying nature and each other's company, what could be better?"

She could have confessed, but instead she doubled down. She doesn't believe she's Themis. *She knows she's Themis*, the titan, daughter of the Earth and Sky, the goddess of law and order, and as if that isn't enough, she went over the top and told them they should pair up and talk about how they feel about doing whatever she asks them to do. Why would they even consider doing whatever she tells them to do? Oh, right, because she's Themis and all must have faith in her. None of this is acceptable to him, but he's not angry this time, he's disappointed, and he's worried.

–Five minutes are up, Pau. What do you say? Partners? Or do I need to fight Clea for Plutarch?

They both break down laughing hard at this. Still smiling, but serious, Hypatia says, "I'm joking, but not really. If you run again, which I am pretty sure you're considering after what Themis said, you're going to mess everything up. Again."

–No pressure.

–Actually, I'm going to apply maximum pressure. You don't trust Themis, fine, but what about me?

–My trust in you is the only reason I'm still here after Themis announced that she knows she is the Themis. I really have a hard time standing by not saying anything while she puts on her show. I know you trust her, though, so I'm doing my best to keep an open mind.

Tell Pausanias that I promise he will laugh again.

What?

Tell him...that I told you...that I promise he will laugh again.

OK.

"I have never trusted anyone more than I trust Themis," Hypatia says, "and she just told me to tell you that she promises you will laugh again. Do you know what that means?"

"She just told you'?" Pausanias is looking at Hypatia with a light hint of panic in his eyes. "You mean, while I was gone she told you that I'd be back and I'd laugh again?"

–No, I mean *she just told me.* It's hard to describe: It's not like a voice echoing in my head. I just hear her and she hears me and we sort of converse. Maybe it's something like the 'remembering' she talks about.

Now he does look panicked. *Hypatia really does hear voices now?* He had brushed off her telling him she heard Themis talking to her in her mind the night they met her, but now she's saying that Themis just talked to her. *Is she having some kind of breakdown? Do I need to stay there to protect her?*

Hypatia can feel Pau's anxiety going into overdrive.

"Stop it, Pau!" she says, her voice like a ruler slapped on a student's desk to wake him. "Stop freaking out! You need to get yourself aligned with what's happening here, OK? I'm not having a psychotic break, if that's what you're thinking. If you can't find a way to trust Themis or me, then you probably should leave. Stop resisting, which you've been doing since you first arrived. You go off on your own every day to explore, but really you're going off to be alone so you don't have to relate to us, don't have to feel anything, so you can maintain your comfort zone of safe detachment. It's no wonder that you chose to spend your life traveling. A transitory life filled with transitory relationships. In case you haven't noticed we weren't called to this place to stay in our comfort zone. We were called here to come together and face the terrible fate of the lawless human race. Together. Don't you get it?! We've been chosen!"

Pausanias has his head down defending himself from Hypatia's intense emotion. She takes his hand, and they sit together in silence. They can hear bird talk echoing faintly within the dome.

Eventually Hypatia says softly, "We've gone way past five minutes. Are we going to be partners or not?

"When did you start 'talking' to Themis like this?" Pau says, stalling for time since he's still unable to think clearly.

–Since we met her. I already told you. Remember how you and everyone else sitting at the table were surprised when she suddenly appeared that evening at dinner?

–I remember.

–I wasn't surprised, because she was talking to me as she came from her hut over to the table. I was the only person who saw her, and she acknowledged that by saying 'hi.'

–What did she say?

–She said 'Hi, Hypatia,' is all......So you don't know what she means about 'laughing again'?

–No idea.

–The way she said it, I thought it would mean something to you. I'm sure it will at some point.

Pausanias is frantically trying to figure out what he should say to Hypatia and what he should do. She is serious about her telepathic connection with Themis and serious about being partners and serious about following Themis to whatever possibly unholy destination she has in mind for them.

He has to decide if his feelings for Hypatia should override his absolute conviction that Themis is taking them for a wild ride, the only question being the degree of wildness, from Disneyland jungle cruise to jumping out of a plane without a parachute. If he promises to be Hypatia's partner, he knows he will honor his commitment, no matter what Themis says or asks them to do.

It's this thought that makes his mind up. When in his life has he ever considered making a serious commitment to anyone?

"OK, Hypatia," Pausanias squeezes her hand. "Let's be partners, then. I'll be there with you for whatever Themis is planning. I promise I won't let you down."

Hypatia smiles wide. "I know you won't, and neither will Themis, you'll see."

* * *

Plutarch and Clea

Clea hands Plutarch a cup of tea. He's sitting at a small round table that is placed next to the cob bench that is built into all three homes. The bench is multi-purpose, serving as a couch, a bed, and most importantly, a source of heat, as it's connected to a rocket mass stove which burns extremely hot, pushing searing smoke through pipes laid in the hollow of the bench.

"Another one of grandpa's designs," Clea says in reply to Plutarch's asking her about it. "We won't have to burn that much wood to get it really warm in here. You'll be surprised." Plutarch notes that she uses the future tense, but he doesn't say anything. He's uncharacteristically not trying to take control of what's happening or dominate the conversation, leaving it up to Clea.

It's his first time in one of the huts, and he's impressed by the elegant simplicity of the design. There's no wasted space in the curvy, circular structure, but at the same time, there seems to be plenty of room. From the outside it seems that inside one might feel claustrophobic, but that's not the case. As in the other huts, there are shelves, nooks, and crannies built into the cob walls and Clea has packed them with books, candles, and an assortment of offerings from nature: crystals, agates, shells, feathers, and driftwood. Most interesting to Plutarch is she has pictures of her family when she was a kid.

"So is this your grandma and grandpa?" he asks, pointing to a picture in a nook at eye level next to him.

"Actually, those are my parents." She takes a picture off a shelf and sits down next to him. "Here is one of grandma and grandpa."

"They look just as I imagined them," Plutarch remarks.

"Hippies, right? Grandma in her tie-dyed shirt. They were amazing people. They saved Themis's life." Clea stops to remember them for a moment and Plutarch keeps quiet.

"It was so nice of Pausanias to bring winter clothes. I'm not sure what we would have done if he hadn't," Clea says.

Plutarch says, "You talk as it's a foregone conclusion that we will be here over the winter."

–It is a foregone conclusion—unless we die, of course.

–You don't mince words, do you Clea?

"You should try it sometime, Plutarch." They both laugh. "I can't help teasing you, sorry. You're just so satisfyingly teasable."

–I expect to be teased. There's something about me that inspires teasing. I'm used to it, and I don't take offense—usually. There's a line of meanness that gets crossed sometimes, and then I object.

–People tease you because they like you, Plutarch, and the ironic thing is that they like you because you are such a good sport about being teased.

–So you like me then?

–Of course I like you. Maybe you haven't registered this yet, but we're partners.

–I've registered that you're assuming we're partners, but I don't know what that means. What, exactly, is the relationship between 'partners' as Themis understands it? Or do we get to decide?

"I honestly don't know, Plutarch. All I know is our pairing up is important as far as Themis is concerned...for several reasons." Clea immediately wishes she hadn't said that. She knows what's coming next.

–Name one.

–Mainly to help us cope with the aftermath of the 'reckoning' as she's calling it.

–How does our being partners help with that?

–Again, I don't really know beyond what anyone might suppose—for comfort, emotional support, that kind of thing.

–How about another reason?

–Now you're teasing me. I think you know, you just want to embarrass me by making me talk about it.

"Well there is one reason I can think of if we truly are the last human beings on earth, or if we are some of the last." Plutarch smiles with genuine affection, and she smiles back.

–Partner, I have to say you have really helped me feel better, and I'm not sure why, but I was more than disgruntled with what Themis said.

–You don't know why I've helped you feel better or why you were so angry at Themis?

–Both, I guess. All I know is that your bringing me here, making me tea, and our talking has made me feel a lot better.

–You were really going off. Everyone was surprised, but we appreciated you losing your disinterested intellectual reserve for once.

–And Themis, she appreciated it?

–More than anyone, Plutarch, because it's important for you to be emotionally open in order to deal with what's coming tomorrow night. Themis just wants us all to be OK. She wants us to be safe, and that means that above all we need to be emotionally prepared. Whatever is going to happen is going to be extremely traumatic.

Plutarch turns to face Clea, and the look on his face scares her. She's not sure she's ready for this. In what might be the first actual spontaneous thing he's ever done, he kisses her. She almost starts laughing because of the absurdity of the moment—it's the first time she's ever been kissed, and it's Plutarch kissing her—and she almost starts crying because of how nice it feels.

Episode 39

Smiling and looking more relaxed than she has in days, Themis acknowledges Hyperides and the couples sitting around the table. They have finished eating dinner, and ceramic cups of tea steam in front of them. No one is interested in their tea. They're interested only in what Themis has to say.

"I don't know if Pausanias found this out in his browsing, but besides being known for representing the Law and for prophesizing, Themis is also known for organizing important meetings—like councils of kings and queens, assemblies of gods and goddesses. Her role is to gather everyone together, making sure everyone who is supposed to be at the meeting shows up. See how happy I am that you're all here, as you're supposed to be, and with your partners! It means I've done my duty." Themis pauses to sip her tea. "This is a good place to start. Today, while talking things out with Pausanias, Hypatia got a little frustrated with him and said, 'Don't you get it? We've been chosen...'"

Hypatia looks at Pausanias to see his reaction. He's clearly agitated trying to figure out how she could know that.

"...and she was right. You may think since I invited you here that I chose you, but it is the Creation that chose you, not me. The Creation always chooses you. We believe we are independent, autonomous actors but how can we be when we are all one? We are chosen every moment—every moment comes into being and out of being simultaneously, the present simultaneously becomes the past and the future. Call it what you want—fate, karma, destiny, God's will—we are chosen again and again and again until we escape the eternal cycle of becoming. People think being chosen is some kind of personal honor, but everyone gets chosen every moment creating an infinite number of causes which create an infinite number of effects. It's not personal; it's just being in some place at some time—being at your particular universal coordinates at any moment of be-ing....Sorry, I'm rambling. It's hard not to be redundant when talking about such things."

Themis stops for a while to gather her thoughts. "Being cho-sen is no honor: it's recognizing what you're chosen for and accepting your duty that makes you honorable. When you do that, you're following the Law, and that's important, that's what makes you important, because it means you're in harmony with the Creation, which needs you to do your work."

"Which is what, Themis?" Hypatia asks.

"To discover who you are, which is the same thing as the Creation discovering itself. It wants to know, and we are how it knows, and it will keep choosing you until you know. You can't escape. There's no way in and no way out. No beginning and no end. How can there be a beginning to eternity? How can there be an end? History is fiction. It's a ruse, a way to control. Convince people that they are born once and die once and the fear that belief generates gives you control. Better do what I say or you're going to end up in eternal torment. What the hell!" Themis laughs at her own joke.

"Did you know, Plutarch—of course you don't remem-ber—that you used to greet people with the phrase 'Thou art.' Think about what that means, 'Thou art.' You recognize your oneness with the other person with that greeting. Thou art, I am; I am, thou art. We are one, not separate. So many human beings are completely deluded by their egos and believe every-thing is personal—everything is about them—and when they are chosen they believe it must be because they are special—just them, not others. If others are special then how are they special? Then when it turns that what they were chosen for has nothing to do with their being special, that it may require sacrifice or suffering, that it may mean they will be humiliated, they turn against the Law and walk away from their duty, making excuses, rationalizing, blaming others, refusing what they were chosen for..."

She stops again to catch her breath and drink tea. "Am I making sense?"

Plutarch says, "Being chosen doesn't make you important or special, it's doing the duty you've been chosen for that makes you important or special."

–Exactly. Thank you. By accepting your duty no matter the pain or sacrifice required makes you a special person and important to the Creation because there are so many who refuse. The Creation cannot exist if everything in the Creation refuses its duty.

Themis pauses, smiling, looking around the table at everyone. "Now I'm finally going to get to the point of this incoherent lecture. I'm going to talk about my life."

That gets everyone's attention. While they are used to and tolerate Themis going on and on about things they don't understand, they are always interested in her personal details. They all lean forward a bit.

"I was a very confused, angry, volatile, precocious, opinionated..."

–Obnoxious, annoying, maddening, depressed...

"...Yes, Clea, I was one messed up child and older sister. Mainly I was angry all the time. I experienced the world I was born into as evil. I woke up every day and the first thing I thought—the first thing I felt deeply—was how wrong everything is, how everyone values the wrong things, does the wrong things, says the wrong things. And sadly, I wasn't so wrong! I was angry about the lies, the hypocrisy, the violence, the selfishness, the entitlement, the injustice, but what I raged about more than anything else was the hatred and humiliation of women, the degradation and disrespect of women by dishonorable, unworthy men who want only one thing—to dominate everyone they encounter, but especially every woman. Justice did not exist in a world that allowed such men to prosper and attain positions of great power. The egos of these men disgusted me: their ridiculous pride, their idiotic self-righteousness, their silly bravado and comical machismo, their deluded belief in their superiority—it was their egos that really set my edge and kept it sharp. If they asked—and when they didn't—I told them what I thought of them, and it was harsh. As you can imagine, I was not a popular or well-liked kid. I was shunned, ridiculed, mocked, and bullied, especially by the children of such men. I was not able to stay in school, and I didn't want to. When the fascist OAP and the Dominionist prosperity preachers took political power I thought I might go crazy from rage...and I was only 12 years old!"

"We knew she was brilliant, but at the same time we thought she was mentally ill," Clea adds. "We didn't know what to do. Themis was pissed off 24/7 and inconsolable. She woke up angry, went through the day ranting about how fucked up everything and everyone was—especially the old sexist white-haired men high up in the OAP—and when she would finally go to bed, she would mumble angrily in her sleep. Luckily, we didn't share a bedroom."

"It's not that hard to imagine, Themis," Pausanias says. "If you are who you say you are, this world is truly a nightmare, except you're not dreaming and can't wake up."

"Thank you, Pau, that's just what it was like for me, a horrible nightmare that I couldn't wake myself up from." Themis, remembering, stops talking for a while. "Finally, grandpa and grandma offered to take care of me at their place. They hoped Nature would work a miracle. Lucky me to have them as grandparents, but luck had nothing to do with it—I was chosen. I felt like I was living in a new world with my grandparents. Not having to see or hear or encounter the injustice, the cruelty, the violence of the world and the egos that drove me mad was the medicine I needed. As I calmed down, I opened up emotionally. My mind became more clear. My body became strong eating good food, breathing clean air, and soaking in water from the center of the earth. I became healthy. I was happy for the first time. And then I started remembering. I was 14."

Themis begins to tear up, and her siblings come over to comfort her. Clea sits next to her and holds her hand, and Trip stands behind her with his hands on her shoulders lightly massaging them. Clea says, "She was just a girl and had no idea what was happening to her, what she was in touch with. She finally feels happy—normal—and then she starts getting messages from the Creation, the universe, God, whatever you want to call it."

"What was it like?" Hypatia quietly asks.

"I was scared. I thought I was probably going to end up in an institution, drugged for the rest of my life." Themis replies, sniffling. "How to describe remembering? An incomprehensible collage of random images, voices, sounds, feelings, and thoughts played at an infinite number of speeds simultaneously. I would find myself in a realm without space or time. It didn't even make sense to think 'Where am I?' because I was nowhere, but at the same time it seemed as if I could be anywhere."

She stops talking, looking as if something has just occurred to her, which it has. "I'll let Plutarch describe it. He wrote about it in one of his many essays. He calls the place I'm trying to describe the 'Plain of Truth'..."

...in which the accounts, the forms, and the patterns of all things that have come to pass and of all that shall come to pass rest undis-

turbed; and round about them lies Eternity, whence Time, like an ever-flowing stream, is conveyed to the worlds.

"...He has a way with words, doesn't he? The transitions from our world to this 'Plain of Truth' and back were sudden and unpredictable. After a while, I started to be able to remember with some intention by forcing myself to focus, especially on sounds. In time I was able to pick out 'voices' and understand sometimes what they were communicating."

Hypatia asks, "What was it like for your grandparents? They must have been worried."

–They were. I appeared catatonic sometimes. Other times it seemed I had no awareness of them. Sometimes I would be talking in a strange language or just spewing incoherent nonsense. Usually after I'd been on the Plain of Truth for a while and came back, I'd be exhausted and go to bed, sleeping for long stretches...but thanks for bringing this up because that's where I need to go in the story now...grandpa had a theory about me. He knew a lot about a lot of things and was very intuitive. He thought I must have a gift, the ability to be in touch with the spirit world, like a shaman or a mystic. He said he thought I was afflicted with what Socrates called 'divine madness,' and that I might be an oracle. He said, 'My daughter didn't learn your name in a dream for no reason, Themis. You were the second oracle at Delphi after your Mother, Gaia.' And he told me what he knew about Themis from browsing the data stream. Can I borrow from Plutarch again? He wrote this about oracles:

The prophetic current and breath is most divine and holy, whether it issue by itself through the air or come in the company of running waters; for when it is instilled into the body, it creates in souls an unac-

*ustomed and unusual temperament, the peculiarity of which is hard to
describe with exactness.*

"I was definitely peculiar with an unusual temperament!"
Themis laughs and stops to drink now cold tea. "To the punchline, I guess. Grandpa and grandma were hippies, remember, and
they smoked weed, but they also took psilocybin mushrooms
every now and then. Actually, grandpa often took small doses in
his morning tea when he needed extra stamina—there is always
a lot of work to do around here as you know."

She looks around at her extended family. The only couple
whose faces show concern are Hypatia and Pausanias, the rest
have heard about the mushrooms. "He wanted me to take a
small dose of magic mushrooms to see if it would help me understand what was going on or to get some direction from whatever
it was that I was in contact with. Grandma thought it was a bad
idea, but grandpa convinced her that it would be safe and possibly helpful. He had a lot of experience using mushrooms, knew
the safe dosage, and felt confident that if he were there with me,
everything would go well."

Triptolemos had slipped away without anyone noticing and
is back now with a jar of honey which he has placed in front of
him.

"This is grandpa's 'blue honey,'" he says, "made blue by bits
of dried mushrooms that over time bleed into the honey. We
have quite a few jars, still. They keep basically forever."

"Trip showed me where the mushrooms are growing,"
Corinna adds. "It's just out in the forest a little ways."

"All right, wait...I'm getting the feeling I'm the only one here
who doesn't know about the magic mushrooms," Pausanias
looks at Hypatia. "Did you know?"

"No, it's a surprise, but I've taken them before, haven't you? I'd like to know what happened."

Corinna jumps in and says, "Before we get on with the story, Trip has something to tell you, Pau. Right, Trip?"

–Uh...yeah...Pausanias...you and Hypatia should know there was a very small dose of this honey in that wine you had the night you went to the dome. It was very small, just meant to help you be more receptive to the effects of the gongs and Themis's singing.

–Themis was singing?

Hypatia puts her hand on Pau's arm to keep him calm. "She was singing, but it blended in with the gongs. I could hear her. It was beautiful."

"No one has a problem with this?" Pau asks, incredulous, looking around at his new family. "No one is concerned that we were given a psychedelic drug without our knowledge or permission?"

"It explains a lot," Plutarch says, "which is good."

Themis gets up from the table and moves around to where Pau is sitting, and Plutarch makes room for her to sit next to him. She starts humming a melody that no one recognizes but which feels utterly familiar, as if their mothers had sung it to them when they were babies. Listening to her, they feel they are with their mother, and she is humming her love for them. The moon, almost full, appears over the trees as if summoned, filling the clearing with light.

Themis stops humming after some time and continues telling her story to the guests, staying where she is next to Pausanias. "I drank tea with some of grandpa's honey in it, and we walked to where the tholos is now. It was his favorite place on the property. He had made a barrier of rocks around the hot spring, creating a pool, and we sat in it together looking out over the ravine. I didn't actually get high from the mushrooms, but grandpa's intuition was right—I rebooted. You know how your computer can have trouble processing when its memory is too full of random crap? Then after you restart it and clear out the memory, it works much better? That's what happened to me. I had been remembering, but slowly, haphazardly, after some hits and a lot of misses, I was sailing, but it was through a jumble of pack ice. After taking the mushrooms I was remembering every-thing, or so it seemed at the time. As I became more accustomed to the Plain of Truth I was able to remember much more. The important thing is I remembered who I am and knew my duty."

Themis is done talking.

Everyone is silent feeling the intense energy generated by this evening under the bright moon moving slowly overhead, ending with Themis humming them back to childhood.

Pausanias breaks the silence. "Something tells me we're all going to drink tea with blue honey in it tomorrow night." No one laughs. They are all thinking about what's supposed to happen tomorrow and no one feels like laughing.

Episode 40

It's near sunset as Clea and Plutarch walk out of her hut on their way to the dome. "Well, are you ready for this?" Clea asks.

"How would I know if I'm ready?" Plutarch puts his arm around her as they walk through the Hobbiton clearing to the trail. "Is being nervous, ready? How about being terrified? Then again I'm excited and happy, too."

–Happy?

–We're doing this together, right? That makes me happy, so I think I must be ready.

–My sister knew what she was doing with the partnership thing. It really does help knowing you have a partner.

–She would say the Creation knows what it's doing, wouldn't she? God forbid she would take credit for anything. Just doing her duty and all.

–She can't help being Themis, you know. Just do your own duty tonight, OK?

The night before, after telling them the story of her 'rebooting,' Themis said she had spent the last two days in the grotto trying to grasp any detail that might provide a clue as to what to expect from the reckoning, and she said the prevailing image she remembers is that of bright light followed by complete darkness. She's sure the bright light is the harvest moon, which is why she thinks that this night is when the reckoning will come.

Pausanias had balked at the ritualistic preparations she said were necessary, but she pushed back forcibly saying that everyone needed to participate to prepare themselves to cope with the 'energetic forces beyond their comprehension' they were going to encounter. They needed to be 'united as one, vibrating at the same frequency, creating a resonance in harmony with the earth.'

Pausanias was not mollified. He said he didn't feel safe knowing that they were all going to be under the influence of psilocybin mushrooms while supposedly trying to survive an apocalyptic event. Themis said, "Will you feel safer knowing that I won't be taking any mushrooms?" She had not used them since the first time; to do so after the mushroom did its duty and helped her realize who she is would be dangerous.

She added, "The mushroom is happy to help us if we sincerely need help but does not appreciate being abused just for our pleasure."

"I don't feel safer knowing you will be in your right mind while we're all high. What about Clea and Triptolemos? Are they abstaining, too?" Pausanias asked.

"I'll be taking them," Clea said. "but I don't really use them anymore. There's no reason for me to, but Themis thinks that I may need them tomorrow night."

"I'll have some," Trip said. "Swinging the rhombus is hard work. I'll need the energy."

"Pau, listen," Clea said. "We all understand your anxiety about this--you're the most sensible person here! Really. It's true that the dose you'll take tomorrow night will be more potent than before, but it will still be a relatively small dose compared to what people normally take. The purpose the mushroom will serve is to make you more receptive to what Themis is going to be trying to do to help us all get through this safely."

"I get that, Clea," Pau said, "but the last tuning by Themis at a lower dose did not go so well for me."

"Everything is always a matter of perspective, Pau," Themis interjected. "You may learn that your tuning went just as it should have."

"Have faith, Pau!" Hypatia pleaded.

Pau answered resignedly, "I know, Hypatia, but it's hard for me to have faith in faith."

"You're right," Hyperides said, master of the last word. "If you don't have faith, you can't understand how anyone can have it, but I can tell you that once you have faith you can't understand how anyone lives without it."

Episode 41

It's early twilight, and as Themis requested, everyone is gathered in the dome. She reminds them that the essential purpose of all of her directions tonight is to bring their vibrations as a group to a resonance that matches that of the earth and keep it there as long as needed for them to come through whatever was going to happen.

As in their first visit, the former guests are all lying on their backs arranged around the omphalos with their heads pointed toward it and their feet pointing toward the walls of the dome. Themis is standing with the earth gong at the northern point of the sun axis that crosses at the omphalos. She is going to strike the gong three times from each direction on the axis as she circumnavigates the dome.

"Please relax your body starting at the top of your head and moving down to your toes," she says, and then guides them in the relaxation exercise as she did on the first night in the dome. "Visualize yourselves connected to the omphalos as if it is the center of a star and each of you is one of its points and then visualize the omphalos as directly connected to the center of the earth."

Themis waits a couple of beats. "When I strike the gong feel the vibration of the sound in your heart and let it ripple from your heart throughout your body."

When Themis strikes the gong, they all gasp. No one had remembered the intensity of the sound of the gong reverberating in the dome, and no one realized how different their consciousness is now compared to then. They are far more receptive to the effect of the sound, and the sensation of the vibrations in their hearts and throughout their bodies is a revelation.

Their hearts expand as the volume of sound reaches its peak, and as the sound echoes throughout the dome, gradually fading away, its vibrations move through their bodies as if their hearts are exhaling a deep breath. Hypatia can actually hear Themis say "now inhale," at the moment she strikes the gong and then say "now exhale," as the sound diminishes in receding waves. She wonders if everyone else can hear her, but she doesn't wonder for long, as Themis again says, "now inhale," and strikes the gong again.

The third time the gong is struck, Hypatia is no longer sensing anything except the sound, which is becoming her body. Themis moves clockwise around the dome to the east axis and before she strikes the gong for the first time from this direction reminds everyone to keep visualizing themselves as the omphalos connected to the center of the earth.

"You are the center" Hypatia hears her say at the moment she strikes the gong, and she visualizes her life energy plunging down into the earth until it merges with the molten core. "Is anyone else experiencing this?" she thinks, almost in a panic.

Everyone else is having a similarly visceral experience, though the details vary. Their bodies are responding to the sound of the gong and the directions Themis gives, and for everyone else except Hypatia, who actually hears her, to the subliminal suggestions she is making.

By the time Themis has struck the earth gong for the twelfth and last time, standing at the west axis of the dome, the initiates are so fully identified with the omphalos and its connection with the center of the earth and with the breathing of their hearts that it feels to them that the earth breathes when they breathe, that when they inhale, the molten core enters into their hearts and when they exhale it flows through their bodies back to the earth's core. Their bodies and the earth are one body.

The reverberation from the last gong strike fades away. Their eyes are closed and their breathing is very slow. While they are lying there on their backs, the harvest moon rises above the treetops filling the candlelit dome with its light.

Startled by the sudden illumination, their eyes open, and they are looking straight up at an orange moon that seems to be floating just outside the dome ceiling like a hot air balloon about to land. The moon is pulling them up toward it, as if the water in their bodies is the ocean. They want to get up, but they can't. Hypatia thinks, "this must be what it's like between the earth and the moon: the tidal relationship, the pull and the resistance, the back and forth, the tension that can't be released."

Themis has been waiting for the moon to appear. She says, "How is everyone doing?"

Corinna answers weakly, "I don't think I can get up unless you tell me to, Themis." And everyone laughs.

"I agree with Corinna," adds Plutarch. "Please order us to get up if that's what we're supposed to do now."

"The moon is mesmerizing," Hypatia says. "I don't want to move."

Themis claps her hands, the sharp, abrupt sound triggering an unconscious instinct in everyone to sit up. "Let's roll up the mats and put them away. It's time to walk to the tholos and get our minds in tune with our bodies."

Episode 42

Triptolemos is standing by the door and in his hand he's holding a thin flat piece of wood that looks like a miniature surfboard. Sanded smooth and painted with geometric designs, it's about a foot long, two to three inches wide at the middle, and gradually narrowed down to a point at each end. There is a long cord attached through a hole drilled in one of the pointed ends.

He is wrapping the cord around the end, preparing for their walk to the tholos. "This is the rhombus I told you about," Triptolemos says. "It's also called a 'bullroarer.' You'll understand when I start swinging it. Grandpa made this. It's an ancient instrument. He said they found one that was almost 20,000 years old. The sound it makes is very low frequency, so it can travel for miles. It was used to send long-distance messages."

"Trip and Themis will go ahead, and I'll come behind," Clea says.

Themis reminds them of what she said last night, "Focus on the sound of the bullroarer as we walk. It will clear your mind."

Trip starts out ahead of everyone as he needs room to swing the bullroarer. He swings it at shoulder height, the cord unwrapping as the rhombus makes a circle around his head. He can modulate the pitch and volume by how fast he swings it, sometimes in a horizontal circle above his head, sometimes at a vertical angle off to his side.

It makes a sound like a bank of propellers as he whips it around and around, at times screaming at a high pitch when the RPMs increase, then when throttled down sounding like the powerful engine of a large boat entering a marina to dock. Depending on how fast or slow or at what angle Trip swings the bullroarer, the sound it makes is more or less similar to these familiar sounds but only because their minds are trying to make sense of the sound by invoking comparisons. The sound it makes is actually not like anything they have ever heard.

At high speed, the rhombus is mind-piercingly loud; it shreds all their thoughts and leaves them on the forest floor; at low speed the rumble it makes seems to gently jostle their vital organs as it travels through their bodies. Following the sound of the bullroarer through the woods lit up by the massive yellow moon does more than clear their minds, it erases them, and the natural world around them takes the opportunity to make its presence felt.

They become acutely aware as they walk of the living being of everything surrounding them, which normally would go unnoticed, blocked by the cluttered contents of their minds and the hubris of their narcissistic egos which assume they are the only beings in existence. The trees on both sides of the trail tower out of sight, humbling them, reminding them of their weakness and short time on earth compared to the strength and long life of the trees and of their forest.

The sound of the bullroarer suddenly stops. Not having the sound to follow, they stop too, confused by the sudden quiet. The bullroarer has disabled their minds. Unable to make decisions, they wait for Themis or someone to tell them what to do. Clea, who had been following some distance behind, catches up to them. "The bullroarer is powerful, huh?" No one is able to use their words and respond, not even Plutarch. Themis realizes the group is waiting for her outside the clearing and comes back to them. "OK, we're here. C'mon then."

She turns back toward the tholos and they trail after her obediently. Plutarch does have a thought while he's following Themis: *Will I get my mind back when this is over?*

Episode 43

It's well past twilight and getting dark, but the moon is high. Triptolemos has lit the candles surrounding the tholos even though their light is not needed. Moonlight reflects off the river below, and they can hear the familiar sound of flowing water. There are bats darting overhead, otherwise it is quiet, and the air is still. "Does anyone need to talk before we start?" Themis looks around the circle the Hyperboreans have made surrounding the tholos, waiting for a response. "Pausanias, how are you doing? You've been quiet tonight."

–I'm good, Themis, don't worry about me. I'm not going to be running off into the woods.

Themis continues to wait. Someone may want to say something.

"It's not that I need to talk," Corinna says, "and it's not that easy to talk right now, but am I supposed to be feeling like my body is not entirely mine anymore? And my mind seems to have shut down." Corinna's comment elicits nods of recognition.

"Yes, hopefully the usual defenses that keep you feeling separate are weakened and you're feeling connected to Nature and to each other. We are always one, never separate and never alone, though we are taught to believe we are. We need to feel physically connected to the earth and emotionally connected to each other tonight—and not just tonight." With a serious expression Themis fixes her gaze on each person for a moment. "Is anyone afraid?"

"I am," Pausanias says, "but I know Hypatia will look out for me."

–I hope all the partners feel the same way. It's important.

After no one else speaks up, the realization that they've reached a point of no return sweeps through the group. Themis gave them a chance to voice their fear and to choose not to go on, and by not taking that chance, they have agreed to surrender to whatever happens. Everyone appreciates Pausanias acknowledging their fear about what may happen at any moment, and his reminding them of the trust he has and they have in their partners sends a surge of love that circles around the tholos comforting them all.

* * *

Clea is distributing the tunics she brought with her to each couple. She explains that grandma taught her the basics of sewing and she made the one-size-fits-all garments just for this ceremony. "I wondered if we'd ever use these," Clea says as she passes them out. They're long-sleeved pullover tunics made of a wool flannel material, all a sort of burlap color. Depending on the person's height, the tunics reach the ankle or the calf.

The night before, Themis had described how the ceremony at the tholos was going to go. The couples are now arranged in a circle around the tholos, standing about 12 feet away. A ring of candles is between them and the bricked-in spring where they will each immerse themselves, couple by couple, before walking to the grotto.

Themis is saying something in a language they don't understand, clearly a benediction of some kind. She repeats it three times, and then stops. "I asked the Mother to bless the tholos and us. Please thank her in your hearts for Her blessing."

Carrying their tunics, Themis and Hyperides approach the brick enclosure surrounding the hot spring welling up from the earth. Themis hands her tunic to Hyperides and strips down, folding her clothes and placing them in a pile near one of the four candles ringing the tholos. She immerses herself in the spring completely, head underwater, holding her breath for a few seconds, and then comes up. After climbing out, Hyperides puts the tunic on her, helping her get her arms through the sleeves and then pulling it down. Themis is almost as short as Corinna and the tunic reaches her ankles. Her shoulder length hair clings to her face, and her eyes are flashing with reflected candlelight. Themis joining them in the ceremony changes the way everyone feels about her. She's no longer the conductor or the queen—she's one of them now—and any reservations anyone had about following her fade away.

Hyperides hands his tunic to Themis and they go through the same ritual: he places his clothes near the candle that Themis chose, climbs in and immerses himself in the hot mineral water, holds his breath for quite a while and pops up noisily, blowing water out of his mouth. He looks a little like how they imagine the god of the sea might look with his wet curly black hair and now rather lengthy beard. Themis helps him with the tunic, which doesn't drape as easily over his thick frame as it did Themis, and they step outside the circle of candles. No one can hear what he says to Themis, but she smiles and takes his hand.

Triptolemos and Corinna follow; then Plutarch and Clea, and finally Hypatia and Pausanias. No one says a word throughout the ceremony. They aren't thinking, only feeling, wishing the bliss of this moment could last forever. Hoping that the reckoning will not come.

Standing near their candles, staring at the tholos, each person remembers going under as one person and coming up as another, and each person understands the reason for leaving his or her clothes behind and putting on identical tunics.

"*We are one,*" Themis says, "*with each other and with the entire Creation. You know that now.*"

And she is right.

Episode 44

Triptolemos is waiting with Themis where the trail to the grotto starts with a flask and a small cup not much larger than a shot glass.

"Please, everyone," she says, "trust me when I say you are going to need the help of the mushroom tonight. I know I haven't been able to describe what we're going to be facing, but I do remember the forces we're going to contend with are going to be extremely powerful. As I said last night, they will be 'beyond comprehension,' and I meant it. I will have great difficulty coping myself. I need your support just as you need mine. We will need the strength that our unity provides, and the mushroom will help us with that. We will need to adapt quickly to changing conditions, and above all you will need to listen to me, heed my voice...I hate to say this, but you will need to follow my orders without hesitation no matter how bizarrely I may look, sound, or act. The mushroom will help you listen to me without your usual doubts and give you a greater reserve of mental and emotional calm and more physical stamina, all of which you will be glad to have. I could continue adding to this list, but the moon is getting lower and we need to get to the grotto before we lose its light." Themis suddenly looks and sounds agitated.

What's going on, sister?

It's coming so fast. We have to get going. You must hurry them along.

Everyone files past Trip for the demitasse of grandpa's blue honey wine and follows Themis down the trail. The moon is no longer high overhead, but there is still enough light to see the trail. Trip and Clea bring up the rear urging everyone to watch their step as they are hurrying to catch up with Themis. They are practically jogging to keep up with her, so it doesn't take long before they are descending down to the river from the bluff above the ravine, having to slow down as the trail gets steeper and rockier.

Everyone stops on the beach, noticing the narrow shallow stream flowing into the river. Themis leads them along the steaming rivulet to the entrance of the grotto where she turns to say, "This is a sacred place. Be grateful for the safety it provides tonight."

Triptolemos has already slipped past them unnoticed to light candles in the grotto's sanctuary. The crystalline sand that lines the stream running down the middle of the grotto sparkles from the rays of the small lantern Clea brought with her.

Their normal inclinations to defend against direct experience are down, and the initiates are wide open to the powerful vibrations of the grotto which literally brings them to their knees as they stop to feel the mineral water that for ages has been carving the rock surrounding them. The water is warm, not hot, but it's warm enough that inside the cave the stream is steaming, making the air moist, heating the grotto.

Hypatia and Pau are kneeling by the water, scooping up the sand. "Is it glowing in the dark" asks Pau, "or is it my dilated pupils?"

"I think it glows a little from the ambient light in here," Hypatia answers. "Your pupils are not dilated."

–Yet.

Hypatia ignores Pau's jibe and thinks, "this must be what it's like to be in the womb."

Corinna is lying on her back in the stream, the water flowing around her almost covering her face. She's remembering what it was like to be little Corinna lying down in a plastic kiddie pool heated by the summer sun. She is enthralled by the patterns created in the rock overhead and the slow dripping of the ferns growing in the ceiling. When a drop hits her face, she winces, but in pleasure.

Plutarch is just sitting in the sand, sifting it through his fingers, not thinking about anything except the sensation of the sand. Clea reaches the amphitheater at the back of the grotto where the spring has been burbling up for eons and notices that she's left the rest behind. "Trip, they stopped following me. They're spellbound by this place." And they go back to retrieve their enchanted partners and friends. Trip gently eases Corinna out of the stream despite her half-hearted objections. Clea gets Plutarch's attention by kissing him on the top of his head and saying, "Let's go. Themis is waiting." Hypatia and Pau follow reluctantly.

Themis and Hyperides are sitting together on ledges in the rock at the back of the grotto. Their stone seats flank the source of the stream, a small waterfall formed from fissures in the rock releasing mineral water from the depths of the earth. They look the part of mythical royalty in their matching tunics; all that's missing are the crowns. Corinna is busy looking around the sanctuary for something she can use to create their crowns, while Pau, still resisting, can't help but laugh to himself, thinking, "if I ever get out of here and back to the real world, I'm going to have the material to write a book."

They all find seats next to their partners in the cavernous room the water has created. The scene is magical and incredibly beautiful. The former guests—except Hyperides who's spent many hours in this place with Themis—have a very hard time accepting that it's real, that they are actually here with a woman who claims mythical heritage and supernatural powers preparing to ride out an apocalyptic event with her.

Plutarch, whose mind has not been working much at all since their walk through the woods following the sound of the bullroarer, is surprised to remember their first night in Hyperborea and how he felt then, what he was thinking about, and he realizes that he is no longer that person. *I'm never the same person. Like Themis said, I am coming into being and going out of being every moment. The present becomes the past and the future simultaneously, and so do I.*

"The effects of the mushroom are greatly enhanced in this place. I hope Triptolemos took that into account when figuring out the dosage." Themis says, smiling. "It is beautiful here."

Suddenly her body jerks violently, as if shaken by the invisible hand of an invisible giant, and she starts to shiver rapidly. She's vibrating so fast it's almost imperceptible, but everyone can see it. Hyperides says, "Don't worry. I've seen this before. This is what happens."

Clea concurs: "It's OK. She's doing what she does. Or it's doing to her what it does, I don't know the right way to describe it. I never know."

Everyone's eyes are fixed on Themis. No one has ever been this focused before. They can feel something invading their consciousness while at the same time rumbling through their bodies.

It's starting, Themis says in her conductor's voice, *I know you can feel it. Remember to stay connected to the earth, to the core, the center—your center, the center we create together.*

Pau can feel the energy surging into his consciousness and through his body like everyone else but he still can't help wondering if Themis is somehow responsible, or if it's just the effects of the mushrooms.

Themis suddenly barks in another voice, one they've never heard before, the voice of the Oracle: **Wind coming, gusts of energy. There are bombs, a shock!**

She continues to vibrate at an unimaginable speed and her face begins to appear electrified, as they have seen before, as if there is a lightning storm being projected onto it. Everyone is completely terrified now, thinking, "bombs? nuclear war?"

Hypatia is especially scared because she can sense how frightened Themis is. She yells out, "Themis, what is happening? What is going on? What should we do?!" Huge swells of energy are coming one after the other, crashing through their minds and breaking over and through their bodies.

Do not fight the waves, the Oracle orders them, *There's nowhere they can take you and nowhere for you to go. They can't move you. Anchor to the core.* Her face is lit up, showering them with sparks.

The shock is coming! Don't try to stop it. You can't. Do not resist!

Suddenly, she is laughing and keeps laughing, almost maniacally, and then in the voice they remember from the night they met, the army of the voice, she says, calmer now, and slowly, as if in a trance:

The Father ends the reign of the fathers.

Like a cosmic wrecking ball of unimaginable size and weight attached to a crane of unimaginable height the shock hits them, and they feel as if they are being slammed back and forth like rag dolls against the rock walls of the grotto. Everything inside them is thrashed out until there is nothing left. The thrashing is the last thing they feel, and the last thought they have is *we're going to die.* All of them, including Themis, are unconscious and lying together on the sand of the grotto.

PART V. EPODE

There be many shapes of mystery,
And many things God makes to be,
Past hope or fear.
And the end men looked for cometh not,
And a path is there where no man thought.

EURIPIDES

Episode 45

The "father" that "ends the reign of the fathers" is the sun, which targeted the earth with two huge comets of plasma formed of billions of tons of ionized gaseous matter laced with highly charged magnetic fields. They were fired out of the sun's corona at many, many millions of miles per hour, going so fast that the first plasma bomb reached the earth in just over 10 hours, and the second followed about 12 hours later. The massive amounts of plasma ejected by the sun formed a trail of ionized matter that stretched across the entire expanse of space between the sun and the earth.

The geomagnetic storm created by the impact of the plasma was, quoting Themis, "beyond comprehension." The earth's magnetosphere, which normally would protect the earth from a solar storm, had been deteriorating for decades and was no match for the impossible strength of the incoming electromagnetic pulses from the sun, which had been aimed with perfect precision by the Father. The surface of the earth became a conductor for voltages on the sun's scale, not the earth's, and after the two plasma bombs made direct hits in the space of 24 hours—the first one literally knocking out the Hyperboreans and everyone else on earth with the energetic shock wave it generated—everything on earth with electromagnetic components of any kind was damaged beyond repair, including copper wiring, which melted.

The transformers of the world's energy grid exploded, and their almost simultaneous combustion created a planetary fireworks show that was briefly visible to those in orbiting space stations and habitats before they died of the intense radiation from the high-energy particles of the plasma. The earth no longer had electrical power of any kind.

Satellites orbiting the earth were kaput, and those in lower orbits fell out of the sky. The data stream was dried up. The GPS system gone. Money that only existed in cyberspace disappeared in an instant, gone forever. Whatever paper money or coins people had in their wallets or purses or under their mattress was worthless. What use is there for capital when there is no longer a capitalist economy? The orbiting habitats which the ultra-wealthy had hoped to escape to when they had finally completed their destruction of the earth's ecosytems, were rendered useless, which didn't matter since their owners no longer had any way to get to them.

All of humanity found out just how dependent they are on electricity, which is entirely and utterly. Now humanity was dependent on three things in this order: potable water, uncontaminated food, and shelter. Winter was just three months away for the Hyperboreans and other survivors in the northern hemisphere.

The darkness that first night was bewildering and terrifying. Very few had experienced such darkness. While the auroral light show all over the world was incredibly beautiful, no one was able to appreciate it since the immediate and very pressing concern was survival, and as the solar storm sent by the Father to chasten the lawless continued, and after the second bomb reached the earth, there were fewer and fewer people left to figure out how to survive the overnight collapse of technological civilization.

Many knocked unconscious by the first shock wave never regained consciousness and died in the fires that started in cities and towns everywhere, fires that could not be contained as firefighting equipment was inoperable and firefighters were not available. The plasma's intense disruption of the magnetic fields of the earth and its atmosphere caused extreme fluctuations in polarity and strength in those fields which caused fatal heart attacks and strokes. People on life support in hospitals died. Some people—and many animals—their neural networks gone haywire, became senseless killers. Many people believed it was the prophesized end times, and when they realized they weren't going to be lifted up to heaven, some in their despair committed suicide.

But the deaths immediately caused by the storm were of many orders of magnitude fewer than the deaths that came in the years following. People in parts of the world where the magnetosphere was weakest were exposed to levels of radioactive particles that eventually led to their death. There was famine and starvation. There was fatal illness due to contaminated water and food. There were violent deaths perpetrated by desperate people who killed for food and water. There were many, many deaths due to the complete lack of medical facilities and personnel.

But not everyone died, and not everyone would die. Survivors, such as the Hyperboreans, were better prepared to cope in the short-term, and some for the long-term. The fury of the Father was not meant to end the human race, it was meant to end the reign of the fathers, the dominion of men over Nature and women.

The Hyperboreans would call it the *Chastisement*. Other survivors and their descendants usually referred to it simply as the "storm."

Episode 46

Themis regains consciousness before anyone else. When she is aware again, she is not worried nor in distress because she remembers now. They would wake up and be OK. They would live. Light had been followed by darkness, as she had vaguely remembered. Humanity had lost its power literally and figuratively. The human magic of electricity, which the sprawling infestation of the earth called civilization relied on, had been snuffed out in minutes by the awesome power surge of the sun, the Father, come to the aid of the Mother.

It made sense in a cosmic family way, not that this understanding brought any solace. Billions of human beings had already died, and billions more would. Untold numbers of animals had been and would be collateral damage. It was a tragic fate made inevitable by the hubris of humankind that if not for the mercy of the Mother would have been much worse.

Themis greets everyone as he or she comes to, assuring them that everyone is going to be fine. When everyone is fully conscious and feeling relatively whole, she says, "It's important for me to finish what I was going to say before being interrupted by that gigantic wave of energy that knocked us all out. Does everyone remember what I said?" No one says anything, but some weakly nod.

–The father is the sun. You should know who 'the fathers' are. Before losing consciousness I was about to say, 'All will live again by the Mother's grace.' You should know what that means, too, and it should give you some hope at least. We live by the Mother's grace, and we will all continue to live by her grace. Hopefully those who survive this...

Plutarch interrupts her saying, "This what?" What just happened?"

–The sun sent a gigantic ball of fire that hit the earth going really, really fast, and another one is coming. The grotto walls and our emotional unity protected us. I don't remember exactly what's going on outside, just that it's devastating. I remember this, us, here.

"We're going to get hit again like that? Are you sure?" Corinna is scared. "How are we going to survive that? I thought I was going to die."

"I have an idea about what happened," Hypatia says. "Is it OK for me to take a look outside?"

–Just look. Don't go outside.

"I'll go with you," Pau says.

Walking together back to the entrance of the grotto, Pau takes Hypatia's hand. "Are you OK? What do you think is happening?"

–I'm OK, just in shock like everyone else. I think it's a solar storm. If I'm right, we should see the northern lights. If we see them this far south, then the whole world is in serious trouble, because that probably means the earth was hit with a massive high-energy coronal ejection.

–A what?

–A plasma bomb.

They reach the opening to the grotto and crane their heads to look at the sky. The light show is mind-boggling. Shifting, colliding, twining shapes of blues, violets, greens, reds, and every shade of these colors, writhing snakes of color changing to solid sheets, and back again, shapes and colors constantly mutating, coming into view and out, replaced by another shape and another color. They are awestruck by the spectacle and are completely unaware that they've been joined by everyone else until Triptolemos says, "Let us have a look, will you?" They move out of the way so the rest of the family can see.

"It's what I thought. A huge solar storm. Actually, much worse than that. The sun must have erupted and sent a gigantic ball of plasma into space going millions of miles per hour that hit the earth. The energy pulse when it hit the atmosphere is what knocked us out." Hypatia looks at Themis: "You're saying another one is coming?"

–Yes, and we have to get ready.

"How do you know all this, Hypatia?" Corinna asks.

–I was an aerospace engineer once, remember? I actually know more or less what happened. Considering the fact we were knocked unconscious by the power of this thing, I'd say that transformers all over the world are blown and the power grid is down. Anything electronic is damaged. The Internet, GPS, ATMs, vehicles, radio—everything is down and out. Plasma has super-energetic magnetic fields that seriously disrupt anything electrical, including our brains and nervous systems. That's what making the northern lights in the sky, the magnetic fields of the atmosphere are getting twisted around, just as you can see."

"You're saying we're fucked." Pausanias says bluntly.

"We're alive aren't we?" Clea says, "so not even close to being fucked. Themis asked me to bring you guys back to the sanctuary. We have to get ready for the next fireball." Corinna doesn't hear, her mouth wide open in amazement at what she's seeing, and Trip has to go back to get her.

Thank you for explaining everything, Hypatia.

I'm scared.

We're going to be OK, you'll see.

Triptolemos takes out a jug of water he brought and passes it around. Everyone drinks thankfully. He then takes out the flask of blue honey wine and takes a swig. "Anyone else? I think it might help."

Clea gives Trip a look and says, "Themis, do you think it's a good idea for us to have some more wine?"

"Actually, yes," Themis says, surprising her, "the closer we are to mushroom mind, the better to withstand the next shock wave."

"Mushroom mind?" Plutarch is getting to the point where his stress is turning into anger at Themis. "I didn't sign up for this," he thinks, petulantly, and then checks himself. "No one did," he argues back to himself. "Get your shit together, fool."

–Mushroom mind is just what we need right now. Mushrooms are like a biological internet in the forest. The network they create allows trees and plants to communicate. We could use our own mushroom mind to keep us anchored against the next wave of energy and its effects. The mushroom will help keep your consciousness from getting as twisted and chaotic as the sky is right now.

Trip hands the flask over to Corinna who takes a drink and passes it on. Everyone has some until it reaches Pausanias, the last person in the circle. He looks at Themis, "Really? This is your advice?" And she says something that makes no sense to anyone except Pau and Hypatia: "Really, Pau, don't you want to laugh again?"

Pausanias snorts, looking at Themis as if to challenge her, and then takes a long drink, swallowing a couple of times. "That ought to do it," he thinks, not having any idea what he means. He's on an edge, an edge that has been getting narrower and narrower since he returned. On one side is surrender, faith; on the other is vindication for not surrendering, not believing, not falling for it. On one side is leaving behind the man his parents named "Michael," the guy "Mike" who went to school and loved to travel and eventually eked out a living writing a blog under the byline of "The Travel Miser," someone he knows as 'himself' and is understandably attached to. It's who he is.

On the other side is an eternity in which he is not himself but something else, always changing but staying the same somehow, a seed, a kernel, nothing but everything. An aspect with an infinite host of names. The edge is getting keener every moment as everything Themis promises happens. Mike can't deny it. Michael is scared. The Travel Miser misses his favorite feeling: hitting the road on another trip to somewhere in his beloved Honda. He doesn't want to choose and he doesn't want to fall.

Episode 47

"I regret not calling my parents now," Hypatia remarks. Themis had finished with her advice on how to withstand the shock wave of the sun's next plasma bomb, which had been pretty much the advice she had barked out hurriedly right before the first one hit, except this time she talked slowly and calmly, emphasizing above all else to stay close to each other physically and emotionally. When the time came, they were to huddle together like Emperor penguins keeping warm and visualize themselves as a group connected as one with the earth. As she put it, "as if we are together in the Mother's womb."

"Me, too," adds Corinna, thinking of her own parents.

Triptolemos would have taken them up to the Eagle's Nest to try to reach their families if they had wanted to, but no one had taken him up on it. "Why didn't you?" he asks his partner.

–To tell the truth, I really didn't think this—whatever it is we're going through—was going to happen. I thought we would eventually leave Hyperborea after a while. Not that I wanted to.

"I guess I thought that, too," Hypatia says, "no matter how much I felt like coming here was destiny, down deep I didn't really believe it. I didn't know what I would say, anyway, considering our situation. 'Hey, mom, I just called to let you know the world is going to end soon according to the prophecies of this woman I just met, and she's telling me I need to stay here or I'll die...so...bye."

Plutarch and Pausanias are nodding in agreement, then Hyperides says emphatically, with obvious emotion, "You were there the night we met Themis. You heard me, saw me. After she spoke, I was not the same person. I couldn't imagine what I would say to my family if I called them. I wasn't me, so who were they? To tell the truth, I haven't thought of them until now. I've been in this strange and unexpected state of wonder and trust, as if I'm a child again. I recommend it. A lot of people would say I've regressed, but I don't know what that means anymore. I'm happy. I never thought I'd be happy. I'm happy to be with Themis and happy to be with all of you. My family."

Everyone is smiling broadly now listening to the new Hyperides talking from his heart. His words penetrate what emotional defenses they still have and evoke in them some of the same wonder and trust.

"We hear you, brother," Corinna says. Themis is smiling, too, and says, "This is probably a good time to tell them, Hyp, since we're feeling so much love, and the more the better right now."

"Tell us what, Hyp?!" Corinna says excited. "You can't not tell us now."

–Themis can tell you.

"Oh no, Hyperides," Themis says, "you tell them. You're the new you, remember?

"Spill it, Hyp," Pausanias orders.

"Well, according to Themis...uh..." Hyperides is as red as the sky is outside the grotto "...I'm going to be a father. She's pregnant."

Clea yelps, "How did you keep this from me, sister?!"

Hypatia wipes away tears that suddenly form. Pausanias is trying to make sense of it—*the alleged goddess is pregnant? Who or what is she anyway?*—but at the same time the news makes him happy, even proud somehow, as if he's going to be an uncle. Triptolemos is trying to corral Corinna, who is jumping up and down in the sand. She dances away taunting him, "No more excuses, Trip! No more excuses!" and then she relents and lets him hold her.

Plutarch just asks, "You're sure?"

"Yes, I'm sure. I remember!" and she laughs. "Her name is Dike."

–So you knew she was coming and her name?" Plutarch asks not as an accusation but in amazement that the story Clea told him seems to be coming true.

–Yes. Maybe Hyperides will tell you about his experience in the dome that night, which will help fill in the gaps.

Hyperides has no choice now, and he gives Themis a pained look which she ignores. He starts out slowly but soon gets on a roll in his telling of the strange tale of traveling through space to the Maiden constellation where he meets the goddess and her child who wants to return to earth.

After hearing what Hyperides went through while listening to the gongs, Pausanias has to re-evaluate what happened to him. He has to admit to himself that what he experienced may not have been just a hallucinatory dream induced by the mushrooms, or at least acknowledge that however bizarre his vision was, Hyperides had—and is still having—one that is far more crazy and potentially far more traumatic, considering it seems to be actually happening. Would Themis actually take her con this far? Really? He couldn't believe it. Didn't want to believe it. Would not believe it.

"Does 'Dike' mean something?" he asks.

"Her name means 'justice,'" Themis replies.

Episode 48

It has been several hours since they regained consciousness and many hours since they left Hobbiton. They have no idea how long they were unconscious. Periodically someone goes to the entrance and checks on the sky, and so far the amazing auroral display has not abated at all. The sun comes up as usual, but its appearance is not welcome. The sight of it climbing over the tree tops fills them with dread. They have no food and only a little water left, so they are torn between hoping the second bomb doesn't hit for a while and wanting to get the shock over with so they can make a run back to their cob settlement.

"Remembering anything, Themis?" Corinna says, hopefully. "Sitting here in the grotto waiting for the next fireball to arrive is kind of like waiting in the dentist's office for a root canal, except a whole lot worse."

–Sorry, I don't know. I just know it's coming. How about I sing something? There's a song that has been going through my head. And Themis suddenly starts to sing, her voice clear, strong, and surprisingly sweet—far from the authoritative voice of the Oracle they have been hearing:

Well, I dreamed I saw the knights in armor coming,
Saying something about a queen.
There were peasants singing and drummers drumming,
And the archer split the tree.
There was a fanfare blowing to the sun
That was floating on the breeze...

Then, astonishing everyone, Pausanias starts singing too, harmonizing perfectly with Themis, the two of them for once in tune...

Look at Mother Nature on the run
In the 21st century.
Look at Mother Nature on the run
In the 21st century.

Themis and Pausanias break down laughing after singing the chorus. Not losing a beat, Themis had followed his lead in updating the lyrics. Each is urging the other to pick up the song, until Pausanias says, "Please, Themis, keep singing. Your voice is soothing for everyone." So she does.

I was lying in a burned out basement
With the full moon in my eyes.
I was hoping for replacement
When the sun burst through the sky.
There was a band playing in my head,
And I felt like getting high.
I was thinking about what a friend had said.
I was hoping it was a lie.
Thinking about what a friend had said.
I was hoping it was a lie.

Pausanias joins in to bring the song home, not harmonizing this time, just singing along, adding his voice to hers...

Well, I dreamed I saw the silver space ships flying
In the yellow haze of the sun.
There were children crying and colors flying
All around the chosen ones.
All in a dream, all in a dream
The loading had begun...

With perfect timing, they both stop singing as if they had re-hearsed this song together many times, pausing for dramatic ef-fect, and then raise their voices again, singing the last two lines at a slower tempo and at the volume of a loud whisper.

Flying Mother Nature's silver seed to a new home in the sun.......
Flying Mother Nature's silver seed to a new home.......

Except for the sound of the waterfall, there is silence, inter-rupted by a few sniffles.

"That was one of Grandpa's favorite songs," Themis says softly. Pau says, "It's one of my favorites, too. One of the few I know all the words to."

Hypatia is looking at Pau as if for the first time, along with everyone else. No one is thinking about the sun or its fireballs or the end of civilization. Themis and Pau singing together has mo-mentarily taken them away in silver ships to some other place and time.

"I said you would laugh again, Pau, and you did. Are you sat-isfied?" Themis says, looking at him with great affection.

Pau gets up from the sand and goes over to where Themis and Hyperides are sitting. "Themis, would you mind standing up?" Smiling, she stands up, facing him. Pau leans over and whispers in her ear, "Do you remember this?" She nods. Pausanias pulls her to him in a hug.

They let go of each other, and Pau says, earnestly, looking into her eyes, "Thank you for your faith, sister."

Episode 49

The shock wave came not long after Pau and Themis had hugged it out, aligning the group's vibrations closer than they had ever been, and just in time. As urgently directed by Themis, they formed a huddle in the sand with their arms around each other creating what might have looked from above like a giant tortoise. Aided by the mushroom, emotionally, they were like a flawless diamond, and when the energy wave from the sun came screaming over the earth and through the grotto, it rolled right over the hard psychic shell they had created. They felt only rolling waves, not the bone-crushing breakers that had knocked them out the first time. Their heads were all together in the middle of the scrum so they could look into each other's eyes, and what they saw was love.

"Is it over?" Hypatia asks while still in the huddle.

–It's over. We can leave now unless Hypatia thinks it's not safe.

–I don't really know if we're safe going outside yet. The rock walls of the grotto should have shielded us from the plasma's high-energy particles, but how much background radiation is out there and how dangerous it is I have no idea.

"Let's wait until we can hear the birds talking," Hyperides says. "They're omens, right? It should be safe then. At least it will feel safe."

Everyone moves to the entrance of the grotto in order to hear the birds, and it isn't long before they hear them chattering, relieved that the storm is over.

* * *

Walking back to Hobbiton, everyone realizes how physically and emotionally exhausted they are. Even though it is the middle of the afternoon, and they haven't eaten in almost 48 hours, having spent two nights together in the grotto, as soon as they are back, they all scatter to lie down, not having the energy or the will to do anything else.

Triptolemos is the first to get up, leaving Corinna to rest. He had not actually fallen asleep, being too worried about the state of the solar energy and communication systems. Nothing is working in his hut. He checks the communal area and the outdoor oven. Nothing. The inverter that services the solar power system at Hobbiton is toast. The whole system is down, as is the system at the lodge. The panels might be OK, but they are worthless without the inverter. They have no electrical power. The last hope for power of any kind is grandpa's back-up biogas system which could run some lights and maybe one refrigerator, if it still works. The turbine generator is mechanical, not electronic, so it might still be operable. He would look at that later.

When Trip gets back from checking the lodge, Hyperides and Themis are up and waiting for him at the agora table with Corinna. "We have no power," he says matter-of-factly, "except I think it's possible the biogas turbine might still work. I'll check that out after I get back from the Eagle's Nest."

"I'll go with you," Hyp says.

"We're on our own, brother, but I know you need to see for yourself," Themis says.

Halfway up the 150-foot climb, Hyperides, out of breath, gasps, "I remember now Themis saying how hard it is to get up here." Trip just grunts in reply, focused on getting to the top and confirming what he expects, which is they are completely cut off from the rest of the world and literally in the dark. How will they even find out what is happening in the rest of the world? What if someone has a bad accident and needs a hospital? Where will be able to get a new inverter? He is getting more and more agitated the higher he climbs.

When he and Hyperides make it back down, they can see that everyone is up now and sitting around the table, except for Corinna and Clea who are cooking something. Soup. The grim looks on their faces tell everyone what Themis has already told them. The outside world is a big black box they have no way of opening except for somehow, some way, someone making a reconnaissance trip of 80 miles or more—and would it even be safe to do that? Probably not.

Pausanias asks Trip if he had tried starting his car. He hadn't, but he's sure the electronic components are fried and the car worthless. "We could use your gas, though, to run a generator if we're lucky. We're going to have to get creative."

They are a somber group sitting around the table eating the bean soup Clea and Corinna made. No one wants to think about the reality of their situation, but no one can stop thinking about it. They may never leave this place. They may die here. How many people are still alive out there in the world? What is going to happen to the survivors? How many survivors are there? How are they coping? It's impossible to control the incessant nagging of anxious fantasies. Nobody feels like talking.

Plutarch, who has been quiet all day, his urge to speak up mysteriously gone, finally says something: "I can't think of a group of people I'd rather be stuck with for the rest of my life than you all."

"That's right, Plutarch!" Corinna says, raising her cup of tea, and everyone toasts, lightly banging their ceramic mugs as the sun dips below the trees. For once they are glad to see it go, but later, as the long winter wears on, they will be yearning for its return every day.

Just then, after Corinna's toast, they hear a woman's faint voice from the edge of the clearing, "Hello...Hi...is Pau here?" Pausanias has heard the voice before and recognizes it. "Kate? Is that you?"

"Yes, it's me. Wyatt's here, too." And Wyatt steps out from behind her. "Hey, man."

Pausanias introduces them all around, using their Greek names without a second thought, which the two visitors accept without comment. They are frightened and confused—traumatized—having been knocked unconscious twice by the fireballs. The light show in the sky was beautiful but terrifying. They had no idea what to do except just stay inside their cabin, which is what they did. It was Wyatt's idea to come to the hot springs place to see if Pau is still around. Maybe he could explain what is going on.

Pausanias, with commentary from the rest of the family, tells them how they made it through what they believe was a huge solar storm, omitting a lot of potentially awkward details which would frighten their guests even more, so the story didn't take long. Hypatia once again explains the phenomenon of plasma bombs erupting from the sun and hitting the earth and the likely effects.

"So we're on our own here? All alone? This happened all over the world?" Kate and Wyatt anxiously ask all the questions anyone would ask after hearing what happened.

"Unless you want to walk out of here," Triptolemos says, "which besides being a very long walk for which you will have to carry water and food for several days, if not weeks, it may not be safe. Actually, probably very unsafe."

Themis, who has been staying in the background not saying anything, jumps in: "You're welcome to stay here with us if you'd like. We have shelter, food, water, heat, and best of all, companionship. The only thing we don't have is power, and Trip will get something rigged up, I'm sure of it."

Kate looks at Wyatt, who nods, and she says, "Thank you. We were really hoping we'd find you here and you would take us in. We're so scared, and our garden is not going to keep us going through the winter. We don't want to be alone right now. Thank you. Bless you."

Corinna blurts out, "Welcome to Hyperborea!"

"Thank you," Kate says, "We won't be a bother. We'll do anything you ask to help."

Plutarch suddenly says, "You're a midwife, aren't you Kate? That's good. We're going to need one."

"I am. But how did you know? Is someone here pregnant?"

Plutarch doesn't respond. He is completely confused and unable to answer, having no idea why he said that and how he knew.

You're remembering, Plutarch. I'll help you.

Huh? What?

Mushroom mind, brother, you don't need hardware anymore. Besides, I'm not immortal, and Hyperborea will need another Oracle.

I heard that, sister. I suppose you remembered this, too, and kept it from me?

Faith, sister!

Episode 50

Lucky and bless'd is he, who, knowing all these things of the spirit,
Toils in the fields, blameless before the Immortals,
Knowing in birds and not overstepping taboos.

HESIOD

The children who are of age are gathered in the sanctuary messing around in the sand and splashing each other with the warm mineral water. They are waiting to begin their initial instruction on the Law, instruction that traditionally begins with the story of their people, the Hyperboreans, which they are all eager to hear, knowing that it has something to do with giant fireballs hurled by the sun at the earth or something like that. Anyway, they are sure it is going to be exciting.

The three wise women—Grandma Justice, born Dike, great granddaughter of Themis, the first Oracle; Grandma Peace, born Eirene, great granddaughter of Hypatia, the first teacher; and Grandma Harmony, born Eunomia, great granddaughter of Corinna, the Bee Maiden, along with the Oracle, born Themis, great granddaughter of Clea—are sitting by the waterfall at the back of the grotto.

"Children, please settle now," Grandma Peace says. "We're ready to start." She waits for them to find places in the sand to sit and to get quiet. "Grandma Justice is going to tell you how the first wise women were chosen by the Creation to live through the Chastisement and establish our home, Hyperborea—a place dedicated to the Law as taught by the Oracle."

Instruction in the Law is Grandma Justice's duty, as it had been for her great, great grandmother Themis, her great grandmother Dike, her grandmother, her mother, and as it will be for her daughter and her daughter and her daughter.

Grandma Justice looks around for Sarah and her son, James, who arrived not long ago from the outside, having been chosen by the Creation to be called to Hyperborea. People from the outside had been showing up more frequently, and as the Oracle remembers, their numbers will continue to increase.

She spots her in the far back. "Welcome, Sarah, and thanks for bringing James here today. Hi, James." She smiles. "Is this your first time in the grotto, Sarah?"

"Yes. It's beautiful." she says shyly. She is still anxious, and understandably so. Hyperborea is always a shock to those from the outside. Those who arrive after a difficult journey have all heard fanciful stories of a hidden river valley, a paradise, a veritable land of milk and honey, a place where life is not a constant struggle, where people sing and dance the night away instead of dropping into their beds, tired after another day of exhausting work on their family farms.

They are told to look for a dinosaur in a tree that marks the way. "You'll know it when you see it. Then go north, following an old, overgrown trail, about 20 miles through the forest," they are told. "If you smell sulfur, you know you've made it."

They hear stories of a mysterious cult, of magic and miracles and mushroom worshippers, and they come a long and hard way through the forest with their expectations and fantasies, but once there, the reality is something else, something entirely other, like it always is.

We are one, Justice begins, and the children respond in unison, *we are one.*

CPSIA information can be obtained
at www.ICGtesting.com
Printed in the USA
FSHW020952230621
82609FS